D0642925

MERIAN C. COOPER'S
KING KONG

★

Also by Joe DeVito and Brad Strickland

KONG: King of Skull Island

MERIAN C. COOPER'S
KING KONG

★

Joe DeVito and Brad Strickland
Illustrations by Joe DeVito

ST. MARTIN'S GRIFFIN
NEW YORK

www.stmartins.com

Book design by Jonathan Bennett

Library of Congress Cataloging-in-Publication Data

DeVito, Joe, 1957–
    Merian C. Cooper's King Kong / by Joe DeVito and Brad Strickland ; illustrations by Joe DeVito.—1st ed.
      p. cm.
    A full rewrite of the original 1932 novel.
    ISBN 0-312-34915-7
    EAN 978-0-312-34915-8
    1. King Kong (Fictitious character)—Fiction. 2. Motion picture industry—Fiction. 3. Apes—Fiction. I. Strickland, Brad. II. Lovelace, Delos Wheeler, 1894–1967. King Kong. III. Title.

PS3604.E8864M47 2005
813'.6—dc22

2005047475

First Edition: October 2005

10   9   8   7   6   5   4   3   2   1

This book is dedicated to the memory of
Merian C. Cooper,
the father of King Kong.

★ FOREWORD ★

"Have you ever heard of . . . Kong?" asked Carl Denham of Engle-horn, captain of the ship taking the adventurer-moviemaker, and his cast and crew, nearer to Skull Island, in uncharted regions of the Indian Ocean. "Why, yes," was Englehorn's measured reply, as if rousing long-dormant memories of the native legends he had heard on his countless voyages in the area. Since the release of *King Kong* in March 1933, very few who have inhabited Planet Earth would need more than a second to respond in the affirmative. *King Kong* has become entrenched in movie lore and culture not only in America, but around the world as well.

The question that, in contrast, remains baffling to many people in the twenty-first century is: Have you ever heard of Merian C. Cooper? What may be surprising to a majority of those who are told about him is that Merian Coldwell Cooper, in addition to *King Kong*, is directly connected to the following: world exploration, many of the classic films directed by John Ford, Technicolor and the increased use of color in motion pictures, the birth of widescreen movies with Cine-rama, the development of commercial aviation, and distinguished service in America's air force in two world wars.

I vividly recall reading the newspaper obituaries, published side-by-side, of Merian Cooper and Robert Armstrong, the man Cooper had chosen, over forty years earlier, to play Carl Denham in *King Kong*. Cooper died on April 21, 1973, and Armstrong the day before. The death of one following so closely on the other reinforced even more to me the degree to which Cooper was the character of Denham. This mingling of Merian C. Cooper into his creations was a trademark of this passionate jack-of-all-trades. Readers of *Merian C. Cooper's King Kong* will discover that Cooper and Denham, in so many respects, are one and the same.

A life that, by ordinary expectations of achievement, would logically be credited to five or six individuals, is, in the case of Cooper, confined to one human being whom famed journalist and broadcaster Lowell Thomas described as "not just a remarkable man, he was incredible." With all of his accomplishments, there is little doubt that it is for the creation of *King Kong* that Merian C. Cooper will be most fondly remembered. *King Kong* was also an outgrowth of the motto that Cooper and filmmaking partner Ernest B. Schoedsack adopted as a litmus test for their future film projects. It was that locations and story elements must incorporate aspects of the distant, difficult, and dangerous.

Cooper was a man with seven-league boots, imbued with the romanticism of exploration, discovery, adventure, and danger more typical of a bygone era. Yet his love of twentieth-century aviation, technology, high finance, and the motion picture industry would, on the surface, seem irreconcilable to his passion for the primitive. Perhaps the most enduring creation resulting from this unique amalgamation of disparate worlds was *King Kong*.

Cooper himself indicated that the elements that became the motion picture *King Kong* began to come together in his mind in 1929, when he was thirty-six years old. The seed was most likely planted, however, at the tender age of six, when an uncle gave him a copy of *Explorations and Adventures in Equatorial Africa* by Pierre Du Chaillu. That, according to Cooper, was when he decided to become an explorer.

In his wanderings, Cooper was in search of adventure in cultures both primitive and modern, while all the time defining his own limits. The arc that brought Cooper to Kong, as chronicled by Mark Cotta Vaz in *Living Dangerously: The Adventures of Merian C. Cooper, Creator of King Kong*, began with his birth in Jacksonville, Florida, in 1893.

An appointment to the U.S. Naval Academy ended in Cooper's embarrassing dismissal before graduation. In his early twenties, Cooper resolved to atone for his apparent casual view of life by losing himself in a cause and "living dangerously." His life-long code of honor crystalized at this crucial time. Cooper became a crack pilot in the U.S. Aero Squadron in Europe during World War I, where he was shot down over Germany and declared dead in 1918, only to resurface in a prisoner-of-war camp.

Following the armistice, Cooper remained abroad, involving himself in humanitarian relief in Poland, then under siege by the Bolshevik Red Russians. There he helped found the Kosciuszko Squadron, a band of freedom-fighters composed mostly of American and English aviators who were brothers-in-arms during the Great War. Cooper became one of Poland's heroes. He was shot down again, this time over Moscow, and escaped a Russian prisoner-of-war camp only to make a perilous trek on foot to freedom, all the way to the Latvian border.

Back in the United States, after stints as a reporter and feature writer on several newspapers, Cooper's wanderlust took him on a round-the-world voyage with Captain Edward Salisbury on the yacht *Wisdom II,* a journey chronicled in *The Sea Gypsy,* coauthored by Salisbury and Cooper. During the voyage, he was reunited with cameraman Schoedsack, whom he had met briefly in Poland when Schoedsack was covering the Russo-Polish War. That adventure ended abruptly in Italy when the *Wisdom II* was consumed by fire. From the ashes of that fire, the partnership of Cooper-Schoedsack was formed and the pair made two landmark drama-documentaries: *Grass* (1925) followed the Bakhtiari tribe in its treacherous semiannual trek over the passes near Zardeh Kuh in the Zagros Mountains to their winter pasture in western Persia, now Iran; and *Chang* (1927), about a family in the jungle of Siam (Thailand) eking out an existence against the everpresent threat of predatory man-eating tigers. Both films were box office hits distributed by Paramount Pictures.

In 1929, following his and Schoedsack's making of *The Four Feathers* at Paramount under the supervision of producer David O. Selznick, Cooper became a New York City businessman and a central figure in the formation of Pan American Airways. Cooper assisted the talented Selznick in becoming head of production at RKO Radio Pictures, and, in the fall of 1931, Selznick brought Cooper into the organization as his assistant. Two years later, Cooper became production head at RKO when Selznick left for Metro-Goldwyn-Mayer. During his tenure at RKO, Cooper paired up Fred Astaire with Ginger Rogers, brought Katharine Hepburn to Hollywood, and began his long association with director John Ford, whom he brought to RKO to make *The Lost Patrol* and *The Informer*. Cooper's stint at RKO also brought him in contact with technical wizard Willis O'Brien, then working on a secret, and ultimately unproduced, project called *Creation*, involving the stop-motion animation of models of prehistoric beasts. O'Brien would prove invaluable in bringing Kong to the screen.

The final link in what would become *King Kong* came out of discussions Cooper had with explorer W. Douglas Burden. Inspired by *Chang*, Burden led a filmmaking expedition to the island of Komodo and brought back two of its indigenous giant lizards for exhibition at the Bronx Zoo. That they eventually became ill and died was an element that found its way into Cooper's beauty-and-the-beast story of a giant gorilla. The final story was classic Cooper, combining elements both primitive and contemporary, and whose premise involved difficulty, distance, and, most certainly, danger.

Popular British novelist Edgar Wallace was brought into the project in December 1932, but died suddenly of pneumonia just over two months later, after turning out a draft script of Cooper's story. The script was more fully developed, under Cooper's supervision, into its final form by James Creelman and Ruth Rose. Cooper, nevertheless, kept Wallace's name on the film and in publicity connected to *King*

Kong, both because of his promise to Wallace and for its publicity value.

At nearly fifty, Cooper, with a wife and three children to care for, could easily have remained safely at home during World War II. However, his innate patriotism compelled him to sign up, as he had done nearly three decades earlier, to serve his country. In China, Cooper was chief of staff to General Claire Chennault of the Flying Tigers, and flew numerous bombing missions with his younger subordinates. Later, in the South Pacific, he was chief of staff to General Edward Kenney, masterminding air operations. At war's end, he was among those on board the U.S.S. *Missouri* in Tokyo Bay at the ceremony formalizing Japan's surrender.

Following the war, Cooper and John Ford formed Argosy Pictures Corporation, and together were responsible for some of that era's best films, including *Fort Apache, She Wore a Yellow Ribbon,* and *The Quiet Man,* as well as revisiting the giant gorilla theme with *Mighty Joe Young.* Ever on the cutting edge, Cooper was a major force in the development, along with Lowell Thomas, of Cinerama, the first commercially successful widescreen movie process, which revolutionized the motion picture industry.

I never met Merian C. Cooper. Photographs of him often show a broad smile of Cinerama proportions. Surviving audio recordings revealed his expansive Southern drawl, and a passion for what he was doing at the moment. My early interest in movies was bolstered by frequent viewings of *King Kong* on Los Angeles television during the late 1950s and early 1960s. Its effect was singularly impressive: the human qualities of Kong; Max Steiner's powerful score, laced with themes for each character; and the derring-do, man-on-the-make Depression-era elan of Carl Denham. At the time, the only accessible publication on Cooper was an excellent article by movie historian Rudy Behlmer in the January 1966 issue of *Films in Review.*

It was in meeting members of his family that I discovered firsthand the Cooper quality of relentless decency and warmth. My association began in 1976, with Cooper's widow, the gracious Dorothy Jordan, at her home on Coronado Island near San Diego, where the couple had retired. I was early in my career as a manuscript curator at the Special Collections department at Brigham Young University. In the ensuing decade, during which Cooper's papers were donated to BYU in 1986, I also enjoyed getting to know their son, U.S. Air Force Colonel Richard M. Cooper. He patiently entertained the countless questions thrown at him as I wound my way through over fifty cartons of correspondence, passports, scrapbooks, photographs, and memorabilia accumulated by Richard's father and seen by no one else.

I must admit to being more than guarded when I heard of a modern adaptation of the original King Kong story. My immediate reaction was to conjure up horrific images of the makeover of the Kong story by movie producer Dino De Laurentiis in the mid 1970s. Leave well enough alone was my unspoken plea. What made me even consider reading this new version was that the request came from Colonel Cooper himself. A subsequent weekend immersed in the typescript erased any concerns I had about heresy, blasphemy, or crassly commercial exploitation of Merian C. Cooper's original story by Mr. De-Vito and Mr. Strickland. After years of being immersed in Cooper's own papers, I emerged from reading the manuscript feeling at home.

The authors' single-minded determination to remain faithful to Cooper's original story has resulted in what is, to me, a seamless tale that authentically derives from the spirit of Cooper's fertile imagination. What they have done is to flesh out the story that Kong devotees so protectively revere, and yet allow the reader to create an authentic theater-of-the-mind experience, not unlike that of old time radio. De-Vito and Strickland convincingly invoke the senses into the voyage of *The Wanderer* to Skull Island and back: the pelting rain, the pungent smell of the jungle, the strained muscles, sweat, and sinews of Carl Denham and Jack Driscoll on the chase for Ann Darrow in peril, the heat and dampness of the tropical isle, and even the acrid aroma of Kong crashing through groves of jungle flora. Of particular interest are their credible embellishments on Cooper's original story, covering the time between the capture of Kong on Skull Island and his exhibition on Broadway, as well as what transpires from Kong's escape and the havoc wreaked in midtown Manhattan until his ascent of the Empire State Building, Ann Darrow in hand.

Venerated stories that have become cultural legends are both formidable in their longevity and, at the same time, highly vulnerable and fragile. Their strength comes from endurance in the culture; their fragility becomes exposed by attempts to alter them. DeVito and Strickland have taken a story—for generations familiar and for decades beloved—and have given it a fresh retelling. They have done their job so convincingly that they reinforce King Kong as myth without disturbing its core time-honored elements. As with Cooper himself, the authors have deftly blended the old with the new in a story that is well within the confines of the term "Faithful." "It's alive!" cried Dr. Henry Frankenstein in the movie about *his* creation that has also become a cultural legend. In the case of *Merian C. Cooper's King Kong,* Cooper's creation is, indeed not only alive . . . but alive and well.

—James V. D'Arc
Curator, Merian C. Cooper Papers
Brigham Young University

ACKNOWLEDGMENTS

Joe and Brad would like to thank
the family of Merian C. Cooper, Randy Merritt,
Barbara Strickland, Danny Baror,
and our editor, Keith Kahla.

MERIAN C. COOPER'S
KING KONG

★

John Weston peered anxiously ahead from the backseat of the creeping taxi. Even in the obscuring twilight, and behind the lightly floating veil of snow, the *Wanderer* was clearly no more than a humble tramp freighter. Weston shook his head. He had imagined a ship of lean grace, all sharply curving contours, straining to embark on a great adventure.

"Sure we're in the right place?" Weston asked the cabdriver.

"Where you told me, pal. Pier four."

The cabbie found a place to park in the shadowed lee of a warehouse. Weston sat for a moment looking through the side window, still not sure. The down-at-heels support of the Hoboken pier certainly matched the rusty tub moored to it. With others of her kind, the *Wanderer* blended into the nondescript background of the unpretentious old town, camouflaged into anonymity. Beyond her, visible in the far distance, twinkled the bright Saturday-evening lights on the Manhattan side of the river. "Lord, I'd never have called that a seagoing craft," Weston muttered. "Don't knock the flag down yet. I want to make sure this is the right place."

"Yeah, sure."

Weston opened the door and lumbered out of the taxi with the short-winded dignity of a fat fifty-year-old man. He saw movement in the shadows next to the warehouse, and then an old watchman stepped out into the light, his head tilted quizzically, his red nose nearly glowing. "Help you?"

Weston pointed. "Yes, Cap. That the moving-picture ship?"

The red nose bobbed up and down in a nod. Weston ducked back into the taxi, read the meter, and handed over the fare from Forty-second Street and Broadway. "Wait here. I won't be long."

"Suit yourself. I ain't gonna pick up nobody in this neighborhood."

Weston shut the cab door and huddled deeper into his topcoat. The watchman switched on a flashlight as Weston scuffed through the light fall of snow. "You another one goin' on this crazy voyage?" the old man asked as Weston neared the foot of the gangway.

Weston stopped in his tracks and gave the watchman a sharp, suspicious look. "Crazy? What's crazy about it?"

The old man shrugged, looking uncomfortable.

"Is it the ship?" Weston demanded. "I expected something a little more modern than this."

"This is it, all right," the watchman said, rubbing his nose. "And the *Wanderer*'s better than she looks. Engines are sound. They'll push her along at a steady fourteen knots, come hell or high water. Hull's in stronger shape than it seems from here. 'Course they say she's had a lot of work done belowdecks, bulkheads ripped out, some kind of steel tank or something put in—I dunno. She'll do, though. Naw, the crazy part is—well, to start with, it's the fellow that's hired her."

The cold was making Weston's ears tingle, but he hunched his head down and said, "You mean Denham?"

"That's him. Fellow that if he wants a picture of a lion, he walks right up to the critter and tells it to look pleasant! If that ain't crazy, what is?"

Weston chuckled. "Yeah, he's a tough egg, all right. But why are you saying the *voyage* is crazy?"

The watchman took a step closer, and Weston caught the scent of bourbon on his breath. "Just is, that's why. You ask anybody on the docks. Let me tell you, there's some mighty smart fellows around here, even if they ain't got such high-and-mighty jobs, and everybody around the docks says it's crazy. They got stuff stowed aboard that vessel I don't believe yet, even if I did see it go aboard with my own two eyes. And take the crew! Old Englehorn's hired on extra hands, three times as many as he needs to sail the ship. Take shoehorns to squeeze 'em all aboard!"

He shook his head, his aromatic breath pluming out on the snowy air. Before he could start again, a man's voice called down from the deck of the *Wanderer*: "Hey, on the gangway there! What do you want?"

"First mate," the old watchman said in a low voice. "Driscoll, his name is."

Looking up, Weston saw a figure at the low rail amidships, outlined in light streaming from a cabin astern and higher up. "What do you want?" the figure repeated in a booming voice.

"Want to come aboard, Mr. Driscoll," Weston yelled back, and he started to climb the wet, slippery gangway cautiously. "Your boss is expecting me."

"You must be Weston, then," the younger man said. "Come on aboard. Watch your step there."

The climb was treacherous and steep, but Weston made it, then stepped onto the deck and got his first clear look at Driscoll. He was a tall young man, strongly built, with reckless eyes and a firm mouth. He held out his hand and Weston shook it, feeling an immediate liking for the young fellow. "Jack Driscoll," the first mate said.

"Broadway's one and only John Weston. The ace of theatrical agents." Weston was puffing a little from the climb, and he grinned. "Even if my wind isn't what it used to be."

"Come aft," Driscoll said. "Denham's wild to hear from you. Have you found the girl?"

In the darkness, Weston's cheer evaporated. He made a wry face but said nothing as he followed Driscoll's swinging stride aft, then up a short ladder to the lighted cabin. Weston blinked in the strong light. In contrast to the rusty sides of the ship, the cabin was spick-and-span, furnished with the Spartan simplicity of seagoing vessels. No decorations, apart from a pipe rack on one wall, a small mirror on the other, and a rack hung with a pea jacket, a civilian overcoat, and a couple of hats. For the rest, four chairs, an oblong map table, an open crate containing black iron spheres smaller than grapefruit but larger than oranges, and a brightly polished brass cuspidor. Two men stood in the cabin, both of them looking expectantly at Weston.

"Visitor, Captain," Driscoll said to one of the men, of no more than middle height. He had a heavy brown mustache touched with gray, and held in his hand a battered old briar pipe. The man was in vest and shirtsleeves, but wore a captain's uniform cap, along with an air of command. The captain's sharp eyes acknowledged Driscoll's introduction, but he didn't speak as he tamped down the tobacco in his pipe and applied a match to it. Puffing, he stepped aside, leaving the stage clear for his companion.

Weston knew this man: Carl Denham, a well-tailored, well-groomed fellow of thirty-five, looking as if he might belong behind a stockbroker's desk—though Weston had to admit he had never met anyone on Wall Street with Denham's air of solid power, of indomitable will. Denham's bright brown eyes, shining with an unquenchable zest for life, flashed at Weston, and in an impatient voice, the film director snapped, "Weston! About time. I was just about to go ashore to ring you up."

Weston's feet were feeling damp and cold from the snow. "If I'd known that, I would've waited in my office."

Denham grinned. "Well, now you're here, shake hands with the skipper. Captain Englehorn, this is John Weston of Broadway."

Englehorn exhaled a cloud of pungent smoke, then extended a hard, rough hand. He didn't say a word, but as soon as Weston had shaken his hand, Englehorn stooped to drag the crate of iron spheres aside to make room at the table for Weston.

"Sit down, sit down," Denham said, sinking into the chair opposite Weston's, but lightly, as if ready to spring up any moment. "I take it you've met the first mate here, Jack Driscoll."

4

"We've met," Weston said, with a smile at Driscoll, who grinned and nodded his agreement.

Denham hardly waited for the answer. "These two are a pair like you've never met on Broadway, old man. Both were with me on my last trip, and I'll tell you right now, if they weren't going along this time, I'd think twice before I started."

Weston took off his hat and set it on the table. Under Denham's intense gaze, he shifted uncomfortably but did not reply. For a moment a silence stretched out, with Denham looking him quizzically in the face. Then Denham leaned forward and said, "Where's the girl, Weston?"

With a sigh, Weston met Denham's gaze. "Haven't got one."

"What!" Denham leaped up from his chair and struck the table hard with the flat of his hand. "Look here, Weston, Actors' Equity and the Hays Office have warned off every actress I've tried to hire, and every agent but you has backed away. You're my last hope. Look, you know I'm square—"

Weston waved a gloved hand. "Denham, everyone knows you're square. But they also know how reckless you are. And you haven't inspired confidence in this picture by being so secretive."

"That's the truth!" Englehorn said around the stem of his pipe.

"Absolutely," agreed Driscoll, his arms crossed. "Denham hasn't told me or the skipper where the old ship is heading. We're under sealed orders, and whoever heard of that when the trip's just to shoot a movie?"

Weston spread his hands, palms up. "There you are. Look, Denham, think of my reputation. I can't ask a young, pretty girl to go on a job like this without even telling her what to expect."

"How about a homely one?" Denham asked with a grin. He waved off Weston's protest. "No, skip it. What do you suppose she has to expect?"

Weston felt his face growing warm with irritation. "All I could tell her would be that she's going on a ship for nobody knows how long to some spot that you won't name, the only woman on a ship full of tough mugs—" He broke off, noticing the stares of Englehorn and Driscoll. Weston coughed. "Of course, I mean the crew."

Denham was pacing restlessly. He paused and smacked his hand down on the table again. "Weston, I'm going on the biggest shoot of my life, and I have to have a girl to put in this picture!"

"You never had an actress in any of your other films," Weston objected. "Not even an actor, for that matter. Why do you need one this time?"

"Not because I want to have one!" Denham paused in his pacing. "It's the public, that's why. The public wants a pretty woman's face. According to them, adventure's as dull as dishwater, there's no romance in it, unless every so often up pops a face to launch a thousand ships. Or is it saps?"

Weston objected, "But in an animal picture, a bring-'em-back-alive—"

Denham overrode him: "Imagine! I work, I slave, I sweat blood to make a good picture. It plays the theaters and makes a dime. But the public says, 'We would've liked it better if there was a woman in it.' And the reviewers say, 'If the film had a love interest, it would have grossed twice as much!' Up to now, I've been on my own, not beholden to any studio. I've arranged the financing for every movie myself—put myself in hock to do it, often enough. There's my wife and son, in a house I've mortgaged to the hilt, waiting for me to succeed. Only now there's a depression on, and the banks won't give me a second look unless I can guarantee a big box office. For that I need—I have to have—a woman in the picture! They want a girl, by george, I'll give them a girl!"

Weston had watched Denham's growling monologue with growing impatience. He stood up and put on his hat. "Well, Denham, I'm sorry, but there's nothing I can do for you."

"You've got to. And you've got to do it in a hurry. We're sailing on the morning tide—have to be away from here by daylight."

The declaration puzzled Weston. "What? You're not due to sail for another week! Why the rush?"

Denham glanced at Englehorn, who shrugged. Then, in the same angry growl, he muttered, "Guess it won't hurt to tell you at this stage of the game. We're carrying explosives and the insurance company's got wind of it. If we don't get away in a jump, the marshal's deputy will be on our necks, and then we'll be tied up in court for months."

"Explosives?" Weston asked nervously.

With a wry grin, Denham reached down to the box Englehorn had set aside and retrieved one of the iron spheres. He tossed it and caught it again, making Weston tense his muscles. Denham barked a short laugh. "Relax. I know how to handle these things. I invented them. This is just to make a point. Weston, I wouldn't lie to you—I wouldn't say any girl who goes with us wouldn't be heading into danger. On an expedition like this, there'll be a little risk now and then. Maybe even more than a little. But take this from me: with a couple of these handy, nothing very serious is going to happen."

Weston found that he had half risen from his chair. He forced himself to sit back down and asked, "What have you got there?"

"Gas bombs, old man! My own design. Or maybe I should say my improvement on an existing design. It's a formula that will knock out a row of elephants, if they get a couple of whiffs of the stuff."

Weston stood then, shaking his head. "Denham, everything you tell me makes me like this proposition less. I'm starting to be glad I couldn't find you a girl."

"Don't talk like the insurance company," Denham snapped, his tone scornful. "Look, as long as men who know what they're doing handle these things—I mean men like me, the skipper, and Driscoll here—the gas bombs are as harmless as lollipops. The truth is that we'll be in more peril from plain old rain and the monsoon season than from anything we're likely to meet up with once we're on land."

"Monsoons?" asked Weston suspiciously.

"They do happen, you know," Denham said, carefully replacing the gas bomb in its crate. "And that's another reason I have to get under way as soon as possible. I've got just six months to get to the location and shoot the film before the monsoon season sets in. Don't look so gloomy, Weston! I could trust the *Wanderer* to get through a blow, and the skipper and Driscoll are dependable. But monsoons bring torrential rain, and rain ruins an outdoor picture. Wastes time, wastes money, and leaves a man with nothing to show for all his work. Every minute the *Wanderer* is moored here takes away from the time we should be using to get our picture."

Weston felt half dizzy from Denham's mile-a-minute speech. He held up his hands to silence the man. "Gas bombs! Monsoons! You make me feel like an accessory to murder!" Weston picked up his hat and clapped it onto his round head. "I'm sorry, Denham, but you'll get no girl from me."

"What?"

Weston headed for the door. "I mean it."

"You do, huh? Well, I'll get one myself!" With a speed surprising in such a solidly built man, he jerked a coat from a hook and a hat from another and shoved past Weston. "You have a cab waiting?"

"Yes, but—"

"If you think I'm going to quit now, just because you can't find me a girl with backbone—"

Weston stepped aside as Denham yanked the door open. "Wait a second—"

But Denham hadn't even paused. "—I'm going to make the greatest picture in the world! Something no one's ever seen, never even dreamed of! They'll have to invent new adjectives when I come back. You wait!"

The door slammed in Weston's face. "My cab!" he said weakly.

Englehorn yelled, "Denham! Where are you going?"

Denham's indomitable voice floated back: "I'm going to find a girl for my picture, even if I have to kidnap one!" His footsteps faded as he hurried down the gangway.

Inside the cabin, Weston buttoned up his overcoat, staring at Englehorn and Driscoll, feeling glad that he had managed to keep out of this whole loony mess. The old watchman was right. Crazy was the word for it. "He's taken my cab," Weston said, feeling a little foolish.

Driscoll and Englehorn both laughed. Driscoll threw up his arms. "Denham usually gets what he wants. What do you want to bet he comes back with a girl?"

"I wouldn't take the bet," Englehorn replied calmly. "All right, all right, Mr. Weston, we'll get you home."

"What kind of girl would be crazy enough—" Weston began, and then broke off in some embarrassment.

Driscoll clapped him on the shoulder. His white teeth flashed as he laughed again. "Hey, Denham would have the nerve to tell me to marry a girl if he decided the script called for it. Come on, Mr. Weston. I'll call you another taxi."

★ 2 ★

Carl Denham roamed Broadway, looking for a face. He jostled through the theatre-hour crowds, eyes alert, and every once in a while he swore impatiently under his breath when some young woman who'd looked promising from a distance proved commonplace as he drew near.

He concentrated on his self-imposed task. If he paused long enough, a world of worries waited to flood in on him: crushing debt, his patient wife waiting for him in their cottage upstate, his little son, Vincent. Denham shrugged off his concerns. They were nothing that a hit movie couldn't fix, and a hit movie was his—if he could find the right face.

His narrowed eyes were like camera lenses, catching countless faces among the crowd: bold faces, frightened faces, sullen faces, inviting faces, pouting faces, expectant faces, painted faces, hard faces, sordid faces, indifferent faces. Not one of them held his gaze or his interest for more than a moment's inspection.

An hour passed, and another, and the crowds thinned. "Maybe I *am* nuts," Denham muttered to himself, feeling the cold through his heavy overcoat. He had traveled toward downtown, passing through Times Square and into the canyons of the lower avenue, leaving behind the glitter and bustle of the theatres. A whipping wind stung his cheeks and lashed snow across his eyes. Still he looked, seeing faces in doorways, faces in breadlines, in passing automobiles. None had the quality he wanted.

Restlessly Denham circled back, leaving Madison Square's benches behind. Fifth Avenue, Park Avenue, swaggering, intimate Fifty-seventh Street, and no luck. The dreary upper West Forties, and he drifted again toward Broadway, where jostling throngs now boiled out of a hundred theatres and movie palaces.

Denham was passing a shop—hardly even that, more like an overgrown booth, scarcely large enough for the bulky proprietor. Outside it on the sidewalk, stands displayed baskets of fruit, lush in the spilled yellow light from inside: oranges, grapefruit, pears, red apples. A slender girl, her back to Denham, stood looking down at the fruit, evidently trying to decide what she wanted.

It happened in an instant. The girl's slim white hand reached softly up to a basket of apples, and before she could even touch one, the proprietor erupted through the doorway, shouting in anger: "Ah-hah! So I catch you, you thief!" He seized the girl's wrist. "No, you don't run. Hey, police!"

"No!" The girl turned and tried weakly to pull away. "No, I didn't take anything! I wanted to, but I didn't. Please let me go."

Denham's head snapped back, his eyes narrowing. He took a half step forward and felt a grin widen his mouth.

The shopkeeper kept his grip on the girl's arm, but with his free hand, he gestured broadly. "Every hour somebody steal. Me, I've had enough. Hey, police!"

Denham put his hand on the man's shoulder. "Shut up. I saw it all. The girl's telling the truth. She was starting to pull her hand away from the apples even before you came out. She wasn't going to steal anything."

The girl turned a grateful face toward Denham. "I wasn't. Truly, I wasn't."

Denham reached into his pocket. "Okay, then. Go ahead and call a cop if you want, friend. But you've got a witness who's dead against you. Here, take this and forget it."

A couple of bills changed the shopkeeper's opinion at once. "Sorry. I didn't know she was with you." He retreated into the shop, out of the cold.

Denham saw the girl totter on her feet, and in an instant he flung his arm around her shoulders. Her head lolled back, and the electric light streaming from the shop shone full on her face. Denham's eyes opened wide, and the grin spread itself across his face, ear to ear. He laughed, guided the girl to the curb, and threw up a signaling hand. "Taxi!"

A Yellow cab that was headed toward the theatre district pulled over with a squeal of brakes. Denham bustled the girl inside and climbed in beside her. "The closest restaurant, and step on it."

Half an hour later, in a white-tiled diner around the corner from the sidewalk stand, he still wore his air of triumph. In the chair on the opposite side of the table from him sat the girl, behind a white barricade of empty china plates and cups. She had hardly spoken since the cab, merely murmuring her thanks, which Denham waved away. He leaned forward on his arms, staring in contentment at the girl's face.

It was a beautiful face, but more than that: she had the kind of well-molded, clearly defined features that the camera loved. Large, incredibly blue eyes, keen with intelligence, looking at him from shadowing lashes. A ripe mouth showing passion and humor. A lifted chin hinting at reserves of courage. Her skin was a delicate, transparent white, and not, Denham decided, because she was undernourished. No, her marvelous complexion went with the kind of hair formed up beneath her shabby hat, hair of pure gold. Denham shook his head. "You know, if I was poetical, which I'm not, I'd say your hair was like something spun out of sunlight."

She smiled, meeting his gaze. "Thanks, I guess."

"Feeling a little better now?"

"I'm a different girl. Thank you again."

"You're welcome. It was a pleasure to watch you dig in. My name's Denham, by the way, Carl Denham."

"Ann Darrow."

Perfect, Denham thought. We won't even have to change it.

Ann Darrow seemed a little nervous. "You've been wonderfully kind," she said in a soft voice.

Denham shook his head. "Don't give me too much credit. I'm not spending time and money on you just out of kindness."

All of the humor drained from Ann's face. She lowered her chin, and her gaze became defiant.

Denham ignored that. "How'd you come to be in this fix?"

Ann blinked as if she hadn't expected that kind of question. "Bad luck, I guess. Times are hard. There must be lots of girls just like me."

"You're wrong there," Denham said, thinking of how he would frame that face for the screen. "Not many have your kind of looks."

"Oh, I could get by in good clothes, I suppose." Ann's smile came back, with a flicker of fear in it. "But when a girl gets too shabby—"

"Got any family?" Denham demanded.

Ann blinked. "An uncle . . . somewhere."

"Ever do any acting?"

With a quizzical tilt of her head, as if she couldn't quite follow Denham's thoughts, Ann said, "A few turns as an extra when they were shooting pictures down at Fort Lee. Once I got a real speaking part, a dozen lines or so. But the studio closed down."

Better and better, Denham thought. A touch of experience, but not enough to give her ideas about how she should be lighted, how she should be shot. He leaned forward, his gaze intent on her. "One more question: Are you a city gal, the kind who screams at a mouse and faints at a snake?"

Ann laughed out loud, looking as if she'd surprised herself. "No, I'm a country gal. I wouldn't pet a mouse, but I'd chase it outside. And I've killed snakes. Well, one snake, anyway."

Denham stood up, squaring his shoulders. "Just what I wanted to hear. Well, Ann Darrow, have I got a job for you!"

Ann stood up, too, her expression cool and determined. She started to speak.

Denham cut her off: "When you're fed up and rested and all rigged out, you'll be just what I need."

Guardedly, Ann asked, "When . . . when does this job start?"

Denham slapped the table. "Right now. This minute. And the first thing we've got to worry about is wardrobe. Come on. Some of the Broadway shops are open late."

"What is this job?" Ann asked, an edge of suspicion in her voice.

With excitement rising in him, Denham replied, "It's money and adventure and fame. It's the thrill of a lifetime. And it starts with a long sea voyage that shoves off at six in the morning."

Ann shook her head and sat down again. Denham could read no fear in her expression now, but instead a good-humored tolerance. "No, I'm sorry. I can't. I don't want a job that badly. I'm grateful to you—I *was* starving—but I can't just—"

"What!" Denham stared at her in baffled amazement for a moment, and then he laughed. "Oh, for the love of mike. I get it. Sister, you've got me wrong. This is strictly business."

"Well," Ann said apologetically, "I didn't want any—any—"

"Misunderstanding," Denham finished for her. "Sure, I know you didn't. It's my fault for getting excited and not explaining. I thought you knew who I was—Denham? Carl Denham? Sound familiar?"

Understanding dawned in those blue eyes. "Yes, I've heard of you! You make moving pictures. In jungles and deserts—"

"That's me. And I've picked you for the lead in my next picture. That's the job, Ann. Want it? You have to make up your mind now. We sail at six."

"Where to?"

Denham bit his lip. "Can't tell you that for a while. It's a long way from New York, though. And before we get there, there'll be a long sea voyage, easy living, good food, the warm sea air, moonlight soft on the water—"

Ann chuckled. "It sounds like a vacation."

With a shrug, Denham confessed, "I'm selling it because I want you in that picture, Ann. But just think, woman! Whatever happens, no matter where we wind up at the finish, it has to be better than being down on your luck in New York. I know what it's like to be broke, believe me. Must be worse for a girl like you, afraid every night that the next morning will find you in the gutter."

Ann looked thoughtful. "You're right," she said at last. "No matter where we wind up at the finish, it has to be better."

Denham offered her his hand, and when she took it, he helped her up from her chair. He held her hand—and shook it. "It's a deal. I'm square, Ann, and I'll be square with you. No funny business."

He let go of her hand and noticed her quick glance down, taking in his wedding band. She looked back at his face. "So you can't tell me yet about what I have to do in your picture?"

"I can tell you this much: keep your chin up and trust me."

Ann looked at him for a long direct moment.

Denham felt himself holding his breath. He had always been lucky, he reminded himself, as his cameraman's gaze again took in Ann's golden hair, her perfect face and lively blue eyes, her graceful, well-proportioned figure.

Ann took a deep breath. "All right," she said, and immediately Denham tossed some money onto the table, gripped her left arm, and steered her out and toward the shops that just might still be open on Broadway.

3

OFF THE JERSEY COAST

DECEMBER 4, 1932

Ann came wide-awake in the narrow berth and for a few seconds could not remember where she was or how she had got there. For those moments, she could only think that this was the first morning in weeks that hunger had not awakened her. Then memory of the previous night's amazing encounter rushed back, and she sat up. She laughed aloud when she saw beside her berth the bowl of apples.

Denham had bought them at the last moment, adding them to a pile of dress boxes, shoe boxes, and hat boxes that overflowed the taxi. Long past midnight the cabdriver had parked near the gangway of the *Wanderer,* and Denham had roused a red-nosed old watchman to help unload the cab. A muscular young man—Ann couldn't remember if she had been introduced or not—came down the gangway to help carry it all, and they had gone on board.

Ann followed Denham's lead down a narrow, dark corridor, toward the stern of the ship. He opened a doorway and said, "This will be your cabin. And here's a bowl to put the apples in." He dumped the fruit into a blue china bowl on a stand next to the bunk. "Here's your key." He set it down with a click next to the bowl of apples. "Okay, pass that stuff in." This was to the burdened young man, who handed over boxes that Denham stacked in a corner. "Sort this stuff out tomorrow. Right now, you get ready for bed. Bathroom's in there, kind of tight, but you'll make do with it. Good night, sleep tight, and make it a long one. You need your rest, and if I see you on deck before afternoon, I'll have the skipper put you in irons."

With that, Denham had stepped out, closed the door, and left her alone. Ann had done as he said, finding the tiny bathroom adequate,

and had put on one of the sedate negligees she had insisted on after Denham had, with an improbable blush, offered to buy her a more daring one. But after climbing into bed, she had spent three or four hours awake, staring at the round porthole with its drifting shadows of snowflakes. At last she had floated into sleep.

Now she brushed her hair back from her eyes and looked at the tiny clock next to the apples. It was just short of eight. She felt it then, the motion of the ship, a long, comfortable kind of roll, and she heard the deep thrum of engines from somewhere far below. She yawned and laughed again. Despite the shortness of her catnap, she was too excited to feel sleepy. And since she foresaw no likelihood of being any less excited for the rest of the day, she decided to risk going out on deck, defying the irons of Mr. Denham's skipper.

Ann swung her slim legs over the edge of the berth, stood up, and went to the porthole. New York had vanished. The snow clouds of the night before had blown out to sea, leaving behind a soft blue sky. Ann opened the porthole and craned to look at the sea. It was calm enough, and the only land she could see was off to the stern, a low, dark, dim line on the horizon. Cool air flooded in, refreshing and brisk. Ann spent some time in sorting her new clothes, shaking her head over Denham's generosity and enthusiasm.

"Buy anything you need, whatever you like, sister," Denham had said. "Believe me, you'll still come in cheap, compared to what I'd have had to pay a leading lady out of Hollywood or off Broadway. We won't be near a shop again for months, so go ahead, shoot the works."

Ann had taken him at his word, buying nightgowns, underthings, stockings, shoes, and even lounging pajamas. She purchased coats, dresses, hats. Denham had interceded only a few times, buying three identical sets of slacks and shirts—"Costume," he explained—and a few other oddments. Now here everything was, in a tottering mountain of boxes that quavered to the throb of the *Wanderer*'s engines.

Ann decided she simply had to unpack and find space for everything in the small closet and the chest at the foot of her berth. As a result, it was well after nine before she closed her cabin door and stepped out into the deserted passageway. Under a new coat she wore her own old dress. She didn't want Denham to think that she was too eager to seize her newly found luxury. Still, underneath the dress, a silken smoothness caressed her body from shoulders to toes. She smiled wistfully, remembering her late mother, who always cautioned her about being prepared in case an automobile hit her. Well, she was ready now. Too bad there were no autos on boats.

Ann emerged blinking onto a sunny deck, almost as deserted as the passageway. Although she was only a lady landlubber, Ann easily guessed that the officers and crew must have cleared away the business of departure and gone belowdecks. Only one person was there, sprawled in a corner shielded from the cool breeze, soaking up the warming rays of the sun. He was an old man, brown, stringy, bald, and he hummed as he tied knots for the benefit of a chattering monkey, bundled up in clothing meant for a doll.

Ann drew close, deciding that the old fellow had a friendly face. The monkey looked around at her and scooted closer to the sailor. She crouched down nearby, and the old man gave her an eyebrow-arched smile. "Morning."

"Teach me to do that," Ann said impulsively.

The old sailor grinned toothlessly. "Yessum! Well, this here's a running bowline. Now, what you do—" He broke off. "But first and foremost, introductions. Me, I'm Lumpy. The monk here, he's Ignatz."

"And I'm Ann Darrow," Ann said.

"Right you are. Mr. Denham told us about you this morning. All right, this here's a running bowline. Up, over, through. Now you try it."

Ann took the rope, but instead of trying the knot, she gazed out over the placid, rolling green sea. "This is wonderful."

Lumpy chuckled. "Well, it's a matter of taste, I guess. I'd rather be having a cold one in Curly's Bar, and Ignatz'd probably prefer clamberin' around in a coconut tree. But the sea's fine when the weather's good."

"I know it won't always be this calm," Ann said, working with the rope.

"No, it goes the other way—behind, see? Well, about the weather, you're right there, too. We'll be headin' into warmer waters, and sometimes that means storms. But this is a good old ship, and you've got nothin' to worry about. We'll get you there safe enough, wherever *there* is. Now you got it!"

A whistle shrilled from somewhere behind them, and Lumpy jumped up with surprising ease. "Keep an eye on Ignatz for me, Miz Darrow. Sounds like there's work to do!"

Before the whistle died away, six more sailors came rushing past, coming from aft, not far from the companionway she had taken.

Lumpy joined them, and a moment later the whistle's owner stepped past her, so intent on his work that he didn't even notice Ann. It was the same muscular young man who had helped carry her things the previous night. Ann frowned, trying to remember if Denham had mentioned his name.

She couldn't recall, but in the light of day, this young man held her interest. His long, well-muscled body, his strong dark face, his general air of being master and knowing it, challenged her. He wore a working outfit this morning, jeans and a heavy black shirt. "Hurry along, man!" the young fellow snapped at a late sailor, who replied, "Aye, aye, Mr. Driscoll."

"Driscoll." Ann mouthed the name. This wouldn't be the captain— too young. He stood with his back to her, and she rose to her feet to see what he was having the men do.

Driscoll wore an officer's cap, and Ann thought he could never have bought his thick woolen shirt on a common sailor's wage. "Rig for stowing," Driscoll shouted, and the men got busy.

Ann looked past him. Whatever the crew was doing dealt with a huge wooden crate near the bows and a tangle of ropes. Bright red letters stenciled across the faces of the container warned DANGER, making Ann wonder what it might hold. Old Lumpy secured lines to the crate, and then waved. Driscoll lifted a hand to his mouth and ordered, "You, Warren, carry that line aft!" He gestured behind him with his left hand, almost hitting Ann in the face. "Aft, you farmer! This way! Aft, aft! Back there!" This time he jerked his thumb back over his left shoulder so furiously that his knuckles brushed Ann's cheek, hard enough to sting. She gasped and jumped backward, scaring Ignatz. The monkey leaped to the rail, chattering madly, as the startled young man swung around, exclaiming, "Who the—" He broke off, his face showing his surprise. "What are you doing on deck? Denham said you'd sleep until noon."

Ann rubbed her cheek. "I just wanted to see," she explained, feeling oddly guilty, like a child that had been spying on grown-ups.

Driscoll let out his breath, which steamed in the cool morning air. "I'm sorry. Did I hurt you?"

Ann smiled and shook her head. "Not really. You surprised me. I'm Ann Darrow."

"Yes, we met last night. My name's Jack Driscoll," he said. "Hang on a minute." He turned back to the work party and shouted orders. They heaved and hauled, lifting the crate, swinging it over an open hatch, and then gingerly lowering it. Some of the crew went below to secure it, and in fifteen minutes the work was over, the hatch cover replaced, and the men scattered.

"Now," Driscoll said, turning back to Ann. "Hope I didn't bruise you."

"It takes a harder punch than that," Ann said, and she laughed.

Driscoll grinned, sheepishly. "So you're the girl that Denham turned up at the last minute."

Ann nodded. "He didn't tell me much. But it's exciting so far. I've never been on a ship before."

With a grunt, Driscoll said, "I've never been on a ship with a woman aboard."

Surprised at his gruff tone, Ann said, "You don't sound like you approve of the idea."

Driscoll shrugged. "Nine times out of ten, a woman on a ship is a nuisance."

Ann's first impression of Driscoll cooled considerably. "I'll try not to be," she said in a level voice.

"I'd appreciate that," Driscoll told her. "When there's work to be done, you'd better stay below and out of the way."

"I wasn't in the way!" Ann protested.

"You were in *my* way," Driscoll reminded her.

Ann couldn't tell whether he was teasing or not. "Do you want me to stay in my cabin for the whole voyage?" She couldn't keep an edge of anger from the question.

Driscoll's solemn face creased into a sudden grin. "I like the way your eyes flash. No, I suppose you can come out now and then. Say, are you sure that sock in the jaw didn't hurt you?"

"I can stand it. Lately I've had a lot of socks in the jaw." Ann heard the bitterness in her voice and bit her lip. She hadn't meant to complain.

Driscoll's gaze softened. "Lot of people have been through a run of hard luck lately," he said. "Okay, we'll have to do something about that. As far as I'm concerned, you can come on deck any time you please."

Something brushed at Ann's left arm. It was Ignatz, still crouched on the rail. Ann extended her hand, and to her surprise, the monkey scrambled up onto her shoulder. The animal sat with one arm around Ann's neck, grumbling at Driscoll, who shook his head. "Well, you've got somebody to guard you, anyhow," he said.

"What are you doing on deck?" The voice of Carl Denham came from behind them, and Ann turned. Denham had just stepped out of the same companionway she had come through. "Ann, I thought I ordered you to sleep the clock around."

Ann laughed. "I couldn't. I'm too excited to sleep."

Denham smiled. "Well, I see you've met a couple of the crew. One of these mugs is first mate, and I don't think it's the one on your shoulder."

"We met last night," Driscoll reminded Denham.

Ignatz was busy stroking and grooming Ann's hair.

"Hope they've been treating you right," Denham said.

Ann squirmed under Ignatz's attention. "Well, the first mate was a little rough, but so far Ignatz has been friendly."

Denham laughed, cocking his head as he watched the monkey comb through Ann's golden hair with its clever fingers. "Beauty and the Beast," he murmured.

"Hey," Driscoll said. "I never claimed to be handsome."

"Not you!" Denham replied with a bark of laughter. "I meant Ignatz. Look how calm he is. He doesn't take well to strangers, and I've never seen him let anybody but Lumpy pick him up."

"He sure seems to like her hair," Driscoll agreed.

"Beauty and the Beast," Denham said again. "Not a bad title, maybe. Good sign, anyway."

"Of what?" Driscoll asked.

Denham smiled. "You'll find out in time, Jack. Ann, since you're up, I'd like to make some screen tests of you as soon as the day warms up a little. Captain Englehorn's in the main cabin, all the way aft. Go see him and tell him I want him to show you where the costumes are stowed. They should fit you well enough, and we've got time for alterations if they don't, but pick one that pleases you and get into it. Think you know what kind of makeup is best for this kind of light, outdoor shots?"

"I think I can do it," Ann said, trying to hide her nervousness.

"Makeup kits are stowed with the costumes. Be sure to line your eyes a little more than you would for street makeup, but don't lay it on so heavy it's like a clown's getup. Go ahead, and I'll get the camera set up."

Ann set Ignatz down, and the monkey immediately made a beeline for a forward companionway. He scrambled up, opened the latch, and vanished, going the same way old Lumpy had gone.

Ann headed back, but as she got out of sight of Denham and Driscoll, she paused. She had heard Driscoll's sharp question: "Do you think she belongs here?"

"What's the matter with her?" Denham asked.

"Nothing. She seems like a fine girl, not the kind you'd find on a trip like this."

"She is a fine girl, Jack. I'd swear to it."

"But I wonder if any girl should be on board, heading for wherever you're taking us."

Ann heard Denham chuckle. "Let me worry about the danger, Jack. Right now you can help me set up my camera."

Before they could step around the corner, Ann ducked through the companionway. At the end of the corridor, she knocked softly at the main cabin door, and Captain Englehorn opened it. His lined face broke into a welcoming smile, and he readily agreed to show Ann where the costumes and makeup were kept.

Denham had been right about the size. Ann wondered if he'd picked her out because she looked as if she would fit the costumes. One of them struck her, and she tried it on. It was primitive in a way, made of iridescent silken strips interwoven with some kind of rustling dried grass, surprisingly soft to the touch. It wouldn't be the most comfortable thing to wear, because it left her arms and legs bare, ivory white in contrast to the brown of the grass and the blue and green of the silk, but Ann thought she could bear the cool of the morning. The sun, after all, was warm on the deck.

Remembering her stints as an extra, she applied a foundation, and then accented her lips, brows, and eyes. She examined the result in a mirror, decided that if it wasn't right, Denham would tell her how to fix it, and then returned to the deck.

Denham, Driscoll, and Englehorn had just finished setting up the camera. "Here she is," Denham said. "Not too cold for that outfit, is it?"

"I can stand it for a few minutes," Ann said. The sun was bright, but the air still held the chill of winter.

"Costume looks good on her, doesn't it?" Denham said to Driscoll.

"Makes her look like some kind of island bride," Driscoll returned.

Denham looked peculiarly pleased. "Sure enough? You really think so?"

Driscoll nodded. "I've seen island weddings, though. She doesn't look like the bride of any ordinary man. Of any man who ever lived. More like a bride of—I don't know."

"It's the Beauty and the Beast costume," Denham said.

24

Ann was shivering. "It's the prettiest one of the lot," she said. "But not the warmest."

"Right!" Denham said. "Let's get the test reel shot so you can get back into something more suited for the weather. Okay, Ann, I just want you to stand over there, near the rail."

Ann took her place, but confessed, "I'm nervous, Mr. Denham. Suppose I don't photograph well enough to suit you?"

Denham was peering through the camera eyepiece. "No chance of that, sister. If I hadn't been sure, you wouldn't be aboard. All we have to worry about is finding the best angles to shoot you from. By the way, don't call me 'Mr. Denham.' Makes me feel like my own grandfather. Call me 'Carl.' That's good, but back half a step . . . right there."

With a hopeful smile, Ann moved in obedience to the director's gesturing hand. From behind Denham, Driscoll grinned at her and silently mimed applause, telling her that she had nothing to worry about—at least in his opinion. Half a dozen sailors, including Lumpy, with Ignatz perched on his shoulder, wandered over and stood at a little distance, watching the procedures. Ignatz hooted softly once or twice. Captain Englehorn himself stood behind them, his drooping mustache lifting briefly as he smiled at Ann. As Denham fussed with his camera, more and more seamen wandered up on deck, until Ann had an audience of more than a dozen.

"Profile shots," Denham ordered. "Let's get the right profile first. Stay where you are, Ann, but face aft. Little more. Hold it! All right, this is just silent stock, so don't worry about saying anything. When I say 'Action,' I want you to look ahead thoughtfully, sort of daydreaming, for a count of fifteen. Then you're going to notice someone coming toward you. Turn, face the camera, and look at me as if I'm someone you recognize. Look surprised—you didn't expect me, but you're happy to see me. Smile. Then you're listening to me talk, all right? Then a nice, friendly laugh. Got that?"

"I think so."

"Good. Ready, then. Camera . . . and action!"

Ann obeyed. It was easier than she had thought, not any different from what she had done at the Fort Lee studio. As far as she could tell, Denham was pleased. He kept muttering, "Good, good."

From behind him, from the loose gaggle of the crewmen, Ann heard other comments: "Don't make much sense to me."

Another sailor agreed: "Yeah, but ain't she a swell looker?"

Denham stopped the camera and beamed at Ann. "That was fine! Okay, relax for a minute. I'm going to try a filter."

Ann hugged herself and rubbed her arms to chase away the goose bumps. "Do you always do the photography yourself?"

Denham didn't look up as he expertly changed lenses. "Have been doing my own shooting ever since my second African picture. We were getting a grand shot of a charging rhino when my cameraman got scared and bolted. Ruined the shot. The fathead! I was right behind him with a rifle, but he didn't trust me to get the rhino before it got him. Anyway, I've never fooled with cameramen since then. Just do it myself. Ready. All right, Ann, stand over there. Little farther. Good, right there. Hold it a second while I focus."

Ann faced the camera, holding still. Behind Denham, she saw Driscoll and Englehorn talking to each other, in voices too low for her to hear, but she saw Driscoll's worried expression and saw how he stabbed a finger toward her twice. Englehorn, looking like a calm old grandfather, patiently replied to whatever the first mate was saying.

Denham said, "Ready. All right, when I start the camera, I'm going to give you a series of directions. Just follow them as best you can, and don't move from that spot. To begin with, I want you to be looking around. You're in a strange place, but it's interesting. You're just taking everything in, you're very calm, you don't expect to see anything. Then just follow my directions. Got that?"

"Yes, Mr.—Carl," Ann replied.

"Camera. Action. Good." Denham's voice tightened, his posture grew tense. "Look around. Strange landscape, but beautiful. Look up. You're calm, you're entranced by the beauty of it all. But there's something in the trees, high above your head—you can't make it out, you can't see it clearly yet, it's dark, it's strange. Look up, higher. Higher. There! Now you see it! You're amazed! You can't believe your senses! Your eyes open wider in shock! It's horrible, but you can't look away! You're fascinated! You can't move—you feel helpless! What is it? It's coming for you, Ann, and you can't get away! You're helpless, no escape! But you can try to scream, it's your one hope, but you can't, you're too terrified! Your throat is paralyzed! Try to scream, Ann! If you don't see it, maybe you can scream! Hide your eyes! Throw your arm across your eyes and scream, Ann! Scream for your life!"

Ann threw her arm over her face and physically shrank away from the imagined danger. And she screamed, her wild, high cry swept up on the soft wind. It was a wrenching scream of pure terror. Ann's heart pounded furiously, and she realized that Denham's direction had done its job. She wasn't simulating fear, but feeling it, so terror-stricken that the crew took a step toward her, and Ignatz shrieked in sympathy.

"And cut!" bellowed Denham. He jumped forward and grabbed Ann's bare arms. "Great, kid, great! Sister, you've got what it takes!" Then he shook his head ruefully. "But your arms are ice cold, Ann. That's a wrap for now. Get belowdecks and change into something more comfortable and warm."

Ann nodded, shivering as much from her own acting as from the cold. Behind Denham, Driscoll suddenly loomed, his face troubled. He tapped Denham's shoulder and said, "Denham, I want to talk to you about what you're planning for Ann. I want to know just what you're getting her into."

"Why, Jack," Denham said, letting go of Ann's arms and turning toward the first mate, "you know you can trust me. Isn't that right, Captain?"

Ann saw Englehorn's eyes flick toward her for a moment. Then the captain said flatly, "I guess so, Mr. Denham. I guess we have to trust you."

Ann left the three of them as she went toward the companionway. Just before returning to her cabin, she turned and looked back. The captain, the first mate, and the director were huddled together in what looked like a tense but subdued argument. She shivered again, wondering what waited at the end of the voyage, and then gratefully closed the door behind her.

4

THE PACIFIC AND INDIAN OCEANS
DECEMBER 15, 1932-MARCH 9, 1933

The *Wanderer*'s blunt, barnacled nose split the warm, oil-smooth water with a matter-of-fact precision. The old ship had made good time on her passage south, and then through the Panama Canal. The weather had changed from the chill of winter to tropical heat, and the *Wanderer* had taken it all in stride, cleaving the foamy crests of waves and leaving a straight, true wake behind her, pounding along to the steady throb of her engines at fourteen knots, twenty-four hours a day, seven days a week. Through it all, Denham was forever on deck, shooting footage of Ann, or else sitting with a sketch pad and pencil— he was an accomplished artist, and the pictures he drew envisioned Ann in a variety of forest and mountain settings, making her look exotic, strangely alluring.

Jack Driscoll had started the trip worried, and his concern increased with every sea mile the ship put behind her. On a sultry Wednesday morning, he met in the cabin with Captain Englehorn and Carl Denham. The agenda for the day was plotting the *Wanderer*'s course—up to a point. "Hawaii, and we resupply and take on more freshwater at Pearl Harbor," Denham was saying. "Then on to Japan, where we'll pick up more coal. Then south by southwest, past the Philippines and Borneo and Sumatra. Then I'll give you the final coordinates."

Englehorn nodded, puffing contentedly on his pipe. "Shore leave?"

"We'll be in port in Pearl Harbor for forty-eight hours, so the men can have a day or so ashore," Denham agreed. "Then in Japan it'll take a little longer. Seventy-two hours is what I'm planning. I want all men back aboard six hours before we're due to weigh anchor in both ports, though."

"I'll take care of it," Driscoll said. Then he gave Denham an irritated glance. "I've come close to asking this a dozen times, Denham, and I'm not going to hold it in any longer. You've got me going with all this mystery. What are you getting us into? What are you getting Ann into?"

Englehorn raised a hand. "Hold on, Jack. We've done all right on two trips with Denham. We'll come through all right on this one, too."

Driscoll choked back an angry response and instead said, "This time it's different. There's a woman on board."

"That's Denham's business," the captain replied coolly.

"That's right, Jack," Denham said, hitching himself up to sit on the edge of the chart table. "I'll promise you this, though: I'll look after Ann. She's a good kid, and I'll take care that she doesn't get hurt. As for the mystery, you and Captain Englehorn will be the first to know— but I mean to tell you the coordinates after all possibility of shore leave for the crew is over."

"Don't want them blabbing about our destination?" Driscoll asked. "Or are you afraid they'd desert if they knew?"

Denham's smile was maddening. "Maybe a little of both, Jack. Maybe a little of both."

And so the *Wanderer* rolled on, logging her constant 330 to 350 sea miles day after day. Hawaii passed as a gentle dream, and the bustling Japanese port as a chaotic tumult with orders shouted in a tongue utterly foreign to Ann Darrow, who took everything in as if captivated.

Then came the long, steady pull to the south and west. The weather grew torrid, and the crew wore barely enough clothes to be decent with a woman aboard. Ignatz flourished, shedding his little jacket and trousers. He had become devoted to Ann, much to old Lumpy's evident liking. Lumpy seemed to like hanging around Ann, too.

Ann confided to Driscoll that she wondered about the film they were to make. So far, Denham hadn't shown her a script or even spoken of one. Driscoll, who had changed his uniform to a white pongee shirt and white ducks, leaned on the rail and chuckled. "Don't let that bother you," he advised. "Denham shoots movies his way. So far, his pictures haven't had much in the way of story—travelogues, more like, showing the folks back home how wild animals live. But he'll shoot miles of film and put together a picture that'll knock the socks off an audience. He'll let you know what he expects when the time comes."

Time was one of the problems. Denham had picked up a crate of books and magazines in Pearl Harbor, all for Ann's amusement. She read steadily through them, sometimes in her cabin and more often on deck, where the sailors were always eager to spread a canvas awning or to bring her a refreshing drink of water. Ignatz sometimes picked up a book and mimicked her, crouching beside her and watching her and turning a page every time she did.

Still, the routine was almost the same, day after day. Sundays were varied by a simple religious service for those who wanted to attend, and they had made a little celebration for Christmas and again for New Year's. On the day when they crossed the equator, there was a kind of party. King Neptune, in the body of one of the biggest sailors, came aboard and ritually inducted the crewmen who had never crossed the line into the fraternity of real seamen—by shaving them with a blunt razor and dunking them into the ocean at the end of a stout line. He waived the dunking for Ann, though, and instead sprinkled her three times with seawater before declaring her an honorary shellback.

But aside from those times, boredom loomed large. Oddly, though, Ann never found herself really jaded. It was all too new, the changing seas, the variable skies, the strange new constellations south of the equator—not to mention the mystery of their destination.

The ship left the Pacific and entered the Indian Ocean, and at their closest approach to land, a few islands lay dim on the far horizon. Ann came on deck one afternoon dressed in a white linen sun hat, a light linen dress, and canvas deck shoes, all of them bought by Denham during the layover in Hawaii. She still felt the heat, and she knew her pale complexion had become ruddy with tan over the past weeks.

Lumpy lay in his usual sunny corner, stripped to the waist. Ignatz sprang up at once and leaped into Ann's arms. She hoisted him to her shoulder effortlessly, his weight now familiar. "Hello, Lumpy," Ann said.

"Nice day, Miz Darrow," Lumpy returned. "Hot, though."

Jack Driscoll walked aft and said, "How about me, Ann?"

"Hello, Jack," Ann replied with a smile.

"Where have you been for so long?"

"Trying on some more costumes for Mr. Denham," she said. "And he says I look very nice in them, too."

"Why not give me a chance to see you in them?"

"You've had chances galore! All the times Mr. Denham has had me here on deck shooting test footage."

"All the times!" Driscoll said with a snort. "Maybe once or twice."

"Dozens of times!" Ann protested with a laugh. "He says it's very important for him to discover which side of my face photographs the best."

Driscoll tilted his head, giving her face a inspection. "I don't see anything wrong with either side."

"You're not a director. I imagine Mr. Driscoll sees dozens of terrible faults."

"Well, both sides look good to me." Driscoll reached out a hand to touch her cheek, but on her shoulder, Ignatz chattered and angrily flapped his front paw at Driscoll's finger. "What do I know?" Driscoll said, lowering his hand. "I'm not a monkey."

"Or a director, either," Ann said.

Driscoll leaned moodily on the rail. "If I were, you wouldn't be here."

His gruffness puzzled Ann. "That's a nice thing to say."

Driscoll looked away, then back at her. "You know what I mean,

Ann. It's all right having you on the ship. I mean it's fine. But what are you here for? What kind of crazy show is Denham planning to put you through when we get to wherever we're going?"

Ann touched his arm. "You told me he was a good director and that I could trust him."

"Sure, you can trust him in that way," Driscoll growled. "He's a good enough guy, married, got a kid and all. And he's aces at shooting footage of wild animals. But he's never used an actress before. I don't know what he plans to do with you when he shoots his movie. Might use you as bait or something, for all I know."

"I can't believe he'd put me in real danger," Ann said.

"*He* doesn't think of it as danger," Driscoll snapped. "Lions and tigers are just good theater to him. Maybe if he'd tell me more about where we're going—I don't know. I don't like this voyage, and that's that."

Ann stood close to him. Softly, she said, "Jack, I don't care what Carl's planning. I don't even care that he's keeping our destination a secret. It doesn't matter where we go, or what happens when we get there. I've had this." She waved her hand, taking in the ship, everything visible from the *Wanderer*'s stern to her bow. "I was down and out, and he held out a hand to help me. No matter what happens from now on, I've had the best time of my life aboard this old ship."

Driscoll tentatively reached for her hand and gave it a gentle squeeze. "Do you really mean that, Ann?"

"Of course I do." Driscoll leaned closer, and Ann averted her face. "I—I mean, well, everyone's been so nice. Lumpy and you, and Mr. Denham, and the skipper. Captain Englehorn's a sweet old lamb."

From the deck, Lumpy gurgled in laughter, and Ignatz clambered down from Ann's shoulder to join him, peering anxiously into his owner's face, making Ann chuckle.

"Lumpy's right," Driscoll said with a grin. "Better not let the skipper hear you calling him a lamb. Come on."

He led her farther along the railing, away from Lumpy and Ignatz. She rested her arms on the sun-warmed rail and looked down into the tropical sea, flashing with pulsating jellyfish, each with a miniature upright sail. "There," she said, pointing. "I've never seen anything like that before. Not one of them bigger than my fist, but they all sail along in the middle of the ocean as if they owned it. What are they?"

"I'm not a biologist," Driscoll said. "Seamen call them sea asters, though."

They stood for a time in companionable silence. Ann reflected on what she had learned about Jack Driscoll. He was reticent in her presence, and yet he had really told her a lot in the weeks since they had left

34

New York. He had confessed that at the age of eighteen, he had run away to sea to escape a terrible fate: college. "My mother wanted me to be a lawyer or a doctor," he had said. "I had other ideas." Ann had learned that his mother had since forgiven him, that his father had died when Jack was in his early teens, and that Driscoll had worked his way up from being a common sailor before the mast to being an officer in the merchant marine, with papers. He had mentioned working with Captain Englehorn since back before the Wall Street crash, and he had even talked about the two voyages Carl Denham had taken aboard the *Wanderer,* to East Africa and to India. Ann had the feeling that Driscoll had faced considerable danger on those trips, but Jack didn't say much about that.

For her part, Ann had told Driscoll about her own life, her parents' dying within weeks of each other during an influenza epidemic, her attempts to find work, her failure, and about the fateful night when, tempted, she had reached for an apple and instead grasped this adventure. She had told Driscoll of her hard times in New York, of her constant hunger and fear.

Now she reflected on that. "Whatever happens from now on, I was lucky that night when Carl found me. I want you to remember that, Jack. I'll always be grateful to Carl Denham."

"Speaking of Carl Denham, may he cut in?" Ann jumped at the unexpected voice. She and Driscoll turned to see the director standing a few feet away, hands in pockets, rocking to the motion of the ship.

"What is it now?" Driscoll grumbled. "More tests?"

"Nope, nothing like that," Denham said. "But I did want to ask Ann for a favor. It's the Beauty and the Beast costume, Ann. I noticed the last time we used it that it's ripped under the left arm. Since we don't have a wardrobe department, except me, and since I'm all thumbs with a needle, I wonder if you could mend it? It's my favorite costume piece on you, and I want it ready when we need it."

"I thought I heard it tear when I was putting it on last time," Ann said. "I'll repair it right away."

Denham gave her an apologetic smile. "I wouldn't ordinarily ask an actress to do something like that—"

Ann tossed her head back and laughed. "I haven't become temperamental yet! I'll see you later, Jack."

Driscoll watched her walk away, feeling again a wave of irritation. Denham took out his cigarette case and offered one to Jack, but he shook his head and put his hands in his pockets. He watched the director light a cigarette, then said doggedly, "Mr. Denham, I'm going to butt into your business."

Denham exhaled a cloud of smoke and looked at him with interest. "What's on your mind, Jack?"

"I want to know when we find out where we're going."

"Pretty soon now."

Driscoll grunted. "You said once we were clear of Japan—"

"Pretty soon, I said," Denham told him. "Calm down, Jack. I've never steered you wrong yet."

With an effort, Driscoll swallowed his annoyance. "Will you at least tell me what happens when we get there?"

Denham squinted against the smoke. "I'm not a fortune-teller, Jack."

Driscoll swore. "You must have some idea of what you're after!"

With a flick of his fingers, Denham snapped his half-smoked cigarette over the rail. "Are you nervous? Going soft on me, Jack?"

"You know I'm not."

"Then why all the fuss?"

Driscoll forced himself to take a deep breath. "I'm not worried about my own skin. It's Ann."

Denham leaned on the rail. "Thought that was it. You're not going soft on me, but on her. Better cut that out, Jack. I've got enough on my hands without having to bother about a love affair between my star and one of the crew."

Driscoll felt his face grow hot. "Love affair? What are you talking about? I'm just—just—"

Denham turned around and gazed thoughtfully up at the radio antenna. "Never fails. Some big, hard-boiled guy meets up with a pretty face, gets to know her for a little bit, and bingo! He cracks up and melts."

"Who's cracking up?" Driscoll demanded. "Look, I've never run out on you, have I?"

"No," Denham said with a chuckle. "No, you haven't. You're a tough guy, Jack, and a good guy. But if Beauty gets under your skin—" He laughed again. "Say, I'm almost making that my theme song."

Driscoll stared at the older man in baffled irritation. "Look, I don't know what the blazes you're talking about."

"Beauty and the Beast, see? It's the idea I'll build this picture on. The Beast is a tough guy, see, tougher than you, or me, or anybody in the world. He could lick an army. But when Beauty comes along, she gets him. He sees her, goes soft, forgets his own code. And once he does that, he's easy pickings. The little guys that were afraid of him can knock him off. That's going to be the heart of my movie, Jack. Think about it."

Before Jack could reply, a young sailor hurried up. "Mr. Driscoll, Mr. Denham, the skipper wants you on the bridge. He wanted me to tell Mr. Denham that we've reached the position he marked on the chart."

"Right, Jimmy," Driscoll growled. "Come on, then. I want to hear what you've got to say now."

"For the love of Mike, that's good timing," Denham said as they walked toward the bridge. "You wanted to know, and now I'm ready to spill it."

They stepped onto the bridge. The helmsman glanced over at them, but Captain Englehorn stood leaning on a chart table and beckoned them over. He tapped a blunt finger on the chart. "Here you are,

Denham. Our noon position was two south, ninety east. This is where you wanted to go. Now maybe you can tell us the rest of it."

Denham flattened the chart with both hands and stooped close to it. "Way west of Sumatra," he murmured. "That's right. Way west of Sumatra."

"Way out of any waters I know," Englehorn put in. "I know the East Indies like the back of my own hand, but I was never around this place before."

Driscoll couldn't contain his impatience. "You said you were ready to spill it, so go ahead. Where do we go from here?"

Denham straightened up. "South by southwest."

Englehorn glanced quickly at Driscoll, then back to Denham. "South by—? Why? It's empty ocean for thousands of miles. How far do you propose to go? How are we supposed to take on more food and water? What about coal? It goes fast when we keep a constant fourteen knots on the old ship."

Denham grinned. "Ease off, Skipper. We're not going much farther. Not exactly around the corner, but not thousands of miles, either." He laughed at Englehorn's expression, then took a wallet from his breast pocket, opened it, and from it took two worn, fragile-looking pieces of paper. He spread these carefully out on the chart table and rapped his knuckles on one of them. "This is the island we're looking for."

Captain Englehorn muttered numbers to himself. "That position is—Mr. Driscoll, bring the big chart."

Jack went to the chart locker and found the large-scale map that was needed. Denham picked up the two smaller pieces of paper to let him spread it out on the chart table. Driscoll pointed to the spot indicated by the latitude and longitude the captain had spoken aloud. "Nothing there, Denham. Nothing but ocean."

"You won't find this island on any chart," Denham said evenly. "Skipper, these two pieces of paper are all we have to go on. This picture and this statement of position. I got them from the captain of a Norwegian bark."

"He must have sold you a bill of goods," Driscoll said. "There's nothing there."

"Listen!" Denham said, his eyes lighting up the way they did when he was coaching Ann through one of her screen tests. "More than thirty years ago, a canoe loaded with natives from this island and one African sailor was blown out to sea. When my Norwegian skipper picked them up, only one man was still alive, and he died before they reached port. But before he died, he gave the captain his map of the island and a pretty good idea of where it lies."

"Where did you come in?" Driscoll asked suspiciously.

"A little more than two years ago, in the fall of 1930 in Singapore," Denham shot back. "I'd known the Norwegian for years, even chartered his bark for one of my early silent films. I'd heard his yarn of having picked up the canoe full of men, and I'd offered to buy the papers six or seven times. For years he didn't want to sell, but the old man needed some quick cash that day in Singapore. I bought the position and the map from him at the price he asked."

"And did he believe the story of the island, the Norwegian?" asked Englehorn.

Denham threw up his hands. "Who cares if he did or didn't? I do! Here, look at the map and tell me if you think a picture as detailed as this could grow entirely out of the imagination!"

He carefully unfolded the second piece of paper, and in spite of his doubts, Driscoll felt impressed by what he saw. It was a highly detailed map indeed, looking more like a European production than an islander's impression. It showed an island surrounded by reefs, through which a tortuous passage had been indicated. On one side of the island a long peninsula curved out, and at the base of the peninsula a steep precipice was sketched. Denham traced this with his fingers.

"The Norwegian told me this cliff is hundreds of feet high. Once it levels off, jungle begins."

The map had been sketched with some degree of care, including clear indications of latitude and longitude, and a complex of soundings indicating water depth.

"Tricky to navigate," Englehorn muttered. "You say this comes from more than thirty years ago? We may have worse problems if any shoals have built up in that time."

"You can do it, Skipper," Denham said.

Englehorn did not reply, but his blunt finger reached down and tapped at the map. At one end of the island lay an extensive peninsula, and across the neck of it the mapmaker had drawn a thick, heavy line. "What's this?"

"It's supposed to be a wall. A barrier to keep something out," Denham said carefully.

"A wall," Englehorn echoed thoughtfully.

"And what a wall!" exclaimed Denham. "Built hundreds, thousands of years ago! So long ago that the natives of the island, the descendants of the builders, have slipped back into savagery. They've completely forgotten the ancient civilization they came from, the one that built the wall that protects them. But the wall's as strong today as it was ages ago. The natives can't build anything like it today, but they keep that wall in good repair. They need it."

Driscoll felt his breath tighten in his chest. "Need it for what?"

Denham wouldn't meet his gaze. "Because there's something on the other side, something they fear."

Englehorn absently took his pipe from his pocket and fingered it. "An enemy tribe, I suppose."

Denham looked sideways at the skipper, his brown eyes flashing. Then he pushed up from the table, paced away, and abruptly turned back again. "Did you, either of you, ever hear of . . . *Kong*?"

Driscoll shook his head, but Englehorn tapped his teeth with his pipe stem. "Kong? Why, yes. It's some kind of Malay superstition, isn't it? Some kind of god, or devil, or something?"

Denham leaned forward. "Something, all right. Neither man nor beast. Something monstrous. All powerful. Not a spirit, something alive. Whatever Kong is, it holds that island in the grip of a deadly fear. It's the same fear that drove the natives' ancestors to build that huge wall."

Englehorn didn't respond. Driscoll gazed from the map to Denham, then back again, shaking his head. "Pretty tall story."

"It's not a story," Denham insisted. "I tell you, there's something on that island. Something that no white man has ever seen. You might call it a legend, but every legend has a foundation of truth, and that's what I'm after."

"Kong," Englehorn repeated softly. "Whatever Kong is, you're going to photograph it."

"Whatever is there. You bet I'll photograph it!"

Driscoll leaned back from the table and crossed his arms. "Suppose," he asked drily, "that it doesn't want its picture taken?"

Denham threw his head back and laughed. "Suppose it doesn't? Why do you think I brought that big crate of gas bombs?"

He walked forward and stood gazing ahead, to the southwest. Englehorn and Driscoll joined him, and Driscoll could not help staring, too. Part of him doubted the tale of the map and the mysterious island, but skeptical as he was, anxious about Ann as he was, he felt rising within him a reckless excitement. Englehorn turned back to the table, made a mark on it with a pencil at the supposed position of the island.

Driscoll turned to watch. The old man was a crack navigator. He clenched the empty pipe in his teeth and hummed to himself as he picked up a pair of dividers and calmly began to lay in the final leg of the voyage, the leg that might—just might, Driscoll thought—lead to an unknown and mysterious island. To *Kong*.

5

SOMEWHERE IN THE INDIAN OCEAN

MARCH 11, 1933

"Don't look down, now."

"I won't," Ann gasped, clinging to the rungs with desperate strength. Why had she asked Jack to take her up here? She swallowed hard and took another step up, and another.

Above her, Driscoll pushed up the floor plate of the crow's nest and clambered through. A moment later he bent back down, extending an arm. "That's a girl. Come on. Not much farther now. Don't give up on me."

"Who's giving up?" Ann demanded. She pulled herself up another two rungs, and then his brown hand closed over her slender wrist firmly, deliberately. He raised her up as if she weighed no more than a bag of potatoes, and then he kicked the trapdoor closed and set her down.

Ann gasped as she swayed to the roll of the *Wanderer*. The peeling, sunbaked deck lay far below, and all around the ship sparkled a glorious expanse of ocean. Ann pushed her golden hair back over her ears, enjoying the cooling breeze. Beside her, Driscoll wiped his damp forehead and beamed his approval. "Looks good. You ought to wear it back like that."

Ann didn't reply. She felt lost in the circle of intense blue ocean, with a clear blue sky overhead. The ship's wake was a white V etched onto the face of the sea, and its motion, noticeable on the deck, was far greater at this height. Ann didn't feel the least touch of seasickness, though. It was exhilarating, almost like flying. She turned in a complete circle and wound up facing forward, facing more or less south. The one interruption in the blank horizon lay in that direction, a low, fleecy cloud lying right on the surface, or so it seemed.

"This is wonderful," Ann said, reaching for Jack's hand. "Why didn't you bring me up here before? I feel like an explorer."

Jack squeezed her hand. "Well, let's see. If an explorer is someone who gets there first, I guess you are. You're the first woman ever to set foot up here."

"And we're going to an island where no one else has ever gone," Ann replied thoughtfully. "It's exciting. When should we get there?"

Jack studied her face solemnly, his expression unreadable. At last he gave her an indulgent smile. "If there really is any such place, we ought to find it by tomorrow at this time. We're certainly no more than twenty-four hours away from the position Denham gave the captain."

Ann looked down at the deck. "Carl's really worked up about it. There he is, pacing back and forth again. I don't think he went to bed at all last night."

Jack slipped an arm around her waist. "Yeah, you're right. I guess I'm kind of worked up myself."

She leaned against him and glanced sideways at his suntanned face. "You? Why, you said you don't even believe there is an island!"

"I hope there isn't," Jack muttered.

Ann laughed. "And you're the one who ran away from home to find a life of adventure! I'd be ashamed of myself, Jack!"

Driscoll took his arm from around her and grasped her shoulders. "Don't you know why I'm worked up? It's not because of any fool island, but because of you, Ann. Denham's blind to risks. What will he expect you to do?"

Ann gazed into his brown eyes and raised a hand to give his cheek a gentle touch. "After what he's done for me, I'll do whatever he says. You're sweet to worry, Jack, but you know you wouldn't really want me to do anything else."

Driscoll shook her very gently. "Yes I would, Ann. There's a limit. Denham's a great guy, but he doesn't think of safety when there's a picture at stake. He doesn't care what happens, who gets hurt, as long

43

as he gets the shot he's after. No, don't interrupt me. I know what you're going to say—that he'd never ask us to do what he wouldn't do, and that's true, and that's okay as far as men are concerned. But with you it's different."

Ann pulled away from him and turned to contemplate the low cloud on the distant horizon. "Well, you don't have to worry yet. And maybe there isn't any island, as you said."

"Maybe not, but—" Driscoll broke off, pounded his fist on the rail of the crow's nest. "Still, I—this is hard for me to—Ann, look at me, all right?"

Ann felt something in her shrink from the request. Instead of looking, she turned partly away from Jack, gazing down at the sea far below. "Jack, I—"

She felt his hand on her arm. "Look at me, Ann. You know why I'm worried. I love you."

Ann felt herself blushing, knew that her face was glowing pink. She bit her lip and could not speak for a moment.

Driscoll put his hands back on her shoulders and turned her around to face him. He pulled her into an embrace. "Ann, that's why I worry," he said in a stifled voice. "I'm scared for you, and I'm scared of you, and we don't have much time. I love you, Ann."

Ann felt tears stinging her eyes, but she lifted a smiling face to Driscoll, and when he leaned toward her, she returned his kiss. After a moment that seemed to go on forever, she forced herself to push away from him. "Oh, Jack."

"Don't say anything," Driscoll said. "Just—just remember what I said." He cleared his throat and pointed to the west, where the sun had sunk down to the horizon. "There's an albatross."

Ann felt a foolish smile on her face. "He's so beautiful," she whispered, but she hardly gave the magnificent wheeling bird a second glance. She leaned back against Jack, and he put his arms around her. "It's all so beautiful," she murmured, feeling warm and safe.

The western sky was ablaze with pink, with indigo, with saffron, peach, and yellow as the sun sank with the swiftness of the tropics. Against the brilliant display, the albatross swung in great arcs, enormous wings outstretched.

And to the south the low cloud had grown to a fog bank, gray to the east, lit with the splendor of the fading twilight on the west. "We'd better get back on deck before it's dark," Jack whispered into Ann's ear.

"Yes," she said. "Yes, Jack."

As they made the climb down, twilight flooded the world. Ahead of the ship, the rolling bank of fog grew, its drifting tendrils shadowed, purple, mysterious. The *Wanderer* never deviated from its course. The prow rose and fell with the waves, rose and fell, but aimed constantly at that distant fog, at whatever lurked at the heart of it.

★ 6 ★

All through the night, the fog thickened. Carl Denham stood, peering into the mist as though trying to dissipate it through sheer will. Doubt assailed him. He had dragged Captain Englehorn and his crew halfway around the world, all based on the Norwegian skipper's incredible map. Had it all been a hope and a prayer, nothing more than a vainglorious attempt to do the impossible? It would have been easy to give in to such misgivings as he stood for hours on end through the muggy night. He shook off his worries and stared into the darkness ahead.

"Don't lose your confidence now. Not when you've come this far," he encouraged himself.

The ship had slowed and was making little more than steerageway. When morning came, she was still creeping through a yellow-white blanket, miles in extent. No garment could keep out the penetrating dampness of the fog. Denham's light tropical clothing became heavy with it, soggy in every fold. Water dripped everywhere, from spars, stays, and walls, and gathering on the bare deck, it trickled in slow, uncertain rivulets.

Denham growled in exasperation. They were sailing blind. At a dozen feet, men and masts and ventilators became vaguely wavering wraiths. At greater distances they vanished behind the soft yellow-white silence. Denham climbed up to the bridge, where Englehorn, Driscoll, and Ann waited. From there he could see nothing of the sailor who heaved the lead in the bow, or of the other sailor who tried to pierce the thick veil from the high vantage point of the crow's nest.

He could hear both men, however. By some atmospheric trick their voices seemed to ring more loudly through the fog than they had ever come through in clear sunlight. "This triple-damned fog!" Denham grumbled in a choked voice. He could barely speak from excitement and frustration. He felt as tense as a man on a tightrope, and he turned away from his effort to stare through the enveloping cloud. "Are you sure of your position, Skipper?"

"As much as I can be," Englehorn murmured placidly as he lit his pipe. "Last night before this stuff closed in, I got a fine lunar sighting."

"Jack!" Ann whispered, and Denham saw she had a firm hold on Driscoll's hand. "If we don't get somewhere soon, I'll explode. I never was so excited in my life!"

"Don't bounce around so much," Driscoll warned her. "Next thing you know you'll be rolling off the ship. And don't keep doing things to get *me* excited. I'm fit to be tied right now. I'd like to throw my cap up into the air and yell blue blazes. But when I think of what we may be taking you into, I've got to keep my head."

Denham shook his head at the first mate's words, thinking, Beauty and the Beast. Aloud, he said, "Well, if your position is right, Skipper, we ought to be almost on top of the island."

"If we don't see it when this fog lifts," Englehorn returned, "we won't ever see it at all. I've sailed for the position you gave me. Either we're within sight of it, or else your Norwegian was having some fun with you and there's nothing but blue water in the place it should be."

The high, intent voice of the leadsman in the bow came sharply up to the bridge: "No bottom at thirty fathoms!"

"Of course," Denham said almost hopefully, "the Norwegian worked out the position from what the natives told him. The black man in the canoe, though, was a sailor, and he gave his best guess. Still, we could be off by a few miles, I suppose."

"If we sight an island, how will we know if it's the right one?" Ann asked.

"We'll know!" Denham rasped impatiently. "The mountain!" He leaned forward, trying to pierce the fog. "The mountain that looks like a skull."

"I'd forgotten," Ann apologized. "Of course. Skull Island, you said the Norwegian called the place."

"Bottom!" The high voice shot back from the bow, and at that triumphant cry they all stiffened. "Bottom, twenty fathoms! Sand and broken white shell!"

"I knew it!" Denham roared.

Englehorn puffed calmly on his pipe. "She's shallowing fast. Dead slow, Mr. Driscoll. Tell 'em!"

Driscoll tore into the wheelhouse and spoke down the engine-room tube. Bells jangled below in reply, and the *Wanderer* dropped off to a speed that was scarcely more than drifting.

"Look!" Ann cried. "Isn't the fog thinner?"

"Sixteen!" came the voice from the bow. "Sixteen fathoms!"

"What does she draw, Skipper?" Denham demanded.

"Six!" For the first time Englehorn lost his customary complacency. He was like Denham now, staring intently, listening even more intently.

"Listen!" Ann whispered.

"What do you hear?" Denham whispered back.

Ann shook her head and with the other three continued to listen. Suddenly, the young, nervous voice of Jimmy dropped down from the crow's nest: "Breakers!"

"Where away?" Driscoll shouted.

"Dead ahead! Not far off, either!"

Driscoll leaped for the wheelhouse and the engine-room tube again. His order came out to the others sharp and clear, and its dying note was followed by the jangle of the engine room's bells and the roll and thunder of the *Wanderer*'s reversing engines.

"Ten fathoms!" called the man in the bow.

"Drop anchor!" Englehorn shouted urgently.

Up forward dim wraiths leaped into action. A chain clanked and rattled through a hawse pipe. An anchor splashed. More bells jangled below. The *Wanderer* suddenly lay motionless and still. Everyone listened.

Driscoll frowned at the muffled sound he heard through the fog. Rhythmic, yes, but with none of the rush and growl of waves crashing into a shoreline. "That's not breakers," he declared roundly.

"No, it isn't. It's the sound of drums," Englehorn murmured, placid once more.

The fog, which had been thinning imperceptibly, tore itself to ribbons on a rising breeze while they listened. Before the edge of a growing wind, it parted and rolled away as though it were a curtain. The blue sea lay exposed under a faintly veiled sun. And a little way off, hardly more than a quarter of a mile, lay a vast wooded island dominated by an eerie skull-like dome. The grisly, gigantic face leered down at them, and Denham had the sensation of slowly waking from a troubled dream. The island dominated by the skull seemed to reach out toward the ship with a long brush-covered finger of sand and rocks.

"We've done it! Skull Mountain!" Denham flung out a victorious arm. "Do you see it? And look at the Wall! The Wall! The Wall!" He struck Englehorn's back with a mighty blow. "See it for yourself, you old sea dog. Do you believe me now?" Just short of hysteria, he shouted to the men at the bow, "Get out the boats!"

Beside him, Ann Darrow stared openmouthed at the green canopy of jungle, the bare gray slope of the mountain. "Jack!" she cried, "did you ever see anything like it? Isn't it wonderful?"

Denham turned to hear his reply, and saw the excitement drain out of Driscoll's face as he looked down at her. Driscoll's mouth tightened somberly. He strode forward to direct the lowering of the boats and the storing of the equipment.

Carl Denham's mind roiled with a thousand details. He hadn't come all this way to miss the opportunity. He had made a dozen pictures before, but none like this one. This one would have it all. "Come with me," he said, grabbing Ann's arm. They half climbed, half slid down the ladder from the bridge to the deck and rushed forward to where the crew was lowering the boats. Denham let go of Ann's arm and laughed. "Man, I can't wait to set foot on that beach!"

Ann gave him a sharp look. "I'm going ashore with you, aren't I?"

Denham laughed. "Are you kidding? Of course! Why do you think I brought you?"

Ann's excitement rang in her voice: "Thank you, Carl!"

Driscoll must have overheard, for he turned away from his work and scowled at Denham. "Should she quit the ship before we find out what's going on and what we're likely to run into?"

Nothing could dampen Denham's mood. With a cheerful shake of his head, he replied, "Look here, Jack, who's running this show? I've learned by bitter experience to keep my cast and my cameras all together and right with me. How do I know when I'll want 'em?"

"Listen, Mr. Denham." Jack took Denham's shoulder and pulled him a few feet away from Ann. Then he lowered his voice: "It's crazy to risk—"

Denham shrugged him off. "It's all right, Jack. Get back to work. Okay, if you're really worried, deal out the rifles and ammunition. See that the men take a dozen of the gas bombs. Oh, and pick me a couple of huskies to carry my picture stuff."

Driscoll shrugged and shot a frown in Ann's direction as he turned to his sailors. Denham shook his head in amiable exasperation and winked at Ann. "I'll have somebody get the costume box up and into one of the boats," he said. "If we're lucky we may get a swell shot right away. Get into the khakis and helmet, Ann. Just in case. And get some makeup on." He hurried back toward the bridge, and behind him, Ann went below.

Captain Englehorn stood sweeping the island with powerful 15×60 binoculars. He had skippered dozens of voyages and knew exactly what to do, what details to oversee. But this one—his eyes scavenged for every detail—this one he felt was different. In the surrounding excitement and clamor, his instinctive composure hid an unaccustomed inner tension.

Englehorn nearly started when Denham, right at his elbow, demanded, "See anything, Skipper?"

The captain made his voice calm as he replied, "Nothing but a few huts at the edge of the brush on the peninsula."

Denham nodded. "I can make 'em out from here. I took a look from the bow and I think there are more and bigger houses back beyond the thicker brush."

Englehorn lowered his binoculars. "Strange, though. This is the first native island I've called on that the whole tribe didn't come down to the beach for a look-see."

Denham braced his hands and leaned on the rail. "The tribe is somewhere close by, though. Hear those drums?"

"Some ceremony, maybe," Englehorn said. A deep, soft clamor rolled across the bay, rising and falling in a swift, importunate rhythm.

"Funny they haven't spotted us yet," Denham said.

That had been bothering Englehorn, too. He replied, "You're right, there. By now, every last native ought to be out and down at the water's edge."

"Maybe they *have* seen us. Drums could be a signal."

"You've heard native drums before, Mr. Denham," Englehorn responded. "You know those aren't signal beats. There's some kind of ritual going on inland. A big gathering, too, if you ask me."

When Denham didn't reply, Englehorn stood wondering just what kind of ceremony could be going on. He remembered Denham's mention of Kong, the god of the island. Though he wasn't a superstitious man, Englehorn couldn't help wondering if the islanders worshiped something real, something physical, under that strange name. But he wouldn't be able to learn the truth standing on the bridge. He scanned the deck for Driscoll. "We'll know soon enough," he said, as if to himself.

"Soon enough," agreed Denham.

Driscoll stood by the davits and supervised as the crew lowered arms into the boats. He glanced up as Captain Englehorn approached from the bridge. "Mr. Driscoll."

"Aye, Skipper."

"Where's the bo'sun?"

Driscoll glanced forward and cupped his hand beside his mouth. "Murphy! Over here!"

The petty officer, a thick, heavy seaman, hurried over. "Yes, sir?"

"Bo'sun, I want you to stay aboard with fourteen men," Englehorn told Murphy. He turned to Driscoll. "You choose the fourteen. All the others will go ashore with us."

Driscoll tried not to show his surprise. The captain's plan would put most of the crew—a small army, with the guns they were taking—on shore. But he nodded soberly and went about the selection. He chose Lumpy first of all, to that veteran adventurer's audible chagrin.

Denham had followed Englehorn. He pushed forward and asked, "Jack, who do you have in charge of my gas bombs?"

"You take 'em, Jimmy," Driscoll ordered.

The young sailor, Jimmy, stooped over the box, hefted it experimentally, looked slightly surprised at the weight of it, and then bore his burden over to the last boat.

"Of course, you're coming, Skipper?" Denham asked.

"No sense in breaking my streak now," Englehorn said with a nod. "Never missed looking over a native island yet, once I caught up with it."

"You're likely to be a big help. You'll probably have to do the talking. In this part of the world, odds are against my having picked up their lingo."

Driscoll didn't like any part of this. To Murphy, he called, "Arm your men, Bo'sun, and keep a sharp lookout. All right, gentlemen, the boats are ready."

Englehorn and Denham climbed down into the first one. Englehorn gave an order, and the crew pushed off. Driscoll motioned the second boat to wait where it swung on its davits. Ann was hurrying across the deck. He helped her in silently, then directed that the boat be lowered. While it settled into the water, he took a last look around the deck.

"Listen for any sign of trouble," he said to the boatswain. "And it wouldn't hurt to do some figuring on the range from here to the island." Without waiting for a response, he swung over the side and joined Ann.

"This is the first time I've ever seen the whole crew together," Ann told him as he dropped into the boat. "I hadn't realized there were so many."

"Twenty men in each boat," Driscoll said. He added gloomily, "We may need 'em."

"But if we don't frighten the islanders, surely they'll be friendly."

"Maybe," Driscoll said shortly. "I don't know, though. Those drums mean some kind of ceremony. I wish I knew what kind."

Ann smiled. "Maybe it's a wedding. Or maybe they're announcing some pretty girl's engagement."

Driscoll suppressed an exasperated smile as he looked at her. She was enough to enthrall any man. She carried the pith helmet in her lap, and her golden hair shone free in the sun and blew about her flushed, excited face. The rhythmic sound of the oars slicing through the pale green water flowed at a steady, calm pace. Everything about Ann struck Driscoll as graceful, like the weightless birds that floated just yards above and behind her head. Suddenly the drums grew louder, and with every tug at the boat's oars, the rhythm grew more distinct and ominous. Then gulls sheered off with menacing shrieks. Driscoll's momentary elation left him. He could not help looking over his shoulder at the island, bobbing in the water as they neared it. No, Driscoll thought. The boat was bobbing, not the island. Bobbing like bait.

As his boat approached the shoreline of the peninsula, Englehorn eyed his surroundings like a wizened owl. He was on the lookout for any clue as to what to expect, details to give him a sense of the island culture. Next to him, Denham held open a map he had painstakingly redrawn from the fragile original, scanning the sketched sandbars and small islets and verifying their position against the real items.

Englehorn needed only a glance to see they were in the channel leading right up to a curved beach on the peninsula. He had sailed over the Indian and Pacific oceans and knew firsthand that scattered remote islands offered more danger than anything imaginable in the civilized world. Once he had landed on Komodo Island, where he lost two of his crewmen to the giant lizards that lived there. Lizards with lethal bites, creatures appropriately referred to as dragons.

Still, up until now he had never really believed Denham's map and his story of the Wall. But seeing was believing, and right in front of him, big as life, reared the great structure. What kind of monster had it been built to keep out? Could *all* of Denham's outlandish story be true? Was there really a Kong, some kind of beast-god? Englehorn settled back, studying the land ahead, trying to glean any detail that might give his party a better chance of survival.

Denham was daredevil enough to risk anything, but Englehorn had known that going out and had signed on in spite of it because Denham was also one of the most resourceful and bravest men alive, and he paid well, too. Very well. And though Englehorn would never admit as much, he felt something within himself that was larger than his comparatively slight frame, something that craved the unknown. Without ever voicing the thought, Englehorn knew that his own reserve nicely balanced Denham's recklessness. They made a good team, and both knew it.

The boat's bow slushed into the beach, and Englehorn rose to leap over the side and help run it up. He consoled himself that this would likely be his last voyage with Denham, but he doubted it. If Denham asked, he would be ready.

★ ★ ★

Denham jumped out of the boat and onto the beach in an instant. He took equipment from the men clambering ashore and within seconds he had mounted his camera on its tripod. "Come on, men." He swung the weight of the camera up onto his shoulder and led the way.

The sights and smells of the village permeated his senses and heightened his awareness: smoldering cooking fires, the scent of broiling fish, the sunstruck beach leading up to a scatter of bamboo huts. This was what he lived for. Every nerve in his being was on fire. The island was real, and he was standing on it! He now believed Kong, whatever he was, was just as real. At the top of the first rise, he held up his hand, and the first party waited until the second boat had grounded. When Denham saw Jimmy climb out, hoisting the crate of bombs, he nodded and beckoned. With the bombs, Denham thought, we're ready for anything.

When Driscoll's crew sprinted up the hill, Denham immediately put them to work. He burdened one sailor with the mounted camera, another with a case of film, and a third with the box of costumes. Meanwhile Englehorn was dividing cases of trade goods among the others. Jimmy grimaced as he shouldered the heavy container which held the gas bombs.

"You stick close," Denham directed Jimmy. "And watch your step. There's enough trichloride in that case to put a herd of hippos to sleep."

"Are we going to see any hippos?" Jimmy asked.

Denham grinned. "Something a lot more exciting, I hope. Where's Driscoll?"

Driscoll came trotting over, followed by Ann. She wore khaki trousers and a short-sleeved tan blouse, and carried her pith helmet—her explorer's costume.

Englehorn, standing close to Denham, turned to his first mate. "Mr. Driscoll, I want an armed man to guard each boat."

"Already attended to, sir," replied Driscoll. Denham heard him add a quick aside: "Stay beside me, Ann."

Denham chuckled and said casually, "Jack, it might be a good idea for you to look after Ann until we find out how we stand."

Driscoll flushed, but he said, "That's fine. What next?"

"Let's see. Skipper, do you think it's safe to go on toward the village?"

Englehorn nodded. "Men, form up, double file. Shoulder your rifles and don't use them unless I give the order. Blast it, Denham, wait!"

Denham had set off, striding vigorously toward the scattered houses at the edge of the brush. He didn't look back, but knew he had automatically become the leader of the march. Just behind him paced the men bearing camera and films, then Jimmy, whose pained face had convinced another crewman to help him with the gas bombs. Next came Englehorn, then Driscoll and Ann.

As the party climbed up the slope from the waterline and achieved some elevation, the Wall began to tower above them, although it still lay far off. Denham realized how enormous the structure really was. The Norwegian skipper's crude sketch had poorly estimated the mighty barrier which ran the full breadth of the peninsula. Off to the sides, trees closed in to hide its base. Giant vines slithered up its sides as if to form some cryptic map of the dawn of time. To Denham, the Wall seemed a great rooted thing, monolithic, eternal—*alive*—the way an ancient, gnarled, apparently dead tree can still manage green leaves on an occasional branch. The vastness of the mighty structure was not dwarfed even by the purple loom of the overhanging precipice. It seemed to be part of the foundation of the island itself.

What it was made of Denham could not exactly tell. Heavy beams, perhaps even whole tree trunks, made up part of it, but soiled or blackened, possibly tarred to preserve them. These stood interspersed between gigantic blocks of something, blocks that made up the bulk of the Wall. "What are those dark masses?" Denham asked.

From behind, Englehorn said, "Maybe volcanic rock. Though the texture doesn't look right, somehow."

"Look at the top," Denham said, pointing up to a ragged row of triangular shapes. "What do you think, Skipper? It's almost Egyptian."

"Colossal, like the Pyramids," Englehorn agreed. He spoke as though in a dream.

Denham's own mind was far away for a moment, remembering the several times he had been around the world. He had viewed many of its wonders but could not quite place this eerie structure. Despite his first impression, it was not really Egyptian. It looked—and then his mind hit on a frightening realization—it looked *reptilian*! He felt an odd chill.

"Who could have built this?" Englehorn asked. "And why?"

Denham shaded his eyes. "As for why, my guess is that it must have been the outer defense of some sizable city on this peninsula, maybe one that even included the two smaller islands out in the bay. Isn't it enormous?"

"But who do you suppose could have built something like this?" Ann asked in an awed tone.

"I went up to Angkor once," Driscoll remarked in solemn admiration. "That's bigger than this. Nobody knows who built it, either."

Denham realized they had all been speaking in hushed tones, like worshipers in an ancient cathedral. His practiced eye saw a panoramic shot that would stun audiences. "What a chance!" he exulted. "What a picture!"

As the group continued along the line of the Wall toward the ceremony, Englehorn muttered, "Listen to that."

Denham nodded. The cadenced drumbeats steadily increased in volume and intensity. And Denham sensed that with them, the party's uneasiness was increasing, too.

They passed the first few straggling huts but saw no sign of an islander. None appeared even when the explorers reached the first outskirts of the village. Denham judged that the settlement would hold a tribe of at least several hundred, filling an area equal to six city blocks. The longhouses lay widely separated, each enclosed and partially masked by the thick brush. Narrow paths through the undergrowth provided the only connecting links. Each building stood by itself in a bare circle of beaten dusty earth smoothed by many feet. One extraordinary detail made the village different from any other that Denham had ever seen. All about lay a scatter of magnificent, broken columns of carved stone—or what looked like stone, anyway—and fragments of skillfully built walls. These ruins stood on every hand, but the majority lay forward, closer to the Wall.

"Part of the original defense during the building of the Great Wall?" Englehorn asked, gesturing at the fallen stones.

"Maybe," Denham replied. "But look at the houses. They're primitive compared to the carvings on the pillars, and they're nothing compared to the Wall. It doesn't add up!"

They pushed through the heart of the settlement, still seeing no one. But suddenly, between two steps, the roll of the drums softened. And now, above their low purring note, voices began to rise in a wildly swelling chant.

Denham swallowed. He must have been wrong in his estimate. The chant sounded as if it came from thousands, not hundreds, of throats. Next to him, Driscoll halted and flung up an arm in warning, and the others stopped dead in their tracks. Ann clutched Driscoll's sleeve, and the sailors looked at one another apprehensively. The sound of the chant came from somewhere close to the Wall. Denham motioned to Englehorn and pointed to an unusually large house ahead.

"If we can edge around that," he said, "I'll bet we'll see everything."

"Do you hear what they're saying?" Ann asked in a soft voice. "They're shouting, 'Kong! Kong!' "

"Denham!" Driscoll called. "Did you catch that? They're at some god ceremony."

"I can hear just as well as Ann," Denham said. "Come on." Moving forward cautiously, he beckoned Englehorn closer. "Think you can speak their lingo?"

"Can't catch any clear words yet." Englehorn paused for a moment, head bowed, listening. "It does, though, sound a bit like the talk of the Nias islanders."

"Let's hope it's close enough to let you talk to them," Denham said.

They reached the last house, and Denham halted, waving the rest of the column to close up and gather near. He himself advanced guardedly to the corner of the house. "Easy now!" he whispered. "Stay here until I see what's going on!"

He stepped around the corner, leaving the others behind. In a moment, he returned, barely containing his excitement. "Holy mackerel!" he whispered. "Englehorn! Driscoll! Get a look at this—but be quiet!" He led them to a vantage point, and all three of them stood transfixed.

The sun had sunk past zenith, and the Wall cast a deep shadow over everything before it. An explosive shout of massed voices rose above a murmurous, hypnotic rhythm. Cries of ecstasy, triumph, awe, and fear rolled thunderously over the gyrating populace.

Above the crowd loomed a towering central structure that dwarfed the Wall itself, which stretched off into the distance on either side. At the center of it all reared a portal, guarded by a pair of immense wooden gates. These in turn bore ornaments, the likenesses of two gigantic prehistoric skulls, their horned faces eerily illuminated by the flickering torches below. A colossal wooden beam ran through each of the obsidianlike masks and firmly barred the doors. One corner of the gate, at the lower right, bore a patch of fresher-looking wood. What force could have broken that mighty structure?

Denham could barely contain himself. He frantically motioned to the camera bearer, took over the machine and tripod, and slowly began to work it to a spot offering the clearest view. While he maneuvered, the drums rolled softly and the chants rose ever higher. Irresistibly drawn to the spectacle, everyone drifted slowly forward until suddenly, without realizing it, they were all standing in plain view of the entire population of the island. The air vibrated with the ongoing chant: "Kong! Kong! Kong!"

7

SKULL ISLAND

MARCH 12, 1933

Ann could only stare. In front of the party lay a double row of huts, with a few unusual artifacts or remnants of different kinds of structures scattered randomly among them. In the far distance, under the shadow of the looming Wall, Ann saw a great beaten square. The tremendous maw of an open gate frowned down on this. Up to the gate's sill rose a series of broad stone steps; and halfway up the steps, on a rude dais covered with skins, knelt a young native woman.

Ann saw at once that the young woman had a lithe and beautiful form. The torchlight gleamed on her bronze skin, which shone as if she had been anointed with oil. Woven strands of flowers, serving as a crown, girdle, and necklace, were her only apparel and increased her soft, frightened charm. On either side of the girl, some on the stairs and some in the square, the chanting natives swayed in ordered ranks.

Ann had an impression of great solemnity. The islanders had not yet noticed the intruders staring at them, for they focused all their attention on the kneeling girl. The leader of the chant seemed to be an ancient man, arrayed in a multitude of leathery skins, decked out with strange long feathers of orange, green, red, and yellow. He swayed as he chanted, his movements jerky, as though he were in the grip of a force more powerful than his own will. Smoldering torches billowed with strangely scented smoke. It was all hypnotic, and to Ann's eyes, every single one of the massed natives swayed spellbound by the old man's voice and movements.

Ann saw, still farther to one side, a strongly built, imposing man, magnificently costumed in furs, grass, and feathers, watching with a kingly detachment. Balancing him on the opposite side of the ceremony, an old woman leaned on a staff taller than herself. Her intense gaze burned on the old man who led the ceremony, but she did not sway, as the others did, and she seemed unaffected by the tide of sound. Ann felt a kind of pity for the woman, who looked like an outcast dressed in rags, though she had the bearing of one who had confidence in her own power.

The witch doctor—that was how Ann thought of the old man leading the ceremony—stood with his arms upraised and his head thrown back. The crowd moaned and chanted, mingling with their repeated cry of "Kong!" something that to Ann sounded like "Atu! Atu!"

Ann saw the old woman suddenly straighten, and she realized that she and the others from the ship had been spotted. Still, the woman made no effort to alert the other islanders. She stood apart, watching the newcomers and waiting.

Ann heard Driscoll quietly ask, "What do you make of this?"

"Oh, Lord," Denham whispered back. "I can only imagine. Look at that old guy in the feathered robe. If he only holds still for a moment until I can focus!" He began to crank his camera.

Driscoll glanced away from the director and motioned for Ann to move behind him. She stepped a little nearer, but stayed where she could see.

Moving close to the girl dressed in flowers, the old witch doctor began an oddly supplicating gyration. In slow, humble gestures, his weaving hands seemed to offer the maiden to a dozen huge and terrifying dancers, who leaped out of the chanting ranks. Broad hollowed furry skulls covered their heads, and rough black skins hid their bodies. Ann couldn't tell whether the fur was actual animal hide or whether it was made of fine strands of dried grass dyed a jet black.

"They look like gorillas," Driscoll muttered. "But there are no gorillas within a thousand miles of here. How did they get that idea?" As if noticing that Ann was still in the open, he moved to put himself more squarely between her and the natives. As though by common impulse, the *Wanderer*'s whole crew grew jostled more closely together, until Ann could hardly see at all. Holding on to Jack's shoulder, she stood on tiptoe to get a better view.

The native chorus dropped into softer and softer tones as the costumed apelike men advanced. The witch doctor moved back and looked toward the king. The old woman standing to the other side had disappeared into the surroundings, leaving the stage to the two men. The king stepped forward, but in that instant his expression changed as he looked beyond the crowd, toward the interlopers, toward Driscoll, Denham, and Ann. "Bado!" he shouted as he raised an arm to point. "Bado! Dama pati vego!"

The chanting, the dancing, all the sound, all the movement, froze to stony silence. Ann tightened her grip on Driscoll's shoulder as he half turned toward Englehorn and asked, "Ever hear that lingo before, Skipper?"

"It's familiar," Englehorn murmured. "That's the leader, the king, talking. I'm pretty sure he's telling the old witch doctor to stop the ceremony, to beware the strangers."

"Looks like we've been found out," Denham said, never looking away from the camera viewfinder.

The massed natives turned as one and stared at the newcomers. Ann had a sense that many of them were drugged, their faces and movements uncertain, glazed, nearly stunned. An errant breeze rolled the smoke from the smoldering torches over the party from the *Wanderer,* and Ann felt a moment's giddiness. Something in the smoke, she thought. Like one of Denham's gas bombs, but not a knockout chemical. Something soothing, hypnotic.

Cries of surprise and outrage brought her attention back. The islanders stared at them with wide, fearful eyes. As if by a silent direction, the women and children had begun to slip away. Many followed the path taken by the old woman who had been standing opposite the king.

Jimmy muttered, "I don't like the looks of this. We'd better beat it or we'll be up to our necks in trouble." He turned, but Ann saw Driscoll's steadying hand reach out to grip his arm.

"Good catch, Jack!" Denham called from his position at the head of the party. "Jimmy, they'll cut us down if we show fear. Nobody run! No use trying to hide now. Everybody stand fast, put up a bold front."

The king made an imperious gesture, and two tall warriors stepped to his side. Slowly, with evident caution but no real fear, he strode forward. Ann saw that the last of the women and children had vanished.

"Look out, Mr. Denham!" Jimmy yelped. "They've got spears—"

"Shut up, you fool!" Driscoll shot back.

"Hold on, everyone," Denham said again. "Skipper, you'll need to translate."

"Jack!" whispered Ann. "Does it mean trouble when the women and children go away?"

"Trouble for them—if they start anything," Driscoll replied, his voice firm and confident. If he was scared, he was hiding it well. Still, Ann clutched his arm more tightly than ever.

Some of the sailors shifted their rifles, their fingers slowly inching toward their triggers. Denham, as though he had eyes in the back of his head, rapped out a warning: "Steady, boys! There's nothing to get nervous about!"

"Hang on, Ann," Jack added. "The chief wants to see if we'll scare. It's all a game of bluff, and I'm betting on us."

Half a dozen paces in front of them the chief paused with his guard. Tall and stern-featured, he stared down at Denham. His broad, strong face glistened with sweat, the deep lines in the flesh accented with ceremonial paint. Above and behind him, the gaunt witch doctor glared at them. Ann had the impression that the older man, the witch doctor, felt more outraged than the king at their intrusion.

For long moments the strongly built chief stood surveying them. His eyes were as clear as glass, yet wide as saucers. His bizarre costume and his expression gave him the look of a terrifying apparition from a childhood fantasy. Still, no one could mistake his authority.

Denham had stopped his camera. He didn't flinch from the island chief's challenging gaze, but said from the corner of his mouth, "Skipper, this would be a good time for a friendly speech."

Englehorn took a step closer, but the king threw up an arresting hand. "Watu! Tame di? Tame di?"

"Ima te bala," Englehorn replied slowly. "Bala! Bala! Friends, Friends!"

"Imbali nega bala, reri tamano alala temo!" the king shouted scornfully. "Tasko! Tasko!"

"What's that about?" Denham asked.

Without looking at Denham, keeping an undisturbed expression on his face, Englehorn replied, "Hard to make out the accent, but I gather he wants no friends. He tells us to beat it!"

"Talk him out of it," Denham ordered. "Ask him what gives with the ceremony."

Ann peeked from behind Driscoll as Englehorn spoke in placid, conciliatory tones and gestured to the flower-clad girl.

"Tapi ani saba. Ani saba Kong!" pronounced the king, and from all the natives came a sighing, worshipful echo of "Saba Kong!"

Englehorn nodded gravely and muttered, "He says the girl is the bride of Kong."

"Kong!" Denham cried exultantly. "Didn't I tell you?"

Denham's use of the word *Kong* drew an instant burning glare from the king. He gave no signal obvious to Ann, but both of his tall guards raised their spears. A murmur ran through the throng. Ann heard hushed voices, sounding dismayed and fearful, repeating "Saba Kong" over and over. The witch doctor quietly said something that Ann could not catch, but his voice rose as he finished, "atu kana ito Kong!"

"He's warning that Kong will be angry," translated Englehorn. Ann could almost have guessed that, for even in the fearless eyes of the chief something flickered, something wary and apprehensive.

At that, the witch doctor suddenly leaped forward, his headdress shaking, his eyes darting fury at both the king and strangers. He cried, "Bar-Atu, te ama si vego! Dama si vego, Bar-Atu! Dama si vego. Punya. Punya bas!" His voice shook with anger—or with fear.

Englehorn took a step back. "We are violating the teachings of Bar-Atu, whatever or whoever that is. We've spoiled the ceremony. None of our kind are supposed to see it. I think we'd better fall back, but carefully."

"Let me try talking to him," Denham said. "What's the word for 'friend'?"

"Bala."

Denham immediately spread his hands and with a grinning, conciliatory step said, "Bala! Bala!" He pointed to himself and then to the king and witch doctor. "Bala! Bala!"

Though he put a smile on his face, Driscoll warned, "Denham, you can't trust these savages. Can't you tell they're drugged on something? The skipper's right. Let's get back on the ship." Ann saw that he made smooth gestures, as though complimenting the natives.

The king cast a cryptic glance in his direction, frowning, and beckoned his guards to stand close beside him. His face was unreadable, but he stared directly into Driscoll's eyes and in a deep voice cried, "Tasko!"

"He understood you," Ann whispered to Jack.

"Couldn't have," Driscoll returned, not looking at her. "How would these birds know any English? Watch it. Men, be ready to defend yourselves." He didn't raise his voice, but behind her Ann heard the clacks of rifle bolts.

She felt fear, but her excitement flooded over every other emotion. She took a step back, and at that moment the king's glance seized on her and her honey-colored hair. He raised his arm in a decisive gesture, and the warriors behind him lowered their spears. The king stared first at Ann, and then turned to the witch doctor as though asking for affirmation.

"M-Malem ma pakeno!" he stammered. "Sita!" He jerked his arm at the witch doctor. His voice took on a quality of hushed awe as he repeated, "Malem! Malem ma pakeno saba!"

The witch doctor hobbled closer, his eyes narrowing at first, then widening as he caught sight of Ann. The warriors on both sides stood enthralled, lowering their weapons until the points touched the ground.

"He's stood them down," Englehorn said. "It's a sign that he wants peace."

"Sabi ma pakeno sati," creaked the witch doctor.

"What now?" Denham asked.

Englehorn sounded nervous: "He said, 'Look at the woman of gold!'"

"It's her hair," Denham said. "Blondes are scarce around here."

Ann saw Driscoll tense. She knew he was not amused, and she touched his arm.

The king's voice rose ecstatically: "Kong! Malem ma pakeno! Kong wa bisa! Kow bisa perat pakeno sati saba Kong," and he turned to the witch doctor as though seeking agreement.

The old sorcerer nodded thoughtfully as Englehorn translated swiftly: "The woman of gold. Kong's gift. The golden one will be a bride for Kong."

"Good Lord!" Denham protested.

The king and the witch doctor advanced on Denham, and the former thrust out his hand in a regal command. "Dama!" he said. "Tebo malem na hi!"

Englehorn's translation followed like pistol cracks: "Stranger! Sell the woman to us!" Ann felt her skin crawl. She dared not speak, dared not ask Denham what their next move should be.

"Dia malem!" the king hurried on.

"Six women!" Englehorn said swiftly. "He will give you six for yours of gold."

Ann gasped and tried to smile. "He thinks a lot of me, doesn't he?"

Driscoll gave her a furious warning look that told her to keep silent. To Denham, Driscoll said, "You got Ann into this! Say the word and I'll put a slug between his eyes!"

"Steady, Jack!" Denham smiled briefly and with an unhurried gesture called up his two carriers.

"Tell him, as politely as you can," he said to Englehorn, "that we'd rather not swap. Tell him, I don't know, tell him our religion does not let us sell our women. It's a taboo."

Ann marveled at the way Englehorn put a solemn, almost apologetic note in his firm response to the king: "Tida! Nem! Malem ata rota na ni! Rota na ni, ka sala mekat. Pakeno malem take mana." To Denham, he muttered, "I've told him our woman is our luck, and we dare not part with her."

Against that refusal, polite though it had been, the witch doctor cried in fury. "Bar-Atu, watu!" he screamed. "Tam bisa pare Kong di wana ta!"

Englehorn took a long breath. "Bar-Atu's teaching tells them they cannot lose Kong's gift."

"That's enough for me," Denham growled. "Tell them again that we're friends, and that we have to leave. I'm taking Ann back to the ship."

"We'd better all slide out," Englehorn said. "Before that smart old witch doctor thinks to send out a war party to get between us and our boats."

Denham nodded. "Fine, but don't leave the old coot so mad, Skipper. Tell him we'll be back tomorrow to make friends and talk things over. We'll bring gifts for them."

"Dulu!" Englehorn promised the chief and the witch doctor gently.

"Dulu basa tika ano. Basa ti ki bala. Bala, bala. Dulu hi tego minah."
He motioned unobtrusively as he spoke, and the camera bearer picked
up the equipment and retreated. The others were slowly backtracking.

"En malem?" the chief insisted. "Malem me pakeno?"

"Dulu pala malem ma pakeno. Dulu basa tika," Englehorn said.

"Get going!" Denham ordered briskly to the crew. "Back away.
And keep smiling, Ann. Don't you realize the chief's just paid you a
whopping compliment? Six for one! Smile at Jack. And keep your chin
up!"

"Dula bala," Englehorn told the chief reassuringly. "Tomorrow,
friend."

The retreat gathered speed, cautiously. No one lagged behind, but
no one ran, either. They made an expeditious, smiling withdrawal. A
half dozen sailors, led by Driscoll, went first, with Ann in their center.
Next the main body moved, rifles held easily, not pointing at anyone,
but ready to fire if need be. Englehorn followed these, and Denham
came last of all.

Ann had to admire Denham's coolness. As a parting sign of friend-
ship he tossed the witch doctor a debonair salute. Then with the same
hand he cocked his hat over one eye, and as the hand dropped, coming
to rest on the butt of his holstered pistol, his lips puckered to whistle a
jaunty marching tune. While the native's eyes widened in surprise he
slipped briskly around the corner of the house and out of the tribe's
sight.

Following the narrow paths among houses, silent and seemingly un-
inhabited, the *Wanderer*'s party came to the edge of the village. Ahead
of them lay the almost treeless slope of land running down to the
beach and the boats.

"Don't tell me there wasn't nobody in them houses," Jimmy
snorted, shifting his box of bombs to the other shoulder. "I heard a
kid squeal once. What a smack his mama handed him. I heard that,
too."

Driscoll, with a half laugh of relief, let go of Ann's hand. He had held it all the way through the march. "Believe it or not," he said with a last backward glance, "nobody is following us. I call that a pleasant surprise."

Bringing up the rear, Denham and Englehorn strode to the crest of the rise.

"I hope," Ann said with a laugh, half at them and half at Driscoll, "that you all know me well enough to understand that I'm no Brunhild. I don't consider myself very warlike or even very brave, but just the same, I want to say that I wouldn't have missed that for the mint. Woman of gold—not a bad compliment at that." With a broad pretense of pride she began to fluff out the hair which had been so much admired.

Driscoll eyed her provocative mouth with an exasperation which did not conceal his admiration for her courage.

"Sister, you were cool as a snowdrift. You can be my leading lady in all the pictures I make from here on in," Denham promised.

Englehorn stood waving them all into the boats. He took his briar pipe from a pocket and clenched it between his teeth, though he did not load or light it. "Tomorrow we'll break out the trade goods. I think, Mr. Denham, a few presents might get us somewhere."

"To the king, you mean," Denham said.

"I think the witch doctor's the better bet," Englehorn told him. "He's the power behind the throne."

8

Launching the boats rasped everyone's nerves raw, though they all tried to look calm. Denham took the lead in that regard, acting purposefully, calmly, as though he didn't anticipate the slightest danger. Still, he and the others knew that spears might come whistling down if the natives had a change of heart and decided to attack. "Let's move it along," Englehorn said in a firm but quiet command.

Denham approved of the efficiency as the men stowed the boats and piled in. Four of the strongest sailors in each boat waited to run the craft out into the low waves of the lagoon before climbing in themselves. Immediately the sailors at the oars put their backs into their rowing. Denham settled back, sure that within seconds they would be beyond spear-cast and safe, at least for the time being.

"No one on the beach," Englehorn muttered. He called to the other boat: "Mr. Driscoll, do you see any sign of the natives?"

"Not a hint," Driscoll shouted back.

"So far, so good," Denham said, already thinking about what gifts he could offer the king and the witch doctor. As long as he didn't tell them what the camera was, he might just be safe. Natives tended to have superstitions against having their images captured.

Denham's musings carried him away from the creak and rattle of the oars in their iron oarlocks, away from the muffled splashing and sizzling of well-churned water. Suddenly Denham became aware that Englehorn had said something to him. "What's that, Skipper?"

"I said, I don't like the look of this island."

Denham turned in his place to look back at the beach and what lay beyond it. In the failing light, the cliffs had taken on a deep purple cast, and etched against it Denham saw the great Wall, leering at them through a misty veil. "Oh, I don't know," Denham said aloud. "Looks like a swell spot for a movie to me. Now all we have to do is figure out how we're going to convince the natives to let us shoot it."

From far behind them, atop the great Wall, an old woman stood at a huge triangular window, its ancient saurian-hide curtain barely parted. She leaned on a tall curved staff carved from bone. She watched as the strangers climbed into their boats, pushed off from shore, and rowed out to the larger craft riding at anchor. Twilight and darkness settled, and still she did not stir. She stood unmoving as night took the village, the Wall, and the great forests and mountains beyond the Wall. Only when she could no longer see even the silhouette of the ship did she move, and then she simply seemed to fade into the night herself.

By twilight, much to Denham's relief, the shore party had safely boarded the *Wanderer*, and as soon as the boats were stowed, he asked Driscoll and Englehorn to talk things over with him. They met in the skipper's cabin. "The men are uneasy," Englehorn said.

Denham grinned. "I kind of sensed that. They seemed glad enough when we got back to the ship."

"Because they knew we got lucky today," Driscoll said. "Now they've got time to think about what we got away from, about how badly we're outnumbered, and about what they saw."

"And heard," Englehorn put in. "Denham, I suppose it's not even worth asking you to give up the idea of filming here. Couldn't you shoot your movie somewhere else?"

"Not a chance," Denham shot back. "For the love of mike, Skipper, isn't your curiosity up? Me, I want to know about this Kong. Who is he? What was that witch doctor jabbering about?"

Denham caught Driscoll's quick glance at Englehorn, a look filled with concern. The mate cleared his throat and said, "Captain, I thought you said this Kong was some kind of myth."

Englehorn shrugged. "And I thought it was. You and I have run across superstitious natives before, Mr. Driscoll. I had no reason to think these Skull Islanders were any different."

Driscoll glared at Denham. "Yeah, but the others didn't keep their superstitions behind a Wall big enough to stand up against a herd of elephants."

A quiet, feminine voice said, "Bigger than that."

The three men turned in surprise. Ann Darrow had come silently in. "I think I ought to be in on this, too. Don't you, Mr. Denham?"

Denham grinned. "You bet, sister. Listen, I'm not going to make you do anything you're not willing to do. But if you're like me, you want to know what this Kong could be."

"Maybe that's their name for the king," Ann said tentatively. "The girl could be meant for him."

Denham nodded thoughtfully, but Englehorn broke in: "No. The king was part of the ceremony, but not the center of it. Besides, you saw how frightened that young woman was. She didn't flinch when the king came near, but she nearly passed out at the mention of Kong's name. It scared her half out of her senses."

"Maybe she was scared of those goons dressed up like gorillas," Driscoll growled. "They were enough to give anybody the heebie-jeebies."

"Men in masks," Denham said dismissively, putting deliberate scorn in his tone. "What's so scary about that?"

"Nothing, but I've got a hunch they were more than that," Driscoll said. "I figure they were acting as living idols. You might say they were the real bridegroom's representatives. Denham, did you look up on top of that Wall during the dance?"

"I was looking through the camera viewfinder," Denham said. "What about the Wall?"

"On the ledge above those huge doors hung a huge drum of some kind, sort of like a gong. A big guy stood beside it with a club. Just before he noticed us, I saw the king look up and raise his hand, as if he was about to give the fellow a sign."

"I think I follow you," Denham said.

Ann looked exasperated. "Well I don't! I'm completely in the dark. Sign to do what?"

"To strike the gong," Denham said. "And maybe that would tell the villagers it was time to give up their sacrifice. Maybe it might even call something from the interior of the island. Most of the island is safely beyond the Wall. What if the king had been about to send the girl out through the gate, alone? What if something was waiting in the forest to hear the drum and come for the girl? What if that something is so strong that they have to get the girl out quick, and then bar the gate again to protect their settlement?"

Ann blinked. "But that's crazy. What could be strong enough, big enough, to require a gate, a Wall, of that size?"

Driscoll put his arm around her waist. Denham began to pace the floor. "That's just it. Beyond the Wall, the wilderness, the jungle. Waiting there is Kong. The girl was a bride, a bride for their god, for Kong. And whatever he is, the natives are terrified of him."

Englehorn murmured, "In ancient China, the emperor built a great wall to keep out the barbarian hordes. Maybe Kong is a fierce tribe."

Denham shook his head. "No, I don't think so, Skipper. I've seen the Great Wall of China. It's longer than this one, but the island Wall is even taller and, from what I could see, broader. Even at the top, it's as wide as a highway. It wasn't built to keep out just a tribe of natives. And this Wall is not just a relic of the past. Those huge doors are obviously still used, and the Wall is kept in a state of repair." Denham paused, swept a hand through his hair. "All these mysteries—some higher culture built that Wall, and what happened to them? My guess is these people are all that's left of them."

73

Suddenly he stopped pacing and banged a fist on the table. "I'm going to get to the bottom of all this. My Norwegian captain didn't steer us wrong. All right, the island civilization has decayed into what we saw. All right, they worship something big, something real, something beyond the Wall. We're going to find it!"

Ann had started when Denham struck the table. "Find what?"

Denham's eyes danced with excitement. "Kong! You heard the chant—Kong, Kong, Kong!"

"Hold on, Denham," Englehorn said. "If you're right, if Kong is something real—well, that pretty little girl wouldn't have been the first of his brides, would she?"

Ann looked sick. "What do you mean?"

Driscoll broke in roughly: "He means that the girl was a sacrifice. When a tribe gives a human sacrifice, it usually does it regularly. Every time the moon is full, or something like that. Skipper, remember that New Guinea bunch? Ritual cannibalism, that was. This is even creepier."

"As it happens," Englehorn said drily, "the moon *is* full tonight."

"Tomorrow we find out what Kong is," Denham said. "Tomorrow we get through the gate, out beyond the Wall."

Driscoll glared at him. "Are you out of your mind? That Wall wasn't built to keep out a lion or a tiger. This Kong has to be something huge. A dozen men represented him, a dozen big mugs decked out like gorillas."

"I never heard of gorillas anywhere but in Africa," Driscoll objected.

"Whatever Kong is, he's not a gorilla," Denham said. "I'll lay you odds that he's big enough to use a gorilla as a medicine ball."

"What could be that big?" Ann asked. "I've never heard of anything that size, except maybe a dinosaur."

Denham grinned. "Holy mackerel! That would explain a lot of the yarn the Norwegian skipper told me. I think you hit it, Ann!"

Driscoll pulled Ann closer to him and exploded: "That's crazy!"

Englehorn shook an unbelieving head.

"Wait a minute. Think about it." Denham started to pace again. "Skull Island's not on any chart. Who knows how long it's been here? Maybe it's the last part of a prehistoric continent still above the sea. It's just the place to find a solitary surviving prehistoric freak."

"Don't get carried away, Denham," Driscoll said. "Nothing like that could happen."

Englehorn tapped his teeth with his pipe stem. "Maybe not, Mr. Driscoll. Maybe not. I've been to the Galápagos Islands off the Pacific coast of South America, and just what Mr. Denham suggests happened there, with a group of modern animals that were cut off from the rest of the world. There are giant tortoises there, and iguanas unlike anything else in the world. Still, that's a long way from a living dinosaur."

"And that Wall is a long way from an ordinary native temple!" Denham shot back. "We've got to find Kong, whatever it turns out to be. And if it's what I think, what a picture I'm going to bring back!"

Driscoll said, "And where does Ann figure into your plans now?"

Denham heard the undertone of anger. He forced himself to laugh. "Hey, Jack, let me run my own show. Remember what I said? I think you've gone soft, after all, and I guess Ann is a plenty good reason. But don't worry about her, and don't try to talk me out of my chance to make the kind of picture that will make us all rich men. It'd be nice to have enough money to—I don't know, settle down, get married, whatever you wanted, right?"

Driscoll flushed, but didn't speak.

"I'm not afraid," Ann put in.

With another laugh, Denham said, "That's a girl!" He tugged thoughtfully at his ear. "Jack has a point, though. Whatever is on the far side of the Wall, it's dangerous. And I'm not about to get you killed, Ann, or myself for that matter. Don't worry, Jack, I enjoy living just as much as you do!"

Englehorn grunted as if in agreement.

Looking at their doubtful faces, Denham said, "I'll tell you what: we'll sign off on everything for now. Let me think this out tonight. By tomorrow morning, I'll have our next step planned."

Englehorn crossed his arms. "In the meantime, Mr. Driscoll, post a half dozen guards with rifles. I don't trust that old witch doctor. If he sends a few canoes out to board us, we'll be ready to send them packing. Hear that?"

Denham tilted his head. "The drums have started again." He felt strangely unsettled. The cadence of the drumming had altered, had changed from the insistent, pounding thunder of the ceremony to a steady, low drone. At this distance, it sounded almost like a mutter of voices, like a crowd of men thinking aloud. Denham wondered just what they were thinking about.

Dinner passed in nervous silence. Afterward, Driscoll went out onto deck and exchanged a few words with the men armed with rifles, who already stood their posts in the bows, amidships, and at the stern. He climbed up to the bridge and found Englehorn standing alone, gazing up at the sky. "Overcast night," the skipper observed.

"Fog's rising again, too," Jack said. "It's going to be a dark night, and that won't make the guards' job any easier."

Already darkness had settled. Jack peered into the gloom and persuaded himself that he could just make out Skull Mountain, its empty sockets and gaping maw wraithlike in the gathering dusk.

"Calm down, Mr. Driscoll," the skipper said quietly. "Are you sure that Mr. Denham isn't right? It seems to me that you have gone a little soft on Miss Darrow. Don't worry, though. A dark night won't hurt anything. We're far enough offshore to keep the natives from making a surprise rush."

Jack leaned on the rail and shook his head. "I just don't like those drums!"

★ ★ ★

76

The insistent droning went on through the night, as the fog closed in and the darkness became complete. Driscoll didn't like any part of this island, and those drums least of all. But he tried to keep any trace of his worry out of his expression as he checked on Ann. She seemed more at ease than he was. Denham was right. Ann was a brave girl.

And as for going soft—Driscoll snorted to himself. Any man could find himself on edge, listening to those monotonous drums. Those mumbling, mysterious drums.

Denham kept them all in suspense until nearly midnight. He was too much of a showman to reveal his plan too early, too much even to realize he was teasing them. In his mind, he was laying the groundwork for the film that would rewrite movie history. At last, though, he called the skipper, Driscoll, and Ann together again in the cabin. "Okay, here's how I've doped it out. We're going ashore bright and early tomorrow with a strong armed party. Skipper, I want your best marksmen. It'll be your job to dazzle these islanders with our trade goods. Shouldn't be hard—we've got stuff they've never seen before. And all the way through, I want you to stress that we're friends, we're no threat. We'll talk our way through that gate, and with our rifles and gas bombs, we'll see what the forest has to hide."

"Not Ann!" Driscoll thundered.

Ann smiled at him. "I'm here to do a job, Jack. I'll go."

"Maybe later," Denham said quickly, before Jack could object again. "You'll stay aboard tomorrow while we get the lay of the land. And Jack will appoint fourteen sailors with rifles to be your body-guard. Well, gentlemen—and lady—we've come all this way to find Kong. Tomorrow we find him."

Ann looked troubled. "I'm ready to go ashore if you need me. I trust you, Mr. Denham—I mean, Carl."

Denham smiled in gratitude. "No, Ann. Ordinarily I'd never sepa-rate my cast from my camera. This time, though, we don't know what we're up against. So you're staying aboard until I know what I'll be getting you into."

"Good idea," Englehorn said.

Driscoll's whole expression changed. "I'm going ashore with you, Denham." He gave Ann a quick sideways glance, and then added, "Let me lead the party that explores the interior. You're right. We won't run into any danger with a strong party. But if you should happen to get hurt, the picture would be held up. If I bump into a tree or something, it won't matter."

A sharp, low cry of concern burst from Ann.

Denham chuckled. "The old college try, eh? Ready to do or die for dear old Rutgers? You're out, Jack. When I organize a parade, I always lead it." He paused and then, with a smile, said, "Still, you might have a point at that. All right, Jack, I take back what I said about your going soft. Maybe you've just got a soft spot, that's all. But I'll tell you what: You'll be in charge of, say, a six-man special guard, with rifles and bombs. Your job is to keep the camera safe. I'll look after myself, but if something eats my camera, I'll take it out of your skin!"

"You've got it," Driscoll said. "As long as Ann stays safe on board."

"Then I'm turning in," Denham announced. "Get a few hours of shut-eye, Jack. I want your eye clear tomorrow!"

"I don't think I'll sleep a wink," said Ann. "All right, Carl. You and Jack make sure the island is safe, but then I expect to get some screen time."

Denham exploded into laughter, so infectiously that Driscoll joined in. Even Englehorn, behind his mustache, managed an amused smile.

But instead of going to bed, Denham went to his cabin and sat pensively turning over what-ifs and what-thens in his head. Let Ann stay aboard tomorrow. The next day, or the day after, it would be a different story. The story of Beauty and the Beast, perhaps. The ceremony had given Denham the glimmer of an idea. If he acted on it, then

Ann's life might be in danger. All of their lives, for that matter.

On the other hand—

"What a picture," Denham told himself, balling his hands into fists. "Oh, man, what a picture that would make!"

9

Past midnight, and the drums never paused. Ann stepped out into drifting mist. Along the deck she could make out the watchful silhouettes of the guards. Low deck lights glowed enough to show her that a few other sailors had come out on deck, seeking relief from the heat and the humidity. Lumpy was one of these. Stretched out on a hatch, in his frayed trousers, he played lazily with Ignatz.

Ann sat on a corner of the hatch. "Hello, Lumpy."

"Evenin', Miss Ann. Ignatz, give her some room." The monkey leaped into her lap, and Ann put up with its scramble to her shoulder. Lumpy said, "Heard you had a touchy time of it ashore."

"Well, I was pretty scared for a while." The monkey put a cool paw on her cheek and peered worriedly into her face. "You would've been scared, too, Iggy."

"It was quiet aboard," Lumpy said, and he gave a gigantic yawn. He seemed too lethargic for conversation, and they sat in silence, Ann feeling soothed by the soft night as Ignatz played with her fingers.

At length, Lumpy asked drowsily, "Miz Ann, mind tellin' me something? What happened ashore to get that cold old turtle so het up?"

Ann said slowly, "I think it must have been the girl. The one they were trying to sacrifice to Kong."

"Oh, yeah. I heard some of the boys talkin' about her. The bride of Kong, they said Mr. Denham called her."

Ann shivered. "What do you think Kong could be?"

Lumpy laughed in scorn. "Ah, don't trouble your head. Just some old heathen god. Every tribe has some kind of god. Could be anything, an old log or a mud statue. I'll bet Kong is just a lump of moss with some dopey idol stuck up on top of it. That bride of his probably never gets within a mile of him. See—" He broke off and then muttered, "Well, that old witch doctor fellow could probably tell you where she goes. See, most of the time the high priest gets what they offer the god—the food and, well, the other stuff, if you get my drift."

Ann realized the bald old sailor was actually embarrassed. She laughed, and as she shifted for a more comfortable position, she accidentally pinched Ignatz's leg. The sensitive monkey squeaked and fled indignantly.

"Oh, I hurt him. Catch him, Lumpy," Ann said. "I didn't mean to sit on him. See if he's all right."

Lumpy got up. "Ignatz! Come here, you varmint!" He shuffled off into the darkness.

Ann sat up and lifted her arms sleepily. An enormous round moon found a break in the overcast, and its light drifted across the deck. Ann became aware that more than one of the guards had turned to gaze at her, and she realized that the moonlight showed her figure to best advantage, made the movements of her light cotton dress almost liquid. Feeling self-conscious, Ann locked her fingers around her knees and stared toward the dark bulk of the island.

Ann thought of Jack and smiled at his reaction to Denham's plan. She pondered her strange turn of fate. Just weeks before she was suffering the cold streets and constant hunger of New York City. And now, well, now she felt rested, relaxed, and falling in love.

Still, they faced the mystery of the island. Ann told herself, Forget about Kong. Old Lumpy is probably right. She had more pleasant things to think about. She stood and lazily made her way aft, to the narrow alley between the rail and the deckhouse.

She hesitated there for a moment, the light spilling from the deckhouse gleaming in her golden hair. The drums swelled for a few seconds to a frenzy, then subsided to their low, rolling murmur again. Ann took a few more steps aft, and the darkness swallowed her.

★ ★ ★

Up on the bridge, a restless Denham found Englehorn just as unable to sleep as he felt. They both turned the moment the drumbeats began to rattle frantically across the bay.

"Listen to that!" Denham snapped. "I tell you, if I could take pictures by firelight, I'd sneak back over there tonight just to get some shots of those drummers."

"Better off here, Mr. Denham."

The drums modulated again, and Denham shrugged. "I know that, but still I hate to miss anything."

A match flared as Englehorn lit his pipe. "I wouldn't mind missing a lot."

"Don't talk like that, Skipper. For the love of mike, it's enough to have Jack Driscoll worrying his heart out."

Englehorn puffed on his pipe. "I'm hardly worrying, and neither is Driscoll, at least not for himself. Still, I'm glad we have guards set. I have half a notion to keep the midnight watch myself."

"I don't think we need the guards," Denham countered. "All the natives are busy ashore."

"Maybe so, but I think I'll stay around just the same."

"Okay, I can't sleep either. I'll keep you company," Denham said with a laugh. "Tell you what, we'll have a good game of pinochle."

The tobacco in Englehorn's pipe glowed cherry red. "I couldn't concentrate. A lot depends on how the chief and the witch doctor receive us tomorrow."

Denham rubbed a hand over his face. "Oh, we'll make friends with them, Skipper. Sure, they didn't like our breaking into their ceremony, but we can convince them that was an accident. Take my word for it, when they get a gander at the stuff I've brought, they'll forget all about it. Something tells me these birds haven't seen many westerners. I've got a ton of costume jewelry, and that ought to get their interest fast enough."

Englehorn grunted. "Denham, don't underestimate these people. They're not idiots, and they're not savages. Not your idea of savages, anyway. They're exactly like us, but their world is different from ours. They all wanted just one thing: to please Kong. You seem to think we spoiled some kind of little show. It's more serious than that."

"All right, Kong's some sort of god to them."

"Even more serious," Englehorn insisted. "If this Kong is what you think he is, some kind of giant or something, and they fear him, the last thing they're thinking about is a handful of trinkets. They wanted to appease Kong, and for that they wanted Ann. It's nothing trivial, Mr. Denham. It's a matter of belief and faith, a matter of sacrifice and blood and death. That's what concerns Driscoll. And me, Mr. Denham. And me."

Denham didn't respond for a few seconds. Then he said, "Suppose they'll do the ritual again tomorrow? If they do, I can get it all on film."

Englehorn took his pipe from his mouth and demanded, "Denham, did you hear a single word I said?"

Denham glanced at him. "Sure, sure I did, Skipper. Don't get me wrong, I'm as concerned for Ann's safety as you are. That's why she stays on the ship tomorrow. If the witch doctor can't get her, he'll use what he has. Kong's got to be appeased, right? And when that whole shindig starts up again, you can bet I'll be filming it."

In the heavy silence that followed, Denham sensed Englehorn's misgivings. Good thing the old man's not a mind reader, he thought to himself.

Ten minutes later, Driscoll entered the bridge, wiping his forehead. "I've just changed the guards. Half the crew is on the foredeck, trying to get some air. Where's Ann?"

Denham shrugged. "In her cabin, or on deck, I suppose. What are you doing, checking on her every half hour?"

"Listen to the drums," Driscoll said. "Denham, I may be soft on

Ann, as you say. But at least I'm not a cold-blooded—ah, skip it." He left the two men and restlessly resumed his rounds, making sure that the new guards were in place and alert. On the crowded foredeck, he heard a chattering and glanced down to see Lumpy lying sprawled on a hatch, Ignatz complaining next to him.

"Lumpy, have you seen Miss Darrow?" Driscoll asked.

"A few minutes ago she was here. Ignatz went runnin' off and I had to chase him down. I thought she'd still be here when I got back, but she's gone."

"How long ago?"

"Dunno, Mr. Driscoll. Fifteen, thirty minutes. I got no timepiece."

Driscoll felt the creeping touch of doubt. "She's probably gone to her cabin." He turned and headed astern. He passed the deckhouse, and in the dark stretch beyond it he stepped on something that crunched underfoot. Curious and a little irritated, he stooped, felt on the deck, and picked it up. He stepped back into the light to see what had been dropped. An instant later, he bellowed, "On deck! All hands on deck!"

Nerves were taut aboard the *Wanderer*. The guard and the hands on the foredeck took up the cry, and feet pounded up the companionway. Old Lumpy, his bald head gleaming in the light from the deckhouse, came running back. "What's wrong, Mr. Driscoll?"

Driscoll held up his find as Englehorn and Denham half climbed and half dropped down from the bridge. "I found this on deck."

"A native bracelet!" Lumpy said. "Them heathens must've come aboard!"

"Who's seen Ann Darrow? Where is she?" Driscoll yelled as most of the crew spilled onto the deck.

Englehorn and Denham looked at one another. Denham took a half step forward. "She has to be in her cabin."

"No, sir!" young Jimmy said from aft. "I heard the call to all hands and went and pounded on her door. She's not there."

Driscoll clenched his hand on the bracelet. "Search the ship! Turn to, you men! Find Miss Darrow!"

The crew scattered as Driscoll made his way to the island side of the ship, Englehorn and Denham in his wake. Driscoll demanded of the guard amidships, "Have you seen anything? Any natives?"

"No, sir!" the man shot back. "Everything's been quiet, except for them drums!"

Denham melted into the shadows as Driscoll questioned the other two guards on this side of the ship, only to learn that neither of them had heard anything. Driscoll felt close to snarling in frustration when Denham returned. "She's not belowdecks, not anywhere."

Driscoll shook the bracelet in his face. "They got her! They came aboard quiet as devils, and they got her!"

Englehorn put a hand on Driscoll's shoulder, and in a command sharp as the crack of a gun, he ordered, "Bo'sun, man the boats. A rifle and fifty rounds of ammunition to every man."

Sound filled the darkness: the boatswain's whistle, shrill and insistent, the creak and thump of davits, the rattle of arms. Voices, too, not frantic, not frightened, but level and purposeful.

Denham was shaking his head. "They must have come in dugouts. How could they have crossed the bay? Our lookouts would have spotted them!"

"Surface is covered with mist," Englehorn said. "And what moon there is comes and goes. Mostly goes. Anyway, we don't have time to find out how they got here. I warned you not to underestimate them." To Jack, Englehorn added, "Mr. Driscoll, before you get into your boat, make sure the ship has been thoroughly searched. Leave fourteen men on watch, and be sure they're well armed!"

Driscoll was already on his way.

★ 10 ★

Powerful hands thrust Ann down to the bottom of the dugout. One of her captors had inserted a gag into her mouth, filling her throat and nose with some pungent, numbing compound, bringing tears to her eyes. She couldn't see a thing, but she felt the dugout leap into motion as paddles bit into the sea. She thrashed wildly, but could send no cry back through the darkness to the *Wanderer*.

Lying pinioned there, Ann thought back to the moment of her capture, when suffocating, pressing hands had seized her. Her first instinct had been to shout for help, but the gag had been ready and had silenced her as the soundless figures had dropped her over the rail, into other waiting arms in the canoe alongside the ship.

Now Ann felt a greater fear than she had ever even imagined. No book she had ever read, no story she had ever heard, could summon the kind of terror which seized her. She writhed with the feeling that her insulted body was alive with crawling, unmentionable things. The gag kept her from shrieking her fear, but she gasped for breath with grim desperation.

She could hear the swoosh of the paddles and feel the flow of the water through the wooden bottom of the dugout. Her nostrils burned with the hot, musky smell of her kidnappers' bodies as they feverishly paddled back to shore. When the dugout grated on the sand and her captors jerked her to her feet on the beach, she could not even stand. Her legs, released at last, refused to hold her weight. She felt dizzy, dimly aware that the sharp-tasting mixture that soaked the gag was drugging her.

Wasting no time, two bulking shadows swung her body to their shoulders and raced off through the shadows toward the village, where ruddy torchlight gleamed through the brush. Several times during the course of the flight someone gave a high-pitched command, and Ann felt herself handed over to a new pair of bearers. The third time she heard the voice give the order, Ann's heart lurched. It was the witch doctor, beyond any doubt. His voice rattled off the incomprehensible island language. Ann could catch only random syllables: *Bar-Atu. Kong.*

Torches spilled bright light across the ceremonial court before the Wall's great gate. The tribe stood massed here, just as it had been in the afternoon. The same ordered rows swayed on either side of the skin-covered bridal dais. The same black-furred gorilla men occupied the two front ranks. The king sat on his same tall stand, clad in the same magnificent feathers, grass, and fur. And the witch doctor, leaving Ann's bearers to stand guard where she had been set down in front of the king, promptly took his own proper position.

The old native woman hovered in the background, supporting herself by leaning on her long staff of curved white bone. With her eyes flashing, she attempted to step forward. Six or eight younger women moved to block her. The old woman's voice rose as she argued with the witch doctor, gesturing at Ann. Anger writhed on the man's features, and he drew his hand back as if to strike the woman, but her helpers, or her watchers, immediately intervened to pull her away, all the while making supplicating motions to the king. More than one man discreetly assisted their exit, and they quickly became lost in the throng of worshipers.

Completely ignoring the distraction, the king spread his arms wide, smiling his approval. He barked orders, and two men seized Ann. Though wild with fear, she felt strength slowly returning to her legs. Still, she would have fallen had the men not held her up as they brought her to the privacy of a torchlit hut. Ann looked desperately behind her, seeing the huge figure of the king making his way after her. The crowd quickly parted for him. He stood at the door and summoned the witch doctor. The witch doctor, in his high, querulous voice, shouted orders, and four native women came into the hut. The two male guards left, closing the door behind them.

"Please," Ann begged. "Please let me go."

The women closed in, smiling reassuringly. All of them stretched out their hands, seeming eager to touch, to stroke, her golden hair. They murmured to her, soft, encouraging sounds, as they crowned her with flowers, as they tied a floral sash around her waist. One of them knelt before her, lowered her head, and spoke what sounded to Ann like an invocation. She understood nothing but "Kong."

Two of the women threw the door open, and the others urged Ann forward. The instant she stepped out, the two male guards seized her arms. Ann knew her eyes were wide, and she felt as though she were bordering on shock. Something, the compound on her gag or the cloying scent of the flowers, made her feel strange, distant, floating on the far edge of consciousness. The king held up his staff, and the people fell silent. The guards dragged Ann forward and forced her to kneel where the day before the native girl had knelt, and she heard the king's voice boom out, "Malem ma pakeno! Kong wa bisa! Koh bisa para Kong!"

As one, the crowd went wild. The guards hauled Ann to her feet, and the throng parted to clear a way for her. Halfway up the broad stone stairs, she saw the bridal dais empty, waiting. She heard a soft voice hiss at her and turned her head to see the old woman. Beside her stood the flower-covered girl of the day before, dressed now as all the other women were dressed. Ann barely recognized her.

The old woman seemed to be trying to tell her something, but what? Hands raised a kind of wooden chalice to her lips, and other hands forced her to tilt her head back. An astringent liquid flowed into her mouth, nearly choking her. She felt herself lifted up onto the dais, but her disorientation grew, blurring everything. Had the old woman tried to signal her not to drink? Ann couldn't think straight. Her senses seemed sharp enough, but she was aware only of sensation, not of coherent thought. When the drums began, she swayed to their hypnotic beat.

★ ★ ★

Ubar-Atu, eldest son of the island's most revered shaman, shouted his orders with nervous haste. Bar-Atu's doctrine had been the way of the island for as long as anyone remembered, and the ancient Bar-Atu, though feeble now, brooked no delay in the ceremonies. The moon hid its face tonight, not a good omen. Still, surely such a fine bride, such an unusual woman, would placate the island god.

As the shaman led the ritual, his speed was not due at all to any fear that the *Wanderer*'s crew would move to rescue the evening's sacrifice. What filled him was the fear of Kong. Kong demanded sacrifice four times a year, when the moon and tides were just so, and that time was almost up. The times of the great sacrifice always brought peril. The opening of the doors left them all vulnerable. During the last sacrifice, the followers of that old woman had caused enough of a disturbance to lead to the brink of disaster.

Ubar-Atu did not have time to consider the old woman's insolence, and he knew that powerful traditions and taboos protected her. Still, he found himself more and more convinced that he would have to stop her, permanently. He finished the final chant, and turned to Bar-Atu. Sweat poured into the old man's eyes as he waited for the king to give the signal for the sounding of the great drum.

The king stood and raised his staff, and the massed natives began a familiar chant. Their serried ranks swayed the torchlight in a hypnotic rhythm. Trying not to appear rushed, the priest performed his supplicating dance. Once more the gorilla men leaped out from the chanting host. The priest's eyes kept straying to the servant atop the wall, his club ready. Hurry, hurry. When Kong saw this magnificent sacrifice, the god would show favor to his people, surely.

The king gave the signal, and the great drum sent its deep, echoing *boom* rolling like thunder over the village, over the forest beyond. Ubar-Atu stepped forward and commanded ten warriors to rush to the two smoothly trimmed beams which held the great gate shut. They laid hands on it and poised expectantly.

Boom!

The crowd moaned. Ann knelt, head thrown back, mouth slightly open, as if only semiconscious.

Boom!

The priest raised his hand, and the men took hold of the beams.

Boom!

The hand swept down, and in a voice that rasped his throat, the priest shouted, *"Ndeze!"*

Ann needed no knowledge of the island language to know that the witch doctor had shouted "Open!" The gate tenders, five warriors at each bar, strained and slowly drew the massive wooden bolts back, one from either side. Each bolt gradually slid through massive, time-pitted black sockets in the form of horned saurian skulls, one at the center of each door. Torchlight gleamed on the bars, showing they had been greased. The men drew the heavy wooden beams onto broad support platforms on each side of the gate.

Below them each of two groups of men began to pull the gate open, thirty men hauling on each half. Each door swung with surprising smoothness for something so large. Chattering came from far above, and Ann became aware that other warriors had swarmed up onto the broad top of the Wall. Torches blazed there. The Wall was thick, much thicker than she had thought at first. As the gates opened, she became aware that one of the larger native houses could easily have been built in the space where the great doors hung. The men hauled with desperate speed, as if everything depended on getting the gate open fast.

Ann dimly wondered if the natives feared that rescuers from the *Wanderer* were on the way. But the thought aroused no hope. Hope had died in her from the moment her first cry had been stifled. Her capture and all that came after was so far removed from anything she had ever experienced or even imagined that she struggled to comprehend. Everyone and everything on the mysterious ancient island had trapped her in some sort of waking nightmare. Suddenly, she heard the king shout, *"Ndundo!"* Overhead, the great drum thundered again and again, shocking Ann's tortured attention into focus for a moment. The signal, Driscoll had said. The signal that Kong's bride was to be offered to the island god. The sacrifice. The sacrifice. *She* was the sacrifice!

At each blow upon the drum the chanting ceased atop the Wall and throughout the village. The massed ranks on either side of the dais broke. With cries of mingled excitement and apprehension, a good portion of the tribesmen, and the women and children as well, raced toward the Wall. Others stayed in their huts and refused to watch.

"Tasko!" the king shouted.

Now the guards picked Ann up, dais and all, and rushed her through the opening gate. At either side a mass of spear-armed warriors joined them, trotting along with shields held ready, spears pointing forward, toward the dark forest.

"Watu!" the king shouted.

Instantly the gate tenders pushed, nearly closing the gate on the heels of the departing group, leaving a gap so narrow that no more than two men at a time could squeeze back through.

"Ndundo!" the king shouted again, and once more the drummer rolled thunder out to the black wilderness.

High on the Wall the islanders raised their torches, as if for a better view. In the uncertain light, Ann had a confused glimpse of the landscape beyond the Wall. For a space of perhaps thirty yards, the land had been kept clear of brush. In the center of this plain, fifty feet from the Wall, stood a stone altar that looked to Ann as ancient as the Wall it faced. Gray lichen spotted its worn steps. A layer of dark moss covered its platform and soaked up the torches' light. The bearers carried her up the steps, up perhaps twelve feet from the ground. Two worn pillars, splendidly carved, rose out of the platform a short arm's width apart.

"Tasko! Tasko!" the king shouted, urgency creeping into his deep voice.

Ann felt her guards lower her to the platform, and hands grasped her arms and hauled her to her feet. Without a word, the men moved her into position between the pillars. Two of them spread her arms while two more tied grass ropes to her wrists, cast loops around the pillars, and drew them tight. Dimly, Ann felt the bite of the ropes, but at a remove, as though she were sedated.

"Ndundo! Ndundo para Kong!" the king's voice exclaimed, and atop the Wall the drummer roused the deafening thunder once more. Ann had been tied facing the Wall, and by raising her head, she could glimpse the torchbearers standing there on the top. The crowd on the rampart swayed in an insane chant that assaulted Ann's ears. She had again that strange feeling of heightened senses, the sharp scent of the jungle mingling with the musky aroma of the burning torches.

Thirst abraded her throat. She moaned, helpless, hanging in the grip of her bonds. Her bearers leaped to the ground and, with fearful glances backward, fled. The gate closed so quickly it almost crushed the last one.

Ann stood alone, beyond help, beyond the protection of the Wall. In the dark, not far off, something moved. From the direction of the precipice came a deep, unreal roar which met the roll of the drum and threw it back against the Wall. Again the drum sounded, and louder the approaching roars answered.

The torch-illuminated mob upon the rampart burst into a great cry: "Kong! Kong! Kong!"

Ann had nearly lost consciousness, but some sense of impending fate lifted her eyelids. It was as if she had awakened from a nightmare, and for a moment, she stared about in bewilderment, uncertain of where she was. Now the pain of her bound arms broke on her, and she writhed, trying to ease the bite of the ropes.

Before her, she became conscious of the dark barrier that was the Wall, with its intricate carvings showing in the flickering light of the dancing torches that crowned it. It seemed to her for all the world like a living thing. Behind her she was eerily aware of a sort of emanating heat, and she heard an unutterably deep and gargled sound, like that of a volcano simmering before eruption. And then she saw the shadow. It came from nowhere, cast by moonlight. It spread over the altar, reached the Wall, and rose like a flood about to engulf it. The natives on the Wall suddenly became mute, as though something had overpowered them, something Ann could not see. She strained to turn her head, becoming suddenly, inexplicably lucid. Then, while her eyes widened, the shadow separated itself from the black cloak of the forest and became solidly real against the moonlight.

Enormous eyes blinked up at the packed Wall. Ann's mind reeled at the sheer size of them, at the size of this creature. Its cry of defiance was nothing short of an explosion; its black furred hands drummed a vast chest, heavily creased and scarred, as if in challenge. In the full glare of the torches, the creature hesitated, stopped, and as though reading the meaning of the thousand hands which gestured from the rampart, turned and looked down at the altar. At Ann.

The altar stood twelve feet above ground level, but the enormous eyes looked *down* at her. With a questioning grunt, the great beast bent over her. High up on the Wall the islanders fell silent, their pointing arms again motionless. The torches seemed frozen, no longer wavering. And then the world moved again, and Ann's terrified screams spread piercingly into the dead silence. Again and again they rang out as she struggled mightily against her bonds. And then, with a gasping echo that the darkness swiftly swallowed, they fell silent.

Kong jerked back a half step and rumbled angrily. The deep lines and scars about his enormous, hideous face revealed a surprisingly expressive countenance. Although he looked as old as time, his features had an unusual expression of youthful desire. Kong tilted his head, and his great hand reached out tentatively, as though with a will of its own, to touch Ann's golden crest. His fingers stopped within inches of Ann's head, and suddenly he reared back, his massive head swiveling to stare up at the Wall in what seemed like deep suspicion. He rose up to his full height and beat his chest with the sound of thunder and claimed his dominance with a deafening roar, as though challenging anyone or anything that dared oppose him. When the crowded natives and all the surroundings remained in subservient silence, and with no sound or further movement from the figure now drooping between the pillars, he renewed his investigation. Ann could stand no more. She felt consciousness fading, and she slipped into a faint.

Kong's interest had been aroused by the unusual look of this sacrifice. In clothing, in appearance, she was unlike anything else on the island. From experience, he knew that he could not simply pluck Ann from her bonds without hurting her. The ropes, however, offered no difficulty. The loops about the pillars were knotted in such a way that with a sharp tug they became undone. Once he had pulled them, the strands fell away from Ann's wrists, and she would have fallen had Kong not supported her with his hand.

Kong frowned, examining the amazing being he lifted from the altar. Shining hair, petal cheeks, tissue garments, puzzling footgear—his giant fingers discovered endless mystery. In intense preoccupation he began to rumble to himself as he gently turned the figure over, this way and that, much in the manner that a human child might curiously turn and inspect a limp, unconscious bird.

When the crowd shouted again, he did not even look up, not even when new voices joined the clamor. With a last, intent look at the pale countenance in his hand, he shifted Ann's form to the crook of one arm and started slowly back into the forest. The heavy creak of the opening gate drew no sign from his receding back. And when a tiny figure plunged through and cried out loudly in challenge, Kong did not hear him. Nor did he hear the shot, or feel something whistle past his ear. He could only think of the jewel he carried as he pushed into the dark, welcoming wilderness.

★ 11 ★

Driscoll's first sight of Kong stunned him. But a glimpse of Ann quickly steeled his nerve, and he yelled out in frustration before attempting to put a bullet in Kong's head. In the darkness the shot went wild.

Denham had taken charge as he raced the rescue boats away from the *Wanderer* and deployed the sailors for the breathless run to the village. But from the moment the crew had hauled the great gate open, Driscoll had seized command. Rushing back through the gate, he immediately set to work organizing the pursuit.

"Jack—" Denham began.

Driscoll turned on him with a snarl of rage. "This is my job, Denham. If you tag along, you'll look to me for orders."

Denham nodded. "We do it together, then. But you call the shots."

"I need a dozen men," Jack shouted. "Who's coming?"

Old Lumpy said, "I'll go!"

Driscoll shook his head. "You stay here and take command of the guard party. I need someone with experience to keep these savages in check. Don't start anything, but don't let them push you around, see?"

"Got it."

Driscoll's finger stabbed out. "I'll take you, and you, and you—"

"Who's got the bombs?" Denham yelled as Driscoll chose his last man.

Jimmy stepped forward, a crate hoisted to his shoulder. "Here!" One of the twelve volunteers reached to take them, but he pulled away. "Mr. Denham, I've carried 'em so far. Take me with you."

"Okay, kid. Skipper, you and Lumpy hold this gate. We're going to need to get through in a hurry when we come back."

"All right, Denham. I'm old for that kind of a run. Don't worry. We'll be here when you need us."

Driscoll couldn't wait. "Single file, all," he ordered. "And don't lose sight of the man in front of you. Come on, follow me."

He set off at a trot, but instead of following, Denham paced him, just beside him. They reached the altar, and Denham sprinted up, holding a flashlight. "No blood, thank God," he said, leaping down again. Driscoll measured the height of the pillars with his eyes, and then looked at Denham incredulously. "Tell me I'm not dreaming. You got a glimpse of him too, didn't you?"

Denham nodded.

Driscoll shook his head as they started off again. "I still can't believe it. I got a fair look. I saw that thing from only the knees up because he was standing on the downside of that slope. Its head was squarely in line with the top of those pillars, and that's twenty feet above the ground if it's an inch." He shivered. "Kong is the size of a small mountain. He must have left a trail we can follow. Look for broken branches, footprints, anything." Immediately he set off with the others following behind, their flashlights scanning the surroundings.

They plunged into the brush, and before long they reached the sheer rise of the precipice. "There's no climbing this," Denham said.

Driscoll gestured. "Listen, off to the left."

"Sounds like water," Denham grunted. "Come on, it may be a break in this cliff."

Driscoll led the way, and in a few dozen steps they found a stream. To the left it flowed in the general direction of the Wall, but it had worn its way through the rock of the cliff off to the right. It tumbled down a steep ravine, the rush of the water drowning out every other sound.

"Kong must have come through here," Driscoll said. "It's the only way, unless he climbed down from the plateau."

"Yeah," Denham said. "But he could wade it without getting his ankles wet. That white water would sweep us off our feet."

"Look around," Driscoll ordered. "See if there's a way up."

Denham plunged off on his own, and after a few minutes, Driscoll heard him call out, "Over here! I've found a track!"

Driscoll jogged over and turned his flashlight on the mark. It was fresh. The moist ground preserved the imprint of an apelike foot so large that even Driscoll stared in unbelief. The imprint marked the base of another cleft in the rock face, this one broader and drier. "It's the old streambed," he said. "It parallels the river. Come on. We can climb it. Move!"

The darkness made the climb cruel going. The brush grew so dense at times that each man had trouble seeing the one in front of him. A cracked shin, a bruising stumble, and the head-jarring impact of unseen branches snapping back from all directions marked nearly every yard of the way. Once a man slipped from the ledge into the swift water and shot down a hundred feet before he found an outcrop to cling to.

"I kept my gun," he gasped cheerfully as they pulled him out.

The last hundred yards became a steep crawl up the shattered face of an ancient landslide, but at last Driscoll stood erect and looked back behind him. A half mile away, the torches on the Wall gleamed like so many fireflies. "Come on," Driscoll said. They had reached the great plateau, but from the very outset they plunged into jungle: enormous trees, and at their base a lush tangle of undergrowth. The stream had widened, leading back into rising country.

"Hard to believe we're on an island," Denham panted. "This place looks like a world all its own."

Driscoll didn't respond, but said, "My guess is we'll find that this plateau slopes gradually back to Skull Mountain. That's a long way off."

They saw no sign of a track. "Look for those prints again," Driscoll ordered the men. "I want to estimate how long his stride is. I'd guess about fifteen feet at least. Use that as a rough guide and look for the logical place the next footprint might be. Fan out in all directions from the last footprint to increase our chances. Make sure you stay in shouting distance, though!"

"Hey, here's a broken bush," one of the sailors yelled. In the beam of his flashlight, the breaks showed fresh white pith contrasting with dark gray bark.

A moment later, another one found a second footprint. The track was in a clear space beyond the broken brush, and once more it pointed upstream. It was clue enough, and as the party converged, Driscoll led the way as fast as he could in the darkness.

Driscoll became aware that the jungle thrummed with life, shrieks and chatters and screeches. Insects, he thought, and birds.

As if catching the thought, Denham said, "Sounds like the whole country's loaded with birds. Birds and bugs. Hey, that means dawn's coming on. Now we'll catch a break, Jack!"

"So let's put on a little speed!" Driscoll shot back.

For some time that proved impossible. They still moved through what seemed utter blackness. Then, slowly, Driscoll could catch shadows at a distance. Gradually, whenever they paused to puzzle out the way, they marched ahead upon a trail grown a little plainer. And finally, unmistakably, Driscoll saw gray light filtering down.

In a slanting shaft of dawn light they found the clearest, most complete footprint so far. Driscoll still had trouble believing his eyes.

Jimmy whistled, shifting his crate of bombs. "Would you look at the size of that thing! He must be as big as a house!"

Denham pushed his cap back. "He came this way, all right."

Driscoll hefted his rifle. "We're still going in the right direction. Come on, and keep your guns ready!"

"Don't worry about that," one of the sailors grunted, and someone laughed in nervous agreement. They continued their pursuit until a wide glade opened up before them.

Driscoll, toes and ankles aching from a thousand stumbles, entered the clearing gratefully. Full daylight had broken, and he ordered a short rest. "Drink some water and take the weight off for a few minutes," he said. "But stay alert."

Except for a thin drifting mist, every tree, every bush, every strand of knee-deep grass, now stood revealed in the light of day. The smell of jungle roiled everywhere, a mixture of fresh morning dew and ages of rotted vegetation.

Driscoll swatted at his neck and smashed something that felt as large as his thumb. "What the—something stung me!"

Denham whistled, looking at the smashed remains. "Looks like a mosquito, but a mosquito that big would just about drain you dry."

Driscoll heard a strange buzzing drone and looked up in time to see a dragonfly as big as a crow swoop over. It flew to the edge of the river, guarded there by a thick growth of reeds, and settled down, its iridescent wings flicking as it perched.

Some of the men reached for sticks, but Denham chuckled. "Don't worry, boys. Those things eat mosquitoes, and with the brand of mosquitoes around here, I'd rather have the dragonflies eating them, not the mosquitoes eating me!"

Driscoll said, "Let's move." They started forward again, and within a hundred steps they came across another footprint. They were still hot on Kong's trail. Driscoll broke into a trot. They left the glade and plunged back into the undergrowth.

Denham suddenly said, "Hold up. What the devil's that? Over there on the right, through the trees!"

Driscoll dropped to one knee and brought his rifle to bear. Something big blundered through the undergrowth. He couldn't see it clearly at first, but from the noise it made, it had to be huge.

"Kong!" someone shouted.

"No. He's taller and darker," snapped Denham.

The brush parted, and an immense brute emerged from the jungle, a four-legged creature with a thick hide, with bony scutes patterned on its flanks, looking like the ornamental armor of a medieval warrior. It carried its long, spiked tail two or three feet off the ground, and it swayed heavily, menacingly, as it advanced. "What is that?" Driscoll whispered.

"Dinosaur," Denham said in hushed tones. "But they were supposed to be sluggish tail-draggers. This thing looks pretty spry to me."

Driscoll could only stare. The creature didn't fit his idea of dinosaurs, either. He'd always pictured them as slow, ponderous lizards, but this creature's movement was graceful and decisive, though its body was huge, larger than any elephant he'd ever seen.

The behemoth had a relatively short, powerful neck ending in a ridiculously small reptilian head, the snout tipped with a powerful beak. It walked on all fours, with its body sloping down from the much taller hind legs to meet the comparatively short and slightly splayed front legs. The great array of plates, larger at their apex atop the hips, gradually tapered in size as they receded toward the front and back. The largest ones, several feet high, swayed from side to side as the creature moved about.

"Stegosaurus," Denham whispered. "Or something like it, anyway. Look at that thing move! If I'd brought—"

"Forget your camera," Driscoll said. "It hasn't noticed us yet. These things eat meat?"

"The books say they're vegetarians," Denham replied. "But I'm starting to think the books are wrong."

Driscoll didn't look at him. "Your learning letting you down? I thought you knew everything, Denham. We'd charm the savages, get them to let you take their picture. Things don't look so sure now, do they?"

"My gut tells me not to be so damned sure of anything in this place," Denham said. "Watch it. It's coming toward us now."

"Where should I put the bullet?" Driscoll sighted, trying to line up the beast's tiny head, but its movements were too hard to follow.

"Maybe I'm not wrong about everything," Denham said. "Jimmy!

Hand me one of those bombs!" He reached back, and Jimmy put the heavy, solid weight in his hand. "When I throw, everyone drop and stay close to the ground, and I mean close!"

The creature grazed in some brush, still apparently unaware of them. Slowly it turned away from them, exposing a barn-sized haunch before it moved off into the trees. Driscoll found he had been holding his breath. He lowered the rifle.

Denham clapped him on the shoulder. "Well, that was a scare we didn't need. Here, Jimmy, take this—"

The attack came without warning. Driscoll heard a crashing, and the beast burst from the concealing vegetation off to the side, charging forward at what must have been its full gait. Driscoll had an impression of immense power. The creature's great bulk swayed, not jerkily, but fluidly. Denham stood in Driscoll's line of fire. He couldn't line up a shot—

The sailors' nerve broke, and they sprinted off toward the river, shouting in dismay. Two of them reached to help Jimmy, staggering under the weight of the crate.

Driscoll snapped off two shots, one into the beast's chest, the other into its head. No effect, other than to madden the monster. It stamped ferociously, letting out a deep-chested hiss like a rasping bellows. Driscoll saw that Denham still held the bomb.

"He's gonna make up his mind in a second. When you drop, keep close to me. Don't get up until I do."

The dinosaur thrashed its head, then lunged forward, like a charging rhino. Denham stood braced until it was seconds away.

Then he threw.

The missile landed squarely in front of the beast's feet. It exploded instantly into boiling blue vapor. The gas completely covered the beast's forequarters, head, front feet, and all.

"Down!" Denham threw himself flat, and Driscoll dropped alongside him, feeling the director's hand on the back of his neck. Before he could protest, Driscoll's mouth was full of moss.

Driscoll inhaled the damp, rich smell of earth, and the sap of growing roots grew bitter on his lips. Just forward of him the ground shook violently from the fall of a great weight. He moved to rise, but Denham's clamped hand refused to release its pressure. Half a minute crept by, seeming to Driscoll like an hour. Then Denham loosed his hold and tapped Driscoll's shoulder twice.

Driscoll stood up. Scarcely the length of his own body away lay the twitching head of the beast, mouth open, tongue lolling, eyes glassy. Behind the head its enormous dome of a rib cage rose and fell spasmodically. Driscoll measured the distance with his eye and exclaimed, "Good Lord! It came fifty feet before the gas finally stopped it."

Denham sounded triumphant: "But I did stop it! Didn't I tell you one of those bombs would stop anything?"

"Is it dying?"

"Not yet," Denham said grimly. "But that's just a detail." He picked up his rifle, walked forward, and put his rifle barrel squarely between the eyes of its triangular head. He pumped in two shots. The great body started convulsively and half rose off the ground before collapsing again with a jolt like an earthquake. Denham hesitated, then for good measure sent another bullet through its saurian head.

Driscoll looked over his shoulder. "My shot just creased the top of its skull. I was beginning to think bullets just bounced off this monster." The sailors had seen it all, and now, as though ashamed of themselves, they were slowly making their way back, their eyes wide at the sight that lay before them.

"What did I tell you?" Denham said to Driscoll. The director crouched beside the grotesque head and reached a tentative hand to touch it. "Prehistoric life!"

The creature was bigger than any land animal Denham had ever seen. Its body still gave signs of movement.

"It takes its sweet time about dying," Driscoll complained. "Look at those spikes in its tail—big enough to cave in a city bus!"

The sailors curiously clustered around the body. A couple of them prodded the flanks with the barrels of their rifles, and the creature jerked in response. "Careful, boys!" Denham warned.

"This isn't getting us closer to Ann," Driscoll said, reloading his rifle and slinging it over his shoulder.

Denham rose to his feet, as if he had only half heard. "Jack, Ann was right last night, but she only had the start of it. She guessed the beast-god was some primitive survivor. But if this thing we killed means anything, Kong isn't the only relic of the past roaming this island. There may be all sorts of creatures that have survived along with Kong."

"That means we have to pick up speed," Driscoll said. "Let's go, men."

Though he didn't voice his fears, Driscoll was growing more and more worried about Ann's fate. The monstrous Kong was fearsome enough, but if Denham was right and the island teemed with living dinosaurs— well, he didn't want to think of it. He led the men at a quick march, as much as that was possible through the heavy growth. Under the canopy of jungle, the air grew green with filtered sunlight. Driscoll could see how Kong could pass through here without leaving much trace. The jungle floor, thick with ancient leaf mold, sprouted little undergrowth. Too dark in the shadow of the trees, he supposed.

Still, the occasional gigantic footprint showed them they were still on Kong's trail. It still led them on a path parallel to the river, but the land now sloped generally downward. Ground mist rose and soon they waded through a lake of curling fog. It rose to their chests, then over their heads. Driscoll groaned in frustration. The drifting mist cut visibility to only a few yards.

From behind, Jimmy said, "Look there, over to the left." Driscoll saw a foggy hollow ahead of them. Thicker, curling mist showed the track of the stream, and concealed within the densest fog something splashed in what sounded like deep water.

"Think it's him?" Denham asked.

"Let's find out!" Driscoll returned, and he raced ahead.

He reached the water's edge ahead of the others and stepped into a depression that proved to be a fresh footprint. He looked down and saw water seeping into the print from the sodden ground, bubbling up as though coming from an underground spring. "Fresh track," Driscoll said as Denham and the others caught up to him. "Kong must have rested around here, and he crossed the river here." He waved toward the streambed.

"Sure has widened out," Jimmy said. "Nearly a lake here. I can't even see the far side."

"We'll have to swim it," Driscoll told them.

Denham grabbed his arm, as if afraid the first mate was about to leap into the water. "That's out. We can't swim, not with our bombs and guns."

Driscoll looked left and right in frustration, and his eye fell on a tangle of tree trunks and branches washed up on a curving line of beach during some recent flood. "All right, then, we'll do better. We'll build a raft."

"Good!" Denham agreed.

Driscoll supervised as the sailors chose the likeliest logs and lashed them together with lianas ripped from the trees lining the waterway. As they worked, he briefly told them about the conclusions he and Denham had reached. He wound up, "The long and short of it is that we don't know what kind of monsters we may run into. You volunteered for this, but if any man wants to turn back now, this is your chance."

One of the sailors looked up from his task of lashing the raft together and gave Driscoll a tobacco-stained grin. "Hell, sir, way I figure, we're far enough out that we got just as much chance gettin' killed going backward as we do moving forward."

"I'm in," Jimmy said, not even looking around, to a general chorus of agreement.

Denham clapped Jimmy on the back. "That's the spirit, boys! I still say that an armed party has nothing to be afraid of. Especially if it's armed with my gas bombs!"

Driscoll nodded, pleased that the crew was sticking with him. He knew that he would rescue Ann or die trying, alone or with an army. Still, something nagged at him, some false touch about Denham's tone, something he could not put his finger on just yet.

★ 12 ★

Driscoll burned with the urge to resume the chase, though the business of lashing together the logs didn't take long. By the time the sailors had finished their work, the craft looked sturdy enough. Jimmy and a couple of others cut long saplings they could use to pole their way across the water, and together the party shoved the raft down the slope, launched it on what looked like a river of fog, and climbed aboard. It was a tight fit, and Denham carefully made sure that Jimmy stowed the crate of gas bombs in the center. "Don't get the guns wet, whatever you do," he warned.

"Shove off!" Driscoll ordered, and the men leaned on their poles. The log raft moved with a jerk and a clumsy roll that made the men at the rear stagger.

Denham gave Driscoll a sardonic sideways look. "This is your first independent command. Guess I'll have to call you Captain Driscoll from now on."

"Stow it," Driscoll said, but not sharply. "Say, this really is wider than I thought. It's not a river here. More like a lake or a lagoon. I still can't see the far side." Driscoll carefully balanced himself, not daring to give in to the uncertain feeling of floating inside a choking fog. He wondered about the nerve of the crew. The dinosaur's attack had shaken them, no question, but none of them had given up. Driscoll recognized their forced jocularity as the response of men under pressure. Building the raft had steadied them, but he knew they all sensed the danger was just beginning.

He knew they cared for Ann, maybe not as much as he did, but to a man they felt protective of the most beautiful woman they had ever seen. He hoped he could call on that devotion if things became rough. Meanwhile, he had other worries. The raft proved a hard craft to manage, and the men grumbled at each other as it dipped and tried to spin. "Easy," Driscoll warned them. "We've got to be careful of the balance. Keep those strokes easy."

The men leaned into their poles—poles that now were more than two-thirds their length underwater at every stroke—and as some of them stuck in the muck at the bottom of the lagoon, the leading edge of the raft bit into the water and a wave washed over Driscoll's ankles.

One edge of the raft went awash. "Close in," he said. "Keep your weight well toward center."

"Gonna have to paddle soon," one of the sailors said. He practically had to kneel to find a purchase with his pole.

The poles were no good as paddles, but Driscoll had thought of that and had thrown a few curved fragments of rotted trunks aboard. He passed these out, and four men knelt to paddle. "Won't be for long," he said. "I think I can see weeds ahead, and we'll find bottom again."

"What's that?" one of the sailors asked in a panicky voice, and Driscoll turned in time to see something dark dip beneath the water, not far away.

The raft grated on something under the surface—a sandbar, Driscoll wondered briefly, or the upward-jutting end of a water-soaked log?

And at that moment, a muffled bellow rolled from just astern. Driscoll felt the raft pitch, rise, and fall. He heard yelps of alarm as some of the men toppled into the lagoon, and then, astern, he saw something rise dripping, a scaly head, with an elephantine trunk writhing, trumpeting eerie blasts. The head rose higher and higher, on a thick, impossibly long neck, and then a mountainous body broke the surface yards beyond it.

"Dinosaur!" Denham exploded in a tone that mingled consternation, triumphant discovery, and awe. "By God, another dinosaur!"

The sailors helped the three men who had fallen overboard, and then they all leaned on their poles, finding bottom again and pushing for their lives. The raft leaped forward, causing Driscoll to lose his chance to fire the rifle he had raised. He lowered the weapon and stared in astonishment at this new threat. The creature's head, vast enough, looked small compared with the rest of the body. It towered above the fog, then bent to sweep the surface of the water in a huge arc. It curved in a curiously swanlike movement and vanished beneath the fog-shrouded water, and a moment later its broad, scaly body sank as well.

"Push!" Driscoll ordered swiftly. "I think it's trying to throw us into the lake! Push, men! Heave! Heave!"

The men bent their backs, but though the raft had glided to within a stone's throw of shore, the creature was faster. Driscoll felt a vibrating thud through the soles of his boots, and the raft pitched wildly.

"The bombs!" shouted Denham, "Save 'em, Jim—"

The world tilted madly, and Driscoll pitched into the water—his last clear impression was of the raft being shattered to its component logs as though by an explosion. Astern, one of the flailing seamen raised a frantic cry in a froth of gargled water and shrieks. Something pulled him under, and he did not reappear. The others struggled toward shore like scattering sheep.

Driscoll struck out at a fast crawl, Denham near him. The raft, overturned from behind, had thrown them both near the shore, and in a moment they were floundering, getting to their feet in knee-deep water. Denham offered a hand to the struggling Jimmy, now free of the weight he had carried.

Driscoll staggered ashore, then turned to see. The half-emerging dinosaur lurched among the fragments of the raft, darting its head to bite at anything that bobbed in the roiling water. Men had reached the shore along a thirty-foot arc, but in the confusion Driscoll could not even count them. Most had survived, anyway, and they were scrambling up the slope when the dinosaur surged forward. It had caught sight of one man, who ran desperately away from shore. The dinosaur heaved itself onto shore and gave chase with elephantine strides.

"Come on, boys," Driscoll yelled. "This way!" He led them on a curving flight up the slope, climbing free of the mist and up onto the humped crest of a long ridge. There he paused, looking ahead to where the terrain sloped down again to a wide morass, a soft, blackish expanse, with areas here and there where the surface had hardened under the sun and cracked into great slabs.

"Hold it, Jack!" Denham yelled, staggering up beside him. "I know what that stuff is—asphalt! There's something like that in California, a pit of tar full of prehistoric bones. This one looks like it's been there since the dawn of time. I'll bet it holds thousands of carcasses, and we don't want to join them. We have to find a safe passage across."

Driscoll nodded. "Before we do anything, let's check our losses. Come on, men! Form up!" Looking back from the crest of the bridge, he had the impression that his men were emerging from a cloud. He could see nothing of the lake below but soft, billowing mist, lit by the morning sun. The scene lay deceptively peaceful, except for the terrified faces of the men who struggled up to join Driscoll and Denham. "Who'd it get?" Driscoll asked as the last of the men made it.

"Jackson," one of the sailors gasped. "He never had a chance."

Driscoll counted heads. "Where's Fredericks? Everybody else is—"

Denham cut him off: "Look!"

Following the line of his pointing hand, on a rise a quarter mile from their own, Driscoll caught sight of a racing figure, fleeing desperately, violently toward a grove of trees. Driscoll recognized "Dutch" Fredericks, the missing man, who must have taken the wrong direction. From the mist the dinosaur burst out in close pursuit.

A couple of the men started downhill, but Driscoll barked a harsh order: "Stand fast! You can't make it in time."

Bile rose in Driscoll's throat as he watched the tragedy unfold.

Fredericks slipped and stumbled toward the closest tree that promised any hope of refuge. By some miracle one was within reach, and with the strength of despair he quickly shimmied around and up into its lower branches, the same way a squirrel spirals up a tree to stay out of the sight of its pursuer.

Driscoll balled his fist. If the man had enough wit, enough courage, to stay quiet, he just might have a chance. For a moment the dinosaur looked puzzled, its great neck swaying as it tried to cope with the fact that its prey had apparently vanished. The creature paused beside the tree Fredericks had climbed, moving its head from side to side as if inspecting the trunk.

A scant few feet above that great stooped head, Fredericks moved from branch to branch, first to the left, then to the right, clearly trying to anticipate the dinosaur's movements. The third time he guessed wrong. Driscoll groaned as he realized the sailor now peered straight into the creature's snarling face.

Denham had somehow hung on to his binoculars. He passed them to Driscoll. "He's caught a break. Look at the eye." Driscoll raised the binoculars, bringing the monstrous head into clear focus. He saw that one eye was blind, withered to a sightless milky orb, from some old encounter. The face showed a series of deep parallel scars. Fredericks had not been seen—

But he had given himself away nonetheless. Even at this distance, Driscoll heard his scream of terror, and so did the dinosaur. Its trunklike snout struck like a cobra, and the horny tip of it, like the top half of a parrot's beak and as big as a man's head, ripped into Fredericks's upper thigh. Driscoll saw the sudden crimson bloom of blood as the dinosaur seized Fredericks's leg and dragged him from his perch. The monster threw the man to earth, out of sight, and then its head bent after him. Driscoll heard a terrible scream, cut short. The dinosaur briefly raised its head, its jaws working, blood dripping, and then bent again.

"I can't believe the books are that wrong," Denham said furiously. "That thing was like a brontosaurus, a plant eater!"

"A hippo's a plant eater, too," Driscoll muttered, handing the binoculars back to Denham. "And hippos kill more people than crocs. Anyway, Fredericks is dead. We can't help him now."

"If I'd saved the bombs—" Jimmy said miserably.

"No use talking," Driscoll said. "We've got our knives and our wits, and that's it. We have to use them, that's all."

No one looked back at the dinosaur, though one of the sailors dropped to his knees and vomited. Driscoll heard another one muttering a prayer, over and over. "Come on," he said. "We've got to get across that, somehow." He led them down the slope, toward the asphalt morass. He had no idea how much farther they had to go, how much longer the men's nerves would hold. Two men dead. And how many more might go before they caught up with Kong?

★ 13 ★

Halfway down the slope, Denham paused and blurted in astonishment, "There he is!"

Driscoll froze, seeing the black form in the distance. Denham was right. The beast-god they were pursuing moved near the center of the asphalt field, coming toward them. Even without the binoculars, Driscoll saw him clearly, something monstrous beyond conception, as hairy as any of the simian creatures of an African jungle. Driscoll had seen apes, though, gorillas and chimpanzees, and Kong resembled them only superficially. The great beast in the distance picked his way with a slow, almost human caution, which made him all the more incredible. "He's walking almost like a man," Driscoll said.

"Not like a gorilla at all," Denham agreed. "Look, he's puzzled."

Kong dropped momentarily, putting one hand down to take his weight, but even in that pose he did not truly resemble a great ape so much as he did a primitive man, tracking some prey and momentarily dropping down to examine its spoor. Denham brought up his binoculars and said, "I see Ann!"

Driscoll almost tore the instrument from his grasp. Yes, there she was, cradled in his left arm like a tiny rag doll. She looked limp, unmoving. Was she—Driscoll cut off the thought before completing it. Kong touched her carefully, lifting her dangling arm and arranging it so that it would not drag in the tarry surface. Driscoll wondered what that meant, that care for his captive. Could Kong's primitive brain value this strange possession for reasons which it could not understand?

Driscoll could not tell, but he was sure that something about Kong's purposeful movements, about his expression, suggested intelligence

113

beyond that of any normal ape. He lost the form in the binoculars, and when he lowered them, he saw that Kong had found his way again. The creature moved confidently, taking long strides over the cracked surface, evidently avoiding weak places. Now he moved away from them.

"What are those things?" Jimmy asked.

Driscoll turned to look. "More dinosaurs!" he said sharply. Three of them this time, armored like tanks, each of them with a gigantic hawklike beak, each with a great curved head-frill armed with three long horns. They emerged from the undergrowth on the far side of the asphalt lake and stood their ground, shaking their heads and bellowing as Kong approached them. Kong roared at the creatures and beat his chest with his free hand. The monsters shook their heads and pawed the earth, like bulls ready to defend their territory.

"Triceratops," Denham said. "Those horns are a couple of yards long and a foot thick at the base! Even Kong is no match for something like that! They must've chased him into the asphalt field, back toward us. Man oh man, if we'd only hung on to the bombs!"

"What did you say they were?"

"Triceratops," Denham repeated. "I may be saying it wrong. I've never heard it, just seen it in books, and I've left the word there. Never expected to see one in person!"

Jimmy, crouched nearby, asked, "What are they?"

Denham shook his head. "Just another of nature's mistakes, son. Dinosaurs. They got their names from the three horns on their heads. They developed those weapons because they had to."

Kong stood now on a dry mound in the center of the morass, and the three dinosaurs had stepped out toward him. Kong had put Ann down on the far side of the mound, out of sight from the ridge.

As the trio of triceratops advanced, the one off to the left suddenly jerked and collapsed slowly, weirdly, onto its side, bellowing in panic. It had walked upon a spot too weak to support its weight. The soft asphalt sucked it down as it struggled to climb out. The other two left it behind, advancing with the menace of gigantic rhinos. They ignored its plaintive bawlings, ignored its thrashing. The creature's efforts made it sink all the faster.

As the other two neared, Kong roared again, bent, and lifted a huge chunk of solid asphalt. His muscles bunched as he raised it clean over his head and hurled it at the two challengers.

As the mass struck and shattered, Denham whistled. "No beast can be that strong! That must have weighed almost half a ton. Look, there goes another!"

Kong had thrown another missile, and this one, though smaller, struck home, smashing off a horn. The hurt creature staggered and Kong redoubled his attack. The second attacking triceratops backed off from Kong's projectiles, swinging grudgingly off to the flank, heading at a diagonal toward the men on the crest. Beyond it, the injured triceratops shook its head, bellowing as it tried to back away. Kong threw another accurate missile, striking it hard on the head. The creature reared onto its hind legs and fell on its side. Kong bellowed in triumph and beat his breast. The jungle reverberated with his roars.

The wounded triceratops tried to heave itself back up. Both of its brow horns had been broken, and now as the dinosaur painfully got to its feet to face the advancing Kong, it lowered its bleeding head. Only the short horn on its snout remained undamaged, and the creature snorted loudly as it braced to meet the attack.

But Kong had pried up another mass of hardened asphalt, the largest one yet, and he crashed his weapon onto his foe with such force that the triceratops fell to its knees as if poleaxed. Somehow, desperately, it managed to rise to meet Kong's onslaught. Without hesitation Kong grabbed its massive skull. For a moment the two brutes stood, straining and frozen, as the ceratopsian fought with its last ounce of energy to resist Kong's hold. Kong roared, his muscles rippling in one supreme effort as he yanked upward with such force that the other creature's entire body shook. The pistol-shot crack of its breaking neck echoed sickeningly, making Driscoll wince.

Kong towered above the carcass, pounded it with such rage that ribs snapped like sticks. He tattooed his chest uncontrollably before looking around as though to dare any creature to challenge him.

"We have to get away from here, but quick!" Driscoll said. "Come on." He led the way into heavy, concealing brush. The lone surviving triceratops lumbered past them, more than a hundred yards away, and did not seem to notice them.

For minutes, it seemed that the surviving triceratops had passed them by. Driscoll could still see it, shaking its heavy head and pacing through growth that would have swallowed a man whole. Kong picked up Ann and made his way straight across the cracked surface of the asphalt lake, climbed a steep ridge, and vanished over the crest.

The earth became mushy beneath Driscoll's feet as they drew close to the lake of tar. A scum of rainbow-hued water covered the margins of the lake, and beneath that lay miry, tarry black earth, of the consistency of thick mud. Driscoll soon saw that in order to venture out onto the lake they had to work their way back toward the triceratops, still snorting and tossing its head near the margin of some brushy woods.

"There," Denham said. "That's the way the dinosaur came out. If it held his weight, it'll hold ours."

Driscoll crouched and motioned, but in the distance the triceratops suddenly wheeled, its head lifted, and sniffed the air. "I think it's scented us!" Denham said.

The creature lumbered toward them. "Run for it!" Driscoll shouted, leaping onto the uncertain surface. The asphalt yielded under his feet, as though it were a thick layer of rubber. In a long, straggling line the men made the dash—but one of them had tried to run through the sedgy margin farther away, and he sank to his waist in the clinging tar. He screamed for help as he turned and frantically clawed at the earth, dragging his legs from the clinging asphalt.

The dinosaur must have heard him, for it wheeled in its run and headed for him. The sailor struggled free and broke into a desperate run, toward the trees that grew at the base of the ridge. Driscoll watched helplessly as the man, looking over his shoulder at the monstrosity thundering toward him, crashed into a low-hanging branch. It knocked him off his feet, and as he tried to pick himself up and swing behind the tree, the charging triceratops smashed into him, bearing him backward. The impact uprooted the tree. The triceratops backed away, and with a wave of nausea Driscoll saw the body of his shipmate impaled on one of the long horns.

"Poor Francisco," one of the sailors said.

"Come on," Driscoll ordered. They picked their way across the hardened asphalt—it bore them up better than it would have Kong or any of the gigantic saurians—past the fallen triceratops, past the bulge in the soft tar that covered the sunken one, and up the ridge that Kong had taken. At the top, Driscoll looked ahead. To his chagrin, half a mile ahead, a ravine cut across their line of march, diagonally from right to left. It looked as though the earth had torn itself apart in a quake, or perhaps a volcanic upheaval had split the stone foundation of the island. Maybe Kong could leap the barrier, but it was too wide for a man.

Denham was scanning the landscape with his binoculars. "There's a kind of bridge," he said at last. "A huge tree fell across it, looks like. We just might be able to get across there."

"What are we waiting for?" Driscoll asked, and they pushed on.

★ 14 ★

Denham thought they made a sorry sight as the survivors of the search party stumbled toward the ravine. Weary and fearful, they showed none of the confidence of the intrepid crew which had set out from the great gate. Yet, he reminded himself, Driscoll had chosen his men carefully. In the past, these men had proved extraordinarily resourceful in the face of danger.

And even now, Denham reflected, they wouldn't turn back. He had to admire that special high courage, the adventurer's final salvation, more potent than any weapon. Cast away in an ordinary wilderness, they would have boldly combined wisdom, experience, and ingenuity and won out. Still, he knew, Skull Island made demands that tested even their tough resolve. Here, for the first time, they learned the meaning of fear, and what it meant to be utterly helpless.

Denham cursed his luck again. This nightmare island presented dangers no man could plan on. He cursed the loss of the arms, though he knew that even if the men still had their rifles, the firearms might not be enough to discourage the denizens of the island. Most of all, Denham regretted the loss of the bombs. Armed with these, they could have fought on with some kind of a chance. Now Denham saw the men as helpless, just like that trapped triceratops slowly suffocating back in the pit.

Now and then someone stumbled and spat out a harsh oath. Denham thought they were on the verge of breaking, of losing their nerve completely. With something like surprise, he noted that his own nerves were steady. Resentment boiled in him, yes, and regret at not having his camera, but under it all he felt more awed than anything else. The books he had read had not prepared him for the reality of these dinosaurs. When he got back, he thought, he'd see to it that some of those books were rewritten. He called the creatures he had seen back to mind and determined to sketch them as soon as he could, before the details faded. Not as good as a photo, not a patch on a moving picture, but he could preserve the appearance of—

"What are we going to do if we catch him?" Driscoll asked in a panting aside.

Denham glanced at the first mate. "What do you mean, Jack?"

"I've been racking my brain for some trick that might free Ann. Kong is gigantic, and the only weapons we have are our knives. Worse than useless! Denham, why don't you go back and bring more men, more bombs?"

"Not a chance," Denham returned. "But we can send a couple of fellows back if you insist. How about young Jimmy and maybe Morgan? They could slip past just about anything if they're quiet enough."

They were within sight of the ravine. "Hear that, you two?" Driscoll asked.

Jimmy could only nod, but the older Morgan growled, "Aye, sir."

"Back you go, then, and be sharp about it."

Denham watched them turn back. Good luck, he thought as they vanished into the undergrowth. They had started out that morning with twelve picked men, Jimmy, Driscoll, and himself—a party of fifteen. Now, with three dead and Jimmy and Morgan heading back, they were down to only ten. As if ten men could do anything against the island god Kong, he reflected bitterly.

The men paused to catch their breath. Driscoll jerked his head, beckoning Denham aside. "How do you figure Kong, Denham?" he asked urgently.

Denham felt helpless. "I don't know how to put it in words, Jack. He's a mystery from the depths of time. What are you asking, exactly?"

Driscoll took a deep, unsteady breath. "He's carrying Ann like a doll. What does he—I mean, what does Kong want with her? I—" He choked in frustration.

Now Denham understood. Driscoll did not dare wrap his mind around the abominations he could imagine.

"Doesn't matter, pal," Denham said. "Because we're going to get Ann back." They had stepped closer to the ravine, a fearful gash in the earth, sheer-sided and far deeper than Denham had imagined. He pointed. "There's our bridge."

Driscoll shouted back to the men, "Come on! Time to move!"

Denham felt far more sympathy for Jack than he had been willing to show. This monster was more than a freak of nature, a subject for his camera. Kong was also a challenge to his spirit. Despite everything, something deep inside Denham reveled in the competition. Kong was the ultimate trophy. I thought I'd bring back the greatest picture the world has ever seen, he thought. Maybe I'll bring back even more than that. Maybe I'll bring back something no one's ever even imagined!

Driscoll saw that the fallen tree had not been placed there by Kong or anything else. It had simply collapsed in some storm or earthquake, and now its huge bole, easily one hundred feet from root to crown, spanned the ravine. They were on the root side, and it would be easy enough to scale the roots, get to the moss-covered top of the trunk, and walk across—

A heavy crashing from back on the trail jerked his attention from the problem. The men had frozen at the sound, and one of them yelped, "That damned three-horned brute is hunting us!"

"It can't cross this log," Driscoll snapped. "Come on!" He gave Denham a meaningful nod.

The director seemed to take his meaning. "Get across, boys," he said, and he waited until last to climb up himself. As Driscoll crossed the giant log, he could not keep from looking down. Heights never bothered him—he had spent his adult life climbing masts. He gazed down into a great depth and saw what seemed to be a thick deposit of mud and slime far below. In heavy rains, no doubt a raging stream flowed there. The nearly vertical walls of the ravine looked volcanic, cut throughout with pits and jagged fissures. Something moved down there, and Driscoll felt the hair on the back of his neck rising in atavistic fear.

A spider like a keg on many legs came crawling out of one of the openings in the far side of the ravine. Jack halted in his tracks, the others stopping behind him, as he watched the creature stealthily climb toward a ledge on which an animal, a gigantic lizard, lay warming itself on a sunny ledge. The spider moved toward it, then hesitated as if intimidated by the size of its intended prey. Then Driscoll blinked as he saw that he had been mistaken. The spider was after something else, a round crawling object with tentacles, like an octopus, that left a trail of slime as it crept along slightly below the level of the sunning lizard. The spider leaped, seized this thing, and dragged it into one of the fissures.

"Like a glimpse into hell," Denham said. "Uh-oh. Here's our old friend again."

Driscoll looked back. The triceratops had apparently trailed them by scent, and now, in its nearsighted fashion, it was blundering about at the edge of the trees. As if impatient or infuriated, the creature thrust its head at one of these and with a jerk ripped the twenty-foot tree right out of the ground. The uprooted trunk fell back and slid off its rough hide. The triceratops tramped in a circle, as if unsure of which way to go. It snuffled the ground, and then, moving uncertainly, the dinosaur advanced slowly in their direction. Ten yards away, it paused, its great three-horned head lifted high, its deep-set eyes peering forward.

At that moment, Driscoll felt the loom of something huge on the far side of the ravine. He saw a dark form burst from the undergrowth on that side and had time to shout, "Look out!" He frantically dived forward, grabbing a vine trailing from the fallen trunk, swung out, and dropped onto a ledge just below the rim of the ravine at the instant Kong attacked.

Kong had caught sight of the men pursuing him not long before. He had paused to find a gnarled, ancient tree, tall and stout enough to offer protection to his sacrifice, and with careful gentleness, he had placed Ann's unconscious form in the notch at its top. Then he wheeled and backtracked to the ravine, determined to defeat this new challenge. The fury roused in him by his confrontation with the three-horned dinosaurs had not died, and now it flared hotter at the thought of these insignificant creatures who dared to follow him. He burst from the forest and roared at the tiny men standing on the log. One dived off, but Kong paid him no attention. On the far side, the last one in line swung himself over and, gripping a root, lowered himself into one of the cavities in the ravine wall.

But the men in the middle of the log could do nothing: to advance against Kong was impossible, and retreat was no less so. The triceratops, sighting his old foe and perhaps mistaking Kong's outburst for a personal challenge, rushed up to the end of the log and growled his defiance.

Kong saw all moving things as potential enemies—the men on the log, the beast behind it. With a menacing shake of his head, he snarled, beat his breast, and pounded the ground. He raised a foot and placed it on the end of the log bridge, but at the same moment, the triceratops plowed into the root end, jarring it. The impact staggered the men in the center. They dropped to hands and knees, frantically clutching the log.

Kong noticed their reaction and stepped back. Reaching down, he seized his own end of the log and knotted his muscles as he gave it an experimental shake. Years of vines had grown over the log, and they broke, one after the other, with loud snaps. The men cried out in terror, clinging to the bark, to each other. With a fierce rumble, Kong slowly pried the log from its web of growth. The triceratops, perhaps fearing that Kong would throw the log at it, backed away, rumbling.

Kong heard one of the men shouting—from directly below him. He couldn't see the one who had swung into a fissure of the ravine wall, but he sensed that the shouts were a desperate attempt at a diversion.

Ignoring the cries, ignoring even the belligerent defiance of the triceratops, Kong curved both of his forearms under the log and strained upward with it. As soon as it tore free in an explosion of snapping vines and flying debris, he jerked it violently from side to side.

Driscoll's shouts, even the rocks he had hurled, had no effect. As Kong pried the log bridge free, Driscoll had to press himself back. Stone and soil rained down on him, and he thought the roof of the fissure he was in threatened to collapse under Kong's immense weight. He could only stare helplessly at the fate of his shipmates on the bridge.

As Kong rocked the log, two of the men lost their holds. One grasped madly at the face of a prone comrade and left bloody finger marks before he plummeted, tumbling into the stagnant silt at the bottom of the crevasse. He had no more than struck when the lizard flashed forward and seized him. Driscoll watched, hoped that the complete lack of movement meant that death had come immediately on impact.

The second man did not die from the fall. He was not even unconscious. He landed feetfirst and sank immediately to his waist in the mud. He thrashed and screamed horribly as three of the great spiders swarmed over him. Driscoll had to look away from the slaughter.

On the far edge of the ravine, the triceratops stamped the ground and retreated, snorting and grunting. Driscoll realized that Kong's rage, and his possession of a heavy projectile, had made the dinosaur think twice. With a last angry huff, it gingerly reared and wheeled around before lumbering away, vanishing beyond the trees.

The men closest to the root end of the log bridge scrambled, trying to leap to safety, but Kong now shook the log, and they went sprawling.

Another man fell and became prey to one of the loathsome spiders. Another jerk and other crewmen followed. By now Driscoll could see twenty or more spiders, boiling out of their dark hiding places at the base of the opposite cliff, eager for blood.

Only one man remained on the log, hanging on with fanatical strength. Driscoll shouted vainly from beneath. Across the ravine, Denham hurled rocks at Kong, but they did no more damage than pebbles. Kong was not to be distracted. He wrenched the log again but could not shake the lone survivor loose. The clinging man shrieked.

The log moved even higher, and Driscoll realized what was about to happen. Kong swung the bridge sideways and dropped it. For a heart-stopping moment, the end caught on the very edge of the ravine. Then it slipped, and the screaming man, the log, everything, smashed down on the feasting spiders below.

Driscoll, staring down in horror, suddenly realized he was about to become a victim. A spider swarmed up one of the heavy vines torn loose by Kong's rage, a vine which now dangled nearly to the floor of the ravine. The climbing creature was so near that Driscoll could see his own reflection in its great black protruding eyes. With seconds to spare, Driscoll drew his knife and sawed desperately. The spider's fangs glistened. Driscoll's revulsion gave him speed, and he hacked through the vine, sending the spider creature plunging back into the ravine. It landed on its back, and one of its kind immediately attacked it.

Though shaking from repugnance and fear, Jack thought again of Ann. Where was she? Everything had fallen silent.

Across the ravine, Denham shouted: "Kong's gone, Jack! He threw the log into the chasm and then beat it. Are you okay?"

"I'm not hurt. Did you see Ann?"

"No. Kong must have left her someplace. Hang on, though. These vines give me an idea. Can you climb out of that hole?"

"I'll try."

"Then you see if you can trail that hairy brute. If we're lucky, Jimmy and Morgan will get back to the Wall. I'll get together another rescue party, and we'll come back here as soon as we can." Denham's head jerked up, and he suddenly yelled, "He's back! Watch out above you!"

Driscoll ducked just in time. Kong's great black questing hand snatched at the air, barely missing him. Driscoll realized that their shouts must have called the giant creature back. Now he seemed intent on destroying his last enemies.

His fingers stretched out, but Driscoll was ready with his knife. He stabbed shrewdly at Kong's dusty, hairless palm, and immediately the beast-god jerked away and roared. Denham threw a rock. Driscoll could not see where it struck, but he heard Kong grunt in anger before the giant hand groped down into the cave again.

This time he snatched quickly, missed, and got clear. He snatched again and missed again. Driscoll stabbed at the fingers, but Kong ignored the wounds.

Driscoll crouched against the back wall of the shallow fissure, stabbing at every chance. Twice huge, curving fingers brushed him; twice he dug his knife in and got away. Kong forced him to the side, cornered him. Crouching lower, making himself as small as possible, he gripped his knife tightly and hunted desperately for an opening.

Then, from not too far away, Driscoll heard a scream—Ann's voice.

A moment later, Denham yelled, "He's leaving, Jack! He must be going to check on her!"

"But she's alive!" Jack yelled back, hope rising in him once more. Ann was alive!

★ 15 ★

What was at first a vague ache became a sharp pain, shocking Ann Darrow back to consciousness. The split branch held her in an uncomfortable grip. At first she saw only the bole of the tree, and above that a glimpse of sky. For long, foggy moments she had not the dimmest idea of where she was or even of what had happened to her. She was aware of being bruised and shaken, and a pall of fear lay heavy on her, but beyond that she could not organize her thoughts. Lingering on the edge of unconsciousness, she lay absolutely still, trying to gather her strength, remembering a vivid dream.

In the dream, Ann could feel the warm press of Jack's lips on hers, and the strength of his embrace made her feel completely safe. But now—groggy, Ann shaded her eyes with a hand against the overpowering light. Gradually, she became aware of the throbbing pain in her back and legs. The dank smell of rotted wood and steaming jungle vegetation filled her nostrils, while a thousand rioting insect sounds assaulted her ears.

Her uneasiness began to give way to terror. She forced herself to sit up and her head began to spin, not only because of weakness but also because of a shocking realization: she was thirty or more feet off the ground, perched in the broad notch of a once mighty tree. It was old and gnarled, and felt solid enough to have been rooted there forever. She was utterly alone. How could she possibly have gotten here?

Slowly, like the slithering, buzzing, chirping noises that had crept into her ears, memory began to steal back as well: Ann remembered screaming, screaming as loud as she could to block out some unimaginable horror . . . she fell back and the clouds whirled above her.

Abruptly, Ann sat bolt upright as the clear memory of Kong filled her mind. She remembered his hot, stinking breath in her face as he gazed upon her with a look that she could not describe. It was intelligent, almost human, but not quite. It was indescribably primeval. And that sent chills up her spine: realizing that it *wanted* her!

She gripped the tree on which she rested, looking hopelessly downward. The thick bole of the tree trunk soared bare and smooth from a tangle of dark underbrush, offering no handholds, no branches, no way down. But where was Kong? Why had she been left high up in a tree? Would the monster come back for her?

Her blood chilled at the thought. Nothing on earth seemed worse than such a fate. Her eyes darted nervously in every direction. She felt naked and vulnerable with nowhere to hide, nowhere to flee. Jumping from her perch would be suicide, and climbing down was impossible. She tried to calm herself, her heightened tension making her forget her aching limbs.

And then the sounds of the jungle sank to a tense silence. She heard a low rumble, then saw a huge, shadowy form that separated itself from the surrounding jungle and became horribly real. It moved like a bird, but on a grotesquely gigantic scale. An ammoniac whiff assaulted her nostrils. The creature's huge head slowly bobbed on a powerful neck. The deep-chested body was horizontally balanced on two heavily muscled legs, and behind the beast trailed a thick tail, held several feet off the ground.

Ann could sense a majesty about this animal, an aura of irresistible power. She felt like nothing in its presence, and in unconscious awe she covered her mouth with both hands. At her sudden movement the creature's head swiveled about, homing in on Ann. It looked directly at her.

She tried not to move, but her chest heaved, and her body trembled. The meat eater's lip curled on one side. Light glinted off teeth like huge, recurved daggers, gleaming with thick, ropy saliva. Its deep-set eyes fixed on her. A growl rolled into a slow hissing roar, and its mouth gaped into a toothed maw large enough to swallow her whole. Slowly, it rose to its full height and arched its neck. Despite her height in the tree, Ann could swear it was looking *down* on her! Suddenly the meat eater hunched back down and advanced toward her. She could feel the vibrations of its pounding feet through the tree trunk, and her screams filled the air as it loomed ever larger.

From somewhere behind, Kong hurtled past her toward the advancing dinosaur. The two behemoths collided with a heavy, cracking thud, both giving voice to deafening roars. Kong's back and arms strained to overcome his equally powerful opponent. Ann could not hear herself screaming, though her throat ached from the effort. She covered her ears to block out the thunder of combat.

The giants separated and stared each other down for an instant. Each refused to give way; each was unaccustomed to being resisted. Kong arched his broad back and rose higher than Ann's perch. He beat his chest in defiance. The great saurian bobbed for a moment, feinting to one side, and then pressed an attack with the swiftness of a striking snake, mouth gaping, teeth flashing.

Knowing that even one bite from that mouth could be lethal, Kong moved swiftly to the side, and the predator's jaws snapped on thin air. Kong's tremendously powerful arms clamped on the creature's head, holding the jaws shut. The dinosaur's two wiry arms dug like steel meat hooks into Kong's thickly furred wrists. Its neck strained against Kong's might, jerking the great ape's entire body from side to side before lifting him off his feet. Suddenly the dinosaur raised one of its legs and used its clawed foot to rake Kong's back. Kong growled in frustration and pain as he lost his grip.

As the meat eater reared back to gain leverage for another bite, Kong lunged forward, grasping his foe under the head with one arm and pounding with the other on its ribs with sledgehammerlike blows. Kong, infuriated by the wound on his back, relentlessly pressed his at-

tack. His clouts forced the flesh eater to take several jerky steps backward, all the while hissing and growling as its jaws snapped constantly. It tried in vain to angle its mouth down to get at any part of Kong's back.

And then with one mighty shove Kong sent the saurian reeling backward. It lost its balance and collapsed on its side. Getting up was not easy for such a giant, and its body and head flailed in an effort to regain its feet. The beast-god stood over his fallen challenger and pounded his chest. Kong's enormous canines glistened in fury. But such tactics would not intimidate his opponent. The creature lashed out with teeth and tail, answering Kong's challenge with a deafening roar of its own.

Realizing the defiance of his enemy, Kong abruptly rushed forward again. The flesh eater, only halfway back on its feet, fell heavily onto its side as Kong rained more blows upon its body. Finally the saurian managed to wedge a huge three-toed foot between its own body and Kong's chest and kicked with all its might. The thrust flung Kong off his feet, and he tumbled backward. As he landed on his heels, the momentum sent him sprawling uncontrollably into the great trunk atop which Ann sat.

Ann held on desperately as the ancient trunk suddenly cracked, the deep roots creaking as if groaning in pain. Slowly, the tree began to topple. Ann clung tightly as the trunk smashed into the undergrowth. The impact jarred her loose and she rolled into springy, thick brush that cushioned her landing. A heavy, short spike of branch had thrust itself into the earth and now kept the entire weight of the trunk from crushing her like an insect. A rush of adrenaline helped keep Ann lucid. She still had a ringside seat, only now she was on ground level and the two combatants loomed above her.

The chest of each giant heaved as each took the other's measure and gathered strength. Kong broke the standoff first, lunging in an attempt to attack his opponent's side again. The saurian spun in an instant, its tail slamming Kong hard across his midsection. Kong caught it but the impact buckled his knees and he roared in fury. The meat eater then frantically tried to shake him off, but Kong held on.

Good, Ann thought. As long as you have his tail, his jaws can't reach you! She realized that as terrifying as Kong was, he had not hurt her. She knew the meat eater would not be so inclined.

Ann sensed that Kong's strength was returning, and while holding the base of the tail with one arm, he mercilessly hammered the narrow hip area of the dinosaur. The creature writhed in pain as it jerked in all directions. Finally, one of the great beast's legs gave way and it landed hard on its knee. Ann heard the loud snap of its thighbone and winced at the sound. Kong let go, and the creature gave out a deep-throated growling hiss. Its sudden inability to stand on two legs forced it to roll painfully onto its side, its one free leg stabbing wildly at the air.

Ann knew the end was near. Kong gave no quarter, and as his tiring adversary attempted to rise, he scrambled onto its back. From behind, he grabbed its head, and twisting its skull with both arms, he forced it to roll agonizingly back down to the ground. Kong quickly maneuvered atop the writhing beast and again wrenched its neck. While leveraging his weight atop the gasping creature, Kong managed to free one arm. Again and again, he smashed his fist against the head of his foe. He shattered enough of its teeth to gain a grip with both hands between the gaping jaws. The monster writhed and hissed as Kong pulled with all his might in an attempt to rip the jaws apart. The dying predator made a last futile attempt to shake Kong loose with a twist of its neck, but it was no use.

Kong's shoulders knotted in effort. Ann screamed as she saw the dinosaur's jaws finally yield. With a sickening crack, the joints gave way. Kong grabbed the upper jaw, twisted it, and pushed down with all of his might, breaking the beast's neck.

At last it lay twitching in its death throes: reflexive jerks, then random shudders, slower, slower. Kong stepped back and grunted. He then advanced and quizzically manipulated the limp lower jaw before dropping the head to the ground. The form lay still. Kong prodded it. No movement. With a growl, he pounded with both fists on the prostrate dinosaur. Nothing.

The island's king threw back his head and, while beating his chest, gave out a triumphant shout that shook leaves from the surrounding trees. He stopped and then repeated his victory cry.

Ann covered her ears as she stared up at him. As soon as Kong stopped, he swung his arms slowly at his side and breathed heavily. He then turned to gaze down and make direct eye contact with her. She saw his hand reach for her. Every nerve in her body tingled. Trapped beneath the ancient trunk, her emotions overtaxed, Ann screamed one last time and lay still.

From fifty yards away, standing on a ledge in the near side of the ravine, Driscoll had seen the whole battle. He felt an agony of concern when the tree collapsed, wondering what had become of Ann. Now he saw Kong lift her limp form from the ground, hoist her to his shoulder, and turn away from the fallen dinosaur. Kong carried Ann like a doll out of the clearing and down the far slope.

Driscoll sensed a clear purpose in Kong's movements. He felt sure the creature was headed for the lair he had not been able to reach before. Now, no longer fretted by the pesky small men who had trailed him from the altar, safely past the morass into which the triceratops had driven him, and secure from the hungry pursuit of the meat eater, Kong seemed intent on bearing his prize home.

Driscoll climbed to higher ground, tracing Kong's progress through the brush by the disturbance the huge creature created, by the sudden bursts of birds from the foliage. He was sure Kong was keeping to a straight line and not moving very fast. He felt equally sure that he could follow the creature. He looked around, angrily wondering where the devil Denham could be. Almost at the same moment he heard a sharp whistle from farther along the rim of the ravine. Driscoll headed for it and soon saw a grinning Carl Denham on the far side of the chasm, holding a coil of vine rope.

Denham held it up and shook it. "I got this ready while the fight was going on!" he shouted. "I figured that if those two killed each other, you could get to Ann, and I could toss you an end of this, and together we could do something."

For the first time since he had left the village Driscoll felt a surge of the old affection for his employer. Whatever else he was, visionary artist, obsessed professional, crazy risk taker, Carl Denham was a man to depend on. He could get a friend into plenty of trouble, sure, but he'd never stop trying to get him back out.

Driscoll yelled, "That stuff may come in handy yet. Throw me one end!"

It took three tries, but finally Driscoll caught the end of the rope. He made it secure to a sturdy tree trunk, and he had Denham tie his end off in a similar fashion. "There, now you've got a way across, if you can find anybody foolish enough to come with you. You shove off back to the village. Arm a party and come back here."

"I hate like hell to leave you, Jack."

"What else can you do? The two of us could trail Kong, but what would we do when we found him? We've got to have some of your gas bombs to bring him down. You go get them. I'll mark the trail from here. We've still got a chance to save Ann."

"I guess that's the only way."

"You know it is."

"Okay, Jack. Good luck!" Denham grinned and waved.

With a grimace, Driscoll returned the wave. "See you later. Maybe."

Denham laughed, then turned on his heel and began to jog back toward the village. Driscoll crossed the clearing, where scavenger flying things, vulturelike but reptilian, had already landed on the body of the fallen dinosaur. They squawked and clattered and tore at the flesh. More wheeled in, and from the edge of the ravine a lizardlike creature more than six feet long appeared, its sharp head lifted, scenting death. The creatures paid no attention as Driscoll passed them by.

Driscoll followed the track of Kong down the slope. As he had expected, he found the trail easy to trace. He hurried along, and before many minutes had passed, he heard a crashing in the brush far down the hillside. Kong was moving deliberately, no longer aware of being trailed.

The screeches of the scavengers faded as Driscoll followed as fast as he dared. He forgot about the horrors he had left behind, the hungry things in the ravine, the fallen monster, the scavengers. Driscoll thought only of the dark enemy ahead, the huge and savage Kong.

★ 16 ★

Denham ran for a hundred steps, then fell into a fast walk for a hundred more. Then more running, more walking. Alone and knowing the lay of the land, he made better time than the rescue party had on the way out. He crossed the stream before it widened into the lagoon, followed its edge, and eventually found the rushing stream that had cut the steep channel through the precipice. Denham scrambled down and then broke through waist-high brush as he made a beeline for the Plain of the Altar. Night was coming on fast, and what had at first looked like low, ruddy stars became the flickers of torches high upon the Wall. Enough daylight was left for Denham to see that the figures holding the torches were not natives, but Englehorn's crew, with the only exception being what looked like an old woman leaning on a staff taller than herself. Denham was too far away to see her face, but her posture showed that she was watching intently, gazing out across plain and forest. She moved, and Denham thought she might have said something.

Then a voice rang out from a structure atop the Wall, one as tall in itself as a single-story house: "Ahoy, Denham!"

Denham released a long-held breath in relief at recognizing Englehorn's strong voice. He snatched the white cap from his head and waved it in acknowledgment, and the red torches blurred as the sailors returned his salute, breaking into an excited gabble. Denham could make out nothing but his own name, and once someone asked a sharp question that ended in "—Miss Darrow?" Denham sagged in relief, recognizing young Jimmy's voice.

Englehorn beckoned Denham forward, and as the exhausted director took his last few stumbling steps toward the Wall, the huge gate be-

135

gan slowly to swing open, just wide enough for him to pass through. Hands reached to help support him, tugged him into the sheltering safety behind the Wall, and he heard the gates slam closed behind him, heard the rasp as the gigantic wooden bars slipped home. For a few moments Denham stood panting at the center of a circle of men, struggling for enough breath to speak. Then Englehorn was at his side, getting an arm around Denham's sagging shoulders. "I've got you," he said. "Can't you men see he's done in? Help me with him."

Denham made a feeble protest, but the sailors all but carried him to a log bench. He sank gratefully down, aware as if for the first time of the aches in his knees, his back, his lungs. He ruefully reflected to himself that he was no longer a young man, though he had forced himself to a speed few younger men could have matched.

"Hey, Denham, where's Mr. Driscoll? Where're all the others?" Jimmy demanded.

Englehorn turned on the man. "Don't worry about that!" he snapped. "Get him some whiskey and some food. And secure the gate so it doesn't open again!"

"No," Denham said with a gasp. "We'll be going through the gate again. Anyway, if Driscoll gets back with Ann, he'll want to come through that gate in a hurry."

Englehorn leaned close, and in a low voice asked, "Where is Driscoll?"

"And Miss Ann?" Denham recognized this voice, too: old Lumpy.

Englehorn shook his head at Denham and said, "Let all that wait until he's rested. Where's that whiskey?"

Someone handed Denham a bottle, and as he tilted it back and let the fiery liquid pour into his throat, he closed his eyes for a moment. After that one gulp he handed the bottle back to the sailor who had offered it. His head was clearing now, and he saw how the men in the torchlit circle were studying him fearfully, taking in his ripped and muddy clothing, his cut and bruised flesh, his sagging, weary face. He sensed they waited with dread to hear whatever fearful story he had to tell. "Morgan and Jimmy both made it back all right?" he asked.

"Just minutes ahead of you," Englehorn told him. "Morgan's taken a launch back to the ship to bring more bombs. I was just about to get up a new party. Where are the others?"

"Tell you later," Denham said, not willing to add to the men's fears.

"Want to get back aboard the ship?" Englehorn asked in a voice that only Denham could possibly hear.

Denham wiped his mouth with the back of his hand and shook his head. "No, but I could use some grub if there's any handy."

Englehorn nodded and barked out a command. One of the sailors turned reluctantly, and Englehorn's voice rasped as he harshly added, "Shove along!"

Denham straightened on his bench, feeling a little better already. He looked at the circle of eyes staring at him, questioning him. "I know you want me to tell you what happened out there," he began.

"Maybe that had better wait," Englehorn said. "Food's on the way." His narrowed eyes signaled a warning, and Denham realized that Englehorn's men were still on the edge of panic, barely under control. Englehorn, Denham thought, must be afraid they'll break and run if they hear any more horrors. But then he'd never asked a man to do anything he wasn't willing to do first, and he realized that not letting them in on the dangers was a kind of betrayal he didn't want on his conscience.

"These guys can take it," Denham said flatly. "And I won't give it to them soft. Listen up, men, and I'll tell you the straight of it. Everyone's wiped out except for Jack Driscoll and Ann Darrow. Jack's gone to help Ann, and I'm going to ask for volunteers to go along with me to help him. All I can tell you is that I've got weapons to deal with the brutes beyond the Wall, and now I've got a better idea of how to handle them. I can't promise that nobody will be hurt, but you men are used to danger, and I don't think there's a man among you that would leave a shipmate and a woman out there alone. Who'll come with me?"

The men looked uneasily into each other's faces, their expressions uncertain in the flickering light of the torches. One of them asked, "What do you mean—'wiped out'?"

"Yeah, what happened out there?" another demanded.

"I mean wiped out!" Denham said sharply. "What do you think I meant? Listen, that hairy giant that made off with Miss Darrow isn't the only dangerous creature on this island. There are other animals out there, and I think we ran into half of them. Here's how it went."

He spoke firmly, without mitigating any of the fear he himself had felt, telling the whole story straight through. He paused only when he reached the tragedy of the log bridge, momentarily overcome by a depressing sense of responsibility for what had happened. He swallowed that back and told the story to the end, with Driscoll setting off to follow the monster and himself running back to the Wall alone.

"I don't get that," one of the sailors muttered. "If there's all these monsters out there, then how in the—I mean you—I mean—" He broke off in a mumble of confused words.

"You want to know how I got clear? That it? How did Driscoll and I manage to survive?" The man nodded, and Denham grinned fiercely. "We kept our heads, that's how! Listen, you men, if you don't panic, you've got a fighting chance, more than an equal chance, against those brutes. I tell you, I've got guns and bombs that can deal with anything this island could throw at us. But you've got to be disciplined, you can't panic. If I'd kept control of the bombs myself, we'd all be all right now, but I didn't, and when we lost them—well, if I'd had just a couple of bombs, we'd all be safe, and we'd have Miss Darrow back with us now. And I was safe from Kong because I was trying to see everyone safely across the log, so I was on this side of the ravine, and Driscoll had the sense to jump onto a ledge."

Englehorn put a hand on Denham's shoulder. "You couldn't have helped what happened. No matter what you did."

Some of the men murmured agreement.

Denham nodded. "You're right. Standing where I was, I couldn't have made a nickel's worth of difference. But I'll tell you boys the truth: I'll never forget I was the one who took them into it. Still, nobody can tell me I let them down. Now, here's something else. I know more about what we have to face out there now, and I've got a pretty good idea of how we can all get through safely. Here's the point, though—if you men don't stick with me and help out now, Driscoll and Ann Darrow don't have a chance."

Old Lumpy shook his head. "We won't never see them again."

Denham leaped to his feet. "The hell we won't! For the love of Mike, haven't you mugs been listening to me? We're not giving up. We'll see 'em both, and sooner than you think. Skipper, where's that grub? I'm gonna eat a bite and then I want another case of bombs. I'll take half a dozen men, no more, all armed to the teeth, and we'll back-track to the ravine. I want men who can do some quick rigging—we have a way across, and in ten minutes we could turn it into a stout enough swinging bridge. Now, who's coming with me?"

To Denham's surprise, Lumpy stepped forward at once. "I'll go, Mr. Denham."

Denham clapped him on the back. "There's a man for you!" he shouted. "Twice the man I am myself! But we need stouter, younger fellows for this! And if nobody volunteers, by thunder, Lumpy and I will do it ourselves! How about it? Aren't you ashamed to let a couple of old geezers like us go alone?"

As if a dam had broken, the whole pack of them stepped forward, to a jumble of assent, casual, reckless, or jovial, depending on the speaker: "I'm in." "Sure, I'll string along." "Hell's bells, why not?"

"You," Denham said, stabbing a finger. "You, you, and you. Jimmy's good with ropes, and he knows the score, so if he wants to go, he's in. One more—you!"

"And me," Lumpy insisted.

"I'd better come, too," Englehorn said.

Denham waved them off. "No, Skipper, we need a strong guard here at the gate. Lumpy, you're out, too. I want you up on top of that Wall with a spyglass, keeping a sharp lookout. When we come back, that gate will have to open quick, and as soon as we're through it, we want it shut and barred again, got me?"

At last the sailor came back with sandwiches, and Denham seized one and wolfed it down.

Englehorn insisted, "You'd better stay here, Denham. I'm fresher than you."

Denham polished off a second ham sandwich, shaking his head. "No good, Skipper. I know the way, and you don't."

"You could draw me a map."

Denham gave a yelp of laughter. "Skipper, don't you know me better? Why, I wouldn't let the freshest man this side of the Indian Ocean take my place on a trip like this, not even if he was the best map reader on the seven seas."

"I see," Englehorn said. "Taking a camera, are you, Denham?"

Denham shook his head. "No camera this trip. Maybe later. But my eyes are as good as any camera lens, and the sketches I'll make—you know how it is."

"I guess I'd say the same if I were in your shoes," Englehorn replied.

Denham turned away from the last unfinished sandwich. "Okay, give me a rifle. I want the six of you to take two rifles each, got me? Ammo belts? Good. All right, there'll be a dozen bombs in the crate when it comes in. Each of you will take two. And remember, all the hell we drew on the first trip was because neither I nor anybody else used the sense that God gave us to hang on to a couple of bombs. I want you lads ready with yours, so don't lose them, and nobody's to throw one until I give the order."

"And these bombs will stop them big brutes?" one of the sailors asked.

Denham looked at the men's expectant faces. "Stop them? I've seen them work. When I call for a bomb, you hand me one, and we'll drop anything in its tracks. One of these babies will knock even Kong right off his feet. Just stick with me until we get close enough to use it, that's all I ask."

"When do you plan to start?" Englehorn asked.

"Right now."

The captain shook his head and took out his pipe. "No, Denham. Too soon." He calmly filled and lit the pipe, puffing on it so the tobacco's red glow lit his craggy face.

"What do you mean?" Denham demanded. "Half an hour ago wouldn't be too soon!"

"Figure it out," the captain returned. "If you leave this second, you'll get to the ravine long before dawn. Then what? My men can't rig a bridge in the dark. All you could do would be to sit around, and maybe get picked off by whatever comes along in the night. You're going to need daylight to follow Driscoll's trail."

Denham bit his lip. "Yeah, that's a point," he admitted reluctantly. "But waiting until we could get to the ravine at dawn means hanging around for four more hours. How I can stand waiting four hours before starting back—well, I don't know."

"Get ahold of that dirty witch doctor," Lumpy growled from the darkness. "While you're waiting, he ought to be able to give you some tips about what to expect out there. And if he ain't willing, I think we can persuade him."

"That's an idea. Where is he?" Denham asked.

Englehorn shook his head. "Haven't seen him since right after you set out. There was some bother when some of them looked like they were going to try to keep you and your party from setting out. We fired a few shots in the air, and in the confusion, I knocked one of the warriors out with the butt of his own spear. All the rest of them vanished. The people seemed scared. They've gone into their huts and have stayed there. I think it's best if we don't bother them. There are more of them than there are of us."

"Any of the men get outside the Wall?" Denham asked. "You don't think any of them are out hiding in the bush waiting to surprise us, do you?"

"None of them went through the gate," Englehorn said. "They're all in hiding, except one old lady. She climbed up on top of the Wall with us. I tried asking her some questions, but she just glared at me. Made me feel like a boy of six caught with his hand in the cookie jar. She was the one who first spotted you coming back, though, and she pointed you out to me. I could almost swear she knew English, the way she seemed to be listening to us up there."

"Well, I guess if any of the natives attack us, we can handle 'em," Denham said.

"They won't," Englehorn said flatly. "They don't think they need to. As far as they're concerned, Kong will take care of you. See it their way, Denham. We've been pretty high-handed with their god, haven't we? We tried to deny him his sacrifice, then chased him after he got her. These people know Kong, and they worship him. To them, we've sinned, and their god will punish us. When he does, they want to be as far away as possible."

Denham nodded. "They're right, too. Kong will be back. If we get Ann away from him, he'll be right on our tails."

"Why?" one of the volunteers asked. "He's just an animal, ain't he?"

"I think Gunnarson's right," Englehorn said. "Seems to me that an animal doesn't have the capacity to think like that, Denham. By this time tomorrow, he'll be foraging for food, not worrying about his sacrifice."

"You're wrong," Denham said slowly. "This island is crawling with monsters, but Kong—well, Kong is the one creature beyond the Wall that's something more than beast. He's smarter, wilier. Call him a monster, too, but he acts halfway human. There's a spark of something more than animal cunning in that huge head of his. To him Ann means something. He won't give her up willingly."

"Oh, come on," Englehorn said.

"I tell you, he's different," Denham insisted. "And if I didn't know that, I wouldn't have one solitary hope of seeing Ann alive again. I saw the way Kong handled Ann, and the way he protected her. He's fascinated by Ann. She's different from the others somehow, and maybe he doesn't have the faintest idea of why she's different or even exactly how she's different. When he saw her, something gave way inside him. It's—well, it's Beauty and the Beast."

"Your movie title," scoffed Englehorn, drawing at his pipe.

"Yes, but that doesn't make it bunk," Denham returned. "You've seen it yourself, Captain. We all have. The tough guy who falls for the soft dame, happens all the time. And nine times out of ten, that's the end for the tough guy. He loses his edge, softens up. That's why I think we've got a chance."

"Just be careful out there."

Denham continued in a low voice, as if he hadn't heard at all: "Kong will lose Ann in the end, one way or another. And after he does, he'll never be the same king of the island again. Brute strength, but strength weakened by a new awareness, and that awareness will be enough to make him hesitate in a clench. Next time he's in a life-and-death fight with one of the island monsters—" Denham shrugged.

"Nice theory," Englehorn said. "But it's moon talk, Mr. Denham. Stuff for your moving pictures. Oh, Kong might have been attracted by Miss Darrow's golden hair, I'll grant you, but only because it was different, it was strange. A magpie is attracted to a shiny stone. And magpies get tired of carrying stones. Kong will get tired, too. Somewhere along the way, he'll drop Miss Darrow. I just hope that when he does, Jack Driscoll is there to pick her up. He's a good man in a pinch. Now you've got some time before you have to start out. Better get some sleep, if you can."

"You're right about Jack. We can trust him," Denham said. He looked at his watch. "As for sleeping, I don't know. I just wish to heaven it were time to do my share. I don't know how I'm going to wait it out."

SKULL ISLAND

MARCH 13–14, 1933

As far as Driscoll could tell, Kong followed no beaten trail, but torn, scattered leaves, broken branches, and the occasional deeply imprinted track in the sodden jungle floor all clearly marked his passage. After an hour or so, Driscoll realized he would have no difficulty trailing the gigantic Kong even without the visible marks he left behind, because the behemoth took no care to move quietly. The cracking and crashing of branches and brush echoed through the darkening shadows of the woods, and Driscoll just had to follow the sound. More, the musky stench of Kong's body, different from the acrid reek of the dinosaurs, hung in the air. Kong's gait had also become leisurely. Ever since he had dealt with the meat eater, the king of the island took his time, apparently fearing no enemy challenge.

Grimly, Driscoll decided that staying *close* to Kong might be his best choice. Surely no other living creature on the island could stand up to Kong, and anything that might try to eat Driscoll would draw Kong's unwelcome attention.

Even so, Driscoll worried that Kong's choice of path meant that more monstrous challenges might lurk in the jungle. Again and again Driscoll crossed clear animal trails, worn through the heavy growth over generations. Most of them were far too narrow to offer Kong a path, but some were both wide and deeply worn. Kong, though, chose to force his way through virgin growth, using no established path that an enemy might discover, offering no place where a wily foe might lie in ambush.

The sun vanished and twilight closed in. Driscoll narrowed the distance between himself and his gigantic quarry, once misjudging his progress so badly that he caught a sudden glimpse of Kong's massive shoulders and head in dark silhouette against a purple sky in which a few stars already gleamed. A flicker of panic made Driscoll crouch and freeze, not through fear for himself, but for Ann. It was too dark for him to see her, but he guessed she was still cradled on Kong's shoulder, still unconscious. He knew his only hope of rescuing her lay in arousing in Kong no suspicion of pursuit. Driscoll had no clear plan and didn't know if he had to try to steal Ann away from her captor alone or whether he would be able to wait until Denham brought reinforcements. Either way, if Kong discovered he was being followed, anything might happen.

Kong's form vanished again, and after a slow count to twenty, Driscoll rose and followed the sounds and scent of the giant creature's progress, taking care to stay well back so that Kong would be unlikely to realize he was so close at hand.

Darkness closed in, and more than once Driscoll went sprawling as a root caught his foot, or felt tears streaming from an eye lashed across by an unseen twig. Eventually, when night had come fully on, the sounds ahead changed in quality, became purposeful. Driscoll crept ahead, wondering what had happened. Had Kong reached his den?

Eventually, Driscoll concluded that the giant had just decided to rest. He seemed to be tearing softer branches from the trees, gathering them into a sort of nest, arranging them in an immense pile against the boles of three ancient trees. Driscoll fell back and found the shelter of a fallen tree trunk. It was so big that he could stretch out under its rounded overhang.

He didn't plan to sleep, but he rested there, aware of every strained muscle, every pulled ligament, every scratch and bruise. He heard Kong's regular breathing, and once another sound, a sound that wrenched his heart. Ann sobbed, just once. Driscoll tensed, but then forced himself not to rise from his position. What could he do in the dark? He couldn't even let Ann know he was nearby. He had to wait it out, though that was the hardest thing he had ever done.

It was a long night, rioting with insect sounds, shot through with the distant screeches and roars of night-hunting animals. Despite himself, Driscoll fell into a series of cat-dozes, none of them deep. Now and again thunder rolled in the distance, and the stars blinked out as clouds slipped across the sky overhead. Eventually, the black sky began to pale into ragged patterns of gray. Thunder boomed in the distance, from back toward the Wall. A cloudy dawn was breaking, and with it Kong stirred. Driscoll heard him rise, grunt, and then break his way through the brush. He had resumed his journey, and Driscoll followed.

Kong topped a ridge, then headed down the far side. From the crest of the ridge, Driscoll caught his first sight of Ann since the battle between Kong and the carnosaur. Kong carried her cradled in his massive left arm, her own left arm dangling loosely. She still lay unconscious, but Driscoll convinced himself he could see her breathing. Her blond hair glowed in the early light, its bright spill contrasting with the dark fur of Kong's arm. Her clothing had been torn, and one round shoulder was bare, a detail that made her look even more helpless and childlike. Fear clutched Driscoll's throat, but he made himself wait until Kong and his captive had moved out of sight before he resumed his pursuit.

Sweat began to sting Driscoll's eyes. The sun still hid behind the cloud cover, but the clouds were like the lid on a simmering pot, holding in moisture and oppressive warmth. He guessed the time as ten o'clock when he once again caught sight of Kong. Driscoll had entered a clearing, and on the far side, he saw the beast-god, fifty yards away, still holding Ann. Her arm no longer dangled free. Driscoll thought she clutched the fur of Kong's chest, but he couldn't be sure.

The vegetation thinned rapidly after the clearing. The trail, which had sloped steadily down from the last ridge, now rose again. Driscoll fell farther back as cover became sparse. At this elevation, the earth became rocky, the soil a thin scatter over dark volcanic stone. The jungle tangle of vines and undergrowth disappeared. The trees here grew more slender, more widespread, towering up with no clustering brush at their roots. As the clouds gathered and the daylight darkened, Driscoll had begun to catch glimpses of a great dome of bare rock, the formation that he thought of as Skull Mountain. Kong picked up speed, clearly heading toward his lair.

Driscoll was at least a mile behind as Kong climbed a rising spur of volcanic rock. On both sides, the stone fell away in steep slopes. Driscoll stared down the left slope. At its base, a more or less level plain stretched, overgrown with grass and almost bounded in by another rocky ridge. Bones littered the floor of this natural enclosure. They had been scattered by scavengers, and green moss filmed many of them. Still, Driscoll thought, they were evidence of titanic battles. He couldn't help wondering if Kong had been one of the combatants.

Following the distant Kong, Driscoll became more and more convinced that the beast-god had a den somewhere on Skull Mountain itself. It made sense: the island's highest peak would offer a retreat available only to a mighty climber. The bare stretches of stone would give Kong an unobstructed view, and the lack of vegetation meant that no herbivores would venture here. In turn, that meant no large meat eaters would have cause to go hunting there. Then, too, Driscoll had seen how Kong fended off challengers by hurling missiles at them, and here were plenty of rocks and boulders to heave at any enemies that might follow him.

As the day wore on, the rising landscape became a jumble of boulders. The sky behind him had become an ugly purplish black, streaked with occasional darts of lightning, but the storm held off. Driscoll doggedly continued, though he was close to exhaustion.

Bruised, battered, and aching, his body throbbed from falls and blows of branches. His belly clenched with hunger. His mouth felt parched with thirst. He stumbled along on legs numb from fatigue. Still he forced himself to follow the distant form of Kong.

Dazed with weariness, Driscoll tardily became aware of something new as he completed a long, slow swing to the left. A great spout of water burst from a dark opening in the side of the mountain, exploding in a white, misty torrent. Over ages it had cut a deep pit into the stone, a boiling lake. It spilled from this into a narrow channel that soon lost itself in the jungle beyond.

The main waterfall rumbled with unimaginable power, but the falling water also fathered a hundred small rivulets that ran in zigzag patterns over the stone or shot out to fall in cascades down to the lake. Driscoll reached one ankle-deep stream, knelt, and scooped up handfuls of wonderfully cool water, slaking the raging thirst that gripped him. He guessed that the waterfall he saw ahead was the source of the stream that, far behind now, widened into the lagoon of the elephantine dinosaur and still farther poured softly over that slide leading down onto the Plain of the Altar. It just might offer a quicker path back, if he could descend to the lake, if the river's banks were not too heavily wooded, if no monsters—

A shadow moved in the corner of Driscoll's eye, and he became aware that Kong was in sight again, on a ledge barely a hundred yards above his head. The giant stared out across the jungle, and Driscoll had a split second to compel his aching muscles to action. He leaped behind a round boulder more than waist high and dropped to all fours as Kong's baleful gaze dropped and swept the ridge on which he stood. Driscoll heard the creature rumble, then move.

He cautiously emerged. The slope up to the ledge was daunting, but he thought he could make it. Hugging the rough volcanic stone, he hauled himself up with arms and legs, at last emerging at the very spot where Kong had stood.

Driscoll realized that his journey had ended. Half a mile ahead, up a much gentler incline, Kong stood on a kind of plateau. Driscoll saw that the mountain's slopes here formed a natural amphitheater. For the moment, Kong had his back to Driscoll. He seemed to be staring downward. Driscoll cautiously edged forward and to the left, and then reached the edge of the plateau. Now he saw that a nearly circular black pool of water occupied most of the plateau. It looked as if a vast underground stream had worn away the stone overlying it. The pool seemed unusually deep, its waters dark, seemingly without source. Ripples and swirls on the black surface hinted at rushing movement far below.

Driscoll now realized that the waterfall that burst from the side of the mountain farther down must have its source here. Ahead, the colossal bulk of Skull Mountain itself blotted out the cloudy sky. A curving cliff half enclosed the pool, and atop the rising cliff a ledge ran up to the opening of a broad, arched cavern.

Kong stood on a narrow, sandy margin of the pool. He had evidently been heading toward the ledge leading up from the pool to the cave when something had stopped him. His shoulder fur bristled as he glared down at the dark water, frozen, alert to some danger that Driscoll could not see.

Driscoll found another spur of rock to hide behind. From this he watched as Kong gingerly set Ann Darrow down. She moved—she was alive! Driscoll saw her huddle against a boulder. Kong didn't give her so much as a glance. Maybe, Driscoll thought, I could—

And then something moved. A serpentlike neck suddenly reared from the dark water of the pool. Driscoll realized that what he had thought of as a black, smooth stone was in fact the body of some water creature—and the monster's head struck at Kong, only a few feet away from the crouching form of Ann Darrow.

Kong lowered his shoulders, as if making ready to meet an onslaught. He struck at the dinosaurian head, but the monster drew back. Kong moved forward, putting his bulk between this threat and Ann, and sounded his challenge.

Again Driscoll heard that thunder of rage, but this time without terror. The battle cry almost shook the stones, and at the same time Kong drummed his fists on his chest. Driscoll searched for an opening, but there was no way he could get past the struggling giants to rescue Ann.

Instead he had to watch in frustration, hoping that she would not be harmed.

The snakelike neck and head had struck again, and this time Kong charged to meet them. Kong's hands seized on the beast's neck and he heaved, but the reptilian horror must have wrapped its tail on some rock at the bottom of the pool. It resisted, pulled back, nearly toppled Kong into the water. Kong fought with flashing teeth and mighty blows of his fists. His feet gripped the uneven rocks at the margin of the pool, withstanding his enemy's attempts to pull him into its own element.

The monster coiled its neck around one of Kong's pillarlike legs and sank its teeth into the flesh of his thigh. Kong snarled in fury and reached to try to grasp the monster's head. The creature had given up trying to haul Kong down. It threw its entire sinuous length out of the pool and wrapped itself around Kong, like a gargantuan constricting snake. Driscoll, hunkered behind his rock, could see no advantage to either side for long moments. The thing from the pool looped its coils around Kong's chest, tried to ensnare his neck. For his part, Kong fought to bring his teeth to bear on those coils, tore at the monster's flesh with his hands, and struggled in a terrible silence. He gave no more challenging roars, but Driscoll could hear the rush of Kong's breath as the monster tried to squeeze the life from him.

Then, suddenly, Kong changed his stance, widening his stride, bending his knees and dropping lower. The move took the creature from the pool by surprise, and it reared its head. Immediately Kong seized that elusive target with both hands. His shoulders knotted with effort, and Driscoll winced as the beast-king crushed the skull. The creature writhed in agony, lost its hold, and its coils thrashed, loosening their clutch on Kong. Kong held the beast's neck in one hand and used the other to peel away the constricting length of the monster. The beast fell into a pulsating mound at Kong's feet, and as if in contempt, Kong threw the smashed head to the top of the pile.

Then Driscoll saw Kong sway, moving as if he were about to collapse. He stood with chest heaving, and then moved his feet from the
loose clutch of the reptile's coils. Kong prodded the dead body and
seemed to shudder. Driscoll nodded. He, too, felt the same horror of
the reptilian monsters of this accursed island. Kong looked around,
reached behind him, and Driscoll saw that he had once again lifted
Ann Darrow. With a surprising tenderness, Kong cradled her form
once more in his arm. With a final snarl at the dead reptile, Kong
mounted the ledge and followed it up toward the cavern opening above
him. He moved heavily, with lowered head.

Sure, Driscoll thought, he's worn out. He's fought monsters, he's
broken a long trail through the jungle with no water and no food, and
he's hardly snatched a wink of sleep. He's not on guard now.

Driscoll broke from cover and hurried after the retreating Kong. He
had to hold his breath near the dead creature—the stench was incredible. Above him Kong toiled up the ledge, his attention wholly occupied by the path before him. Driscoll drew his knife, no longer fearing
detection. Still, he did not dare attack. Kong might have exhausted
himself in fighting that reptilian horror, but those big hands retained
more than enough strength to rip him to shreds. Kong reached the
cavern and did not even pause before vanishing inside.

A few moments later, Driscoll stood just outside the opening, gazing inside. The vaulted cavern seemed to meander in three or four different directions, and Kong was nowhere to be seen. One path led
upward, but it seemed to have been blocked at some time in the past.
Now a spill of huge stones lay before it, and it stretched up into darkness and obscurity. Kong might have taken that route, or he might be
lurking in the shadows within the cave. Driscoll could not tell.

He sank down and sat with his back braced against the cave wall,
wondering if Denham had made it back to the Wall, if he was somewhere on the trail with weapons and reinforcements. Then he heard a
drumming sound from overhead. He edged out and gazed up the steep

face of Skull Mountain. Another round cavern gaped far up there, one of the eye sockets of the skull's face, and at its base a shelf of rock projected a short way out. Kong stood on this, sending his defiant cry out over the island. He had reached his lair, and now he claimed mastery.

Something bright moved at Kong's feet—Ann, set down and trying to creep back into the cave, away from the edge, away from Kong. Driscoll made up his mind. He went into the lower cavern and picked his way up the rubble-strewn ramp that led upward into the gloom, upward toward Kong—and toward Ann.

In the darkness, Driscoll must have taken a wrong turn. Following a gray gleam of dim light, he emerged, but not into the eye cavern. Instead, he found himself standing in a narrow crevice a few feet below the eye socket. The sky was darkening as the threatening clouds built up, and above him, Driscoll could hear the shuffling of Kong. Thunder, closer than it had been, vibrated the very stone of the mountain under Driscoll's grasping hands.

He got a grip and pulled himself up, cautiously. When his head cleared the edge of the rocky shelf, he saw that Ann had retreated to just inside the cavern entrance. Kong stood before her, tilting his head, looking down at her quizzically. Ann struggled to rise to her feet.

And then something screamed, something higher up, in the sky. Driscoll whipped his head around. The largest of a flock of pterodactyls that had been wheeling against the ragged sky came spiraling down in a long swoop. Kong must have seen it at the same instant, because he bellowed out a savage challenge. The diving pterodactyl came within Kong's reach, and he struck at it, but it wheeled away, just out of Kong's grasp, to be borne up again by a rising gust of air.

Driscoll heard Ann shriek, just as she had when the carnosaur threatened. He pulled himself up onto the ledge, no more than twenty feet from Kong. If Kong noticed him now—

But Kong's attention was all on Ann. The beast-god stooped over Ann, and a huge hand reached forward almost fondly. One of the great fingers brushed Ann's golden hair, with an oddly affectionate tenderness, as if the monster were trying to comfort her. Ann sobbed brokenly.

Driscoll's weary muscles failed him, and he sagged back into the crevice just below the eye socket, but he caught himself at a point where he could still see. Ann tried to shove the monstrous finger away and screamed again. Kong closed his great hand around her form and lifted her into the air. Driscoll saw the gleam of Ann's bare shoulder as Kong held her as though she were a curious little doll.

Driscoll gripped the stone as he watched Kong caress Ann with clumsy fingers. He seized her dress, pulled at it, tore half of it away, and rubbed the fabric between two fingers before letting it fall. If Kong's expression had been threatening, Driscoll would have risked everything, would have attacked Kong with nothing more than his knife. The huge creature showed no sign of aggression, though, but instead seemed merely puzzled and interested. Ann struggled, crying out weakly.

Abruptly, Kong stiffened, swinging around with a jerk that made Driscoll flatten himself against the stone. Then he realized that Kong had not sighted him at all, but another enemy. The pterodactyl, perhaps attracted by Ann's bright hair, had swooped in again. Kong swept an arm at it, and without looking, he set Ann down behind him.

The flying creature screamed and soared away, then seemed to tilt up, stand still for an instant as it balanced in air on the tip of one outstretched wing, and then began a long plunge downward, plainly trying to attack Ann. Kong moved to block this new adversary. The flying creature apparently was intent on spearing Ann with its long, sharp bill, swooping in for a lightning-quick strike before Kong could stop it.

Driscoll clenched his teeth. The flying monster didn't have a chance—but it offered his first real hope of rescuing Ann. He saw her struggle to her feet behind Kong.

"Ann!" Driscoll risked a loud whisper. She heard him and sprinted toward him. Above her head, Kong seized the body of the pterodactyl. The great wings beat the air with leathery flaps, and the flying monster screeched again.

Ann reached the edge of the platform just as Driscoll dragged himself onto her level. Visibly struggling not to cry out, she gasped, "Jack!"

"I'm here, Ann." They embraced, but briefly. Kong had killed the pterodactyl. Now he hunched over it, using his teeth to rip gobbets of flesh from the body, wolfing them down.

Ann whimpered. "Don't let him touch me again, Jack." She wore only tatters of her dress and scraps of her underthings now, and she clutched these rags close to her.

Kong must have heard her. He swung his heavy head toward them, his mouth bloody from his meal. He threw the remains of the pterodactyl over the edge of the rocky shelf and roared. A horrible low, rolling growl rumbled from his chest. The look in Kong's eyes was unlike anything Driscoll had ever seen, had ever imagined. The monster advanced, trapping them at the edge of the cliff.

Cold fear gripped Driscoll. Kong would let nothing stand between him and what he desired. If not for Ann, Driscoll might have stood utterly frozen, but he had to save her. Looking wildly around, he realized that they stood directly above the dark pool—far above it. "Jump!" he yelled, but he gave Ann no choice, pulling her with him. With his arm locked around her waist, they plunged over the edge of the shelf and down, down, toward the black and waiting water.

★ 18 ★

Ann had time to gasp in one deep breath before she and Jack plunged feetfirst into the black pool. The impact jarred her, but the warmth of the water startled her. She had braced herself for a stinging chill, but the pool felt nearly blood-warm, soothing against her scratched, bare skin. She felt Jack close by, tried to swim in his direction. Everything was black, and she had no sense of direction, no idea of which way led up to air, to life.

A hand closed gently on her wrist and pulled. She was rising—at least she was moving—and then an arm wrapped around her waist, and she knew that Jack had her. Her lungs were close to bursting with the urgent need to breathe, but she trusted Jack, gave herself into his keeping. He was scissoring his legs, and she tried to kick, too, helping him as much as she could.

Then, miraculously, her head broke the surface, and she threw it back and breathed, breathed deeply, hearing Jack gasp from somewhere close beside her, panting quickly, deeply. "All right?" Jack's voice shouted. "Ann, are you all right?"

The lightning-streaked clouds had become so thick that even in afternoon, the land lay in a kind of twilight. Ann could see Jack's strained, concerned expression as he trod water. His hair lay plastered to his skull, and streams of water crept across his forehead and down his cheeks.

"Yes," Ann said when she had breath. "I can swim. Jack, I can't believe you've come!"

"I wouldn't let you get away from me. Do you see Kong?"

"Not yet. He wouldn't jump in, but he'll come down through the tunnel. What will we do?"

155

Jack jerked his head. "This way." He swam toward what looked to Ann like a whirlpool, an eddy of water on the far side of the pool. She followed, and from behind them Ann heard the outraged screams of Kong.

"This is a long shot, but a better chance than we'd have at his hands," Jack said. "Three deep breaths, then dive. I'll hold your hand the whole way."

Now Ann heard the drumming of Kong's chest, and she knew he was on the ledge, charging toward the pool. "I'm ready."

"I'll be right beside you. Breathe three times, then dive!"

They both jackknifed and slipped beneath the surface. Ann kicked as hard as she could, sensing Jack driving himself down beside her with the strength of his legs. They were too far from their objective, and they had to rise for air. The instant they did, Ann heard Kong's growl as he threw himself forward to stop them. This time she shouted, "Dive!" They both bent at the waist and slid into the depths again. Ann heard a muffled roar and felt the *whump* of Kong's hand as it thrust into the water, grabbing for them.

But suction caught them and pulled them beyond Kong's reach. The strong current swept them ever deeper. The water pressure filled Ann's ears, made the sinuses in her cheeks creak and sting. Darkness ahead, then dim, gray light. She gave in to the current, no longer swimming but swept along, and she crossed her arms, cradling and protecting her head. Where was Jack?

Ann felt herself pulled into what seemed to be a tunnel, one worn smooth by the passage of water over eons of time. Her right knee banged painfully against stone, but she barely had time to register the jolt before finding herself tumbling in a white spray of foamy water. Jack—where was he? She couldn't see him anywhere—

The fall ended as she splashed into a churning pocket of roiling water and bubbles, spinning heels over head. This time she popped to the surface like a cork, whirling madly as she drew breath into her tortured lungs. Then the swift current swept her along between two tall, sheer walls of stone.

"Jack!"

Two times, three times, she repeated her shout, turning onto her back to float, briefly lifting her head. In the riverbed, a gloom almost as thick as night had fallen. She could see nothing. She rolled over and started to swim against the current. Fear rose in her again, fear of being alone, but even worse, fear for what might have happened back at the falls. If Jack was hurt—

"Here!" he shouted in her ear. "I'm okay, Ann!"

She felt his arm around her waist again. "Thank God!" she cried, and then was busy treading water. The swift river ran deep here.

"Just what we need," Jack said. "Follow me!" He struck out downstream, and Ann followed. After half a dozen exhausting strokes, she felt Jack grab her wrist and pull her forward. Something rough, bobbing—a tree trunk, or perhaps just a lightning-blasted branch from a huge jungle tree—floated high in the water, and Ann clung to it gratefully.

"This is the ticket," Jack said from behind her. "This river leads right back to the Wall, and if we can stay with it, it's the quickest way back. Kong will be after us, but he'll have to come overland, through the forest. We must be drifting at ten or twelve knots. We can beat him."

"Are—are you hurt?" Ann asked.

"Kong made a grab for me just as I made that last dive. Anyway, his nails tore some skin from my scalp, I think. It's not deep. I'll do."

She reached blindly, caressed his face, then felt the cut in the flesh above Jack's ear. It seemed to be a couple of inches long, and the warmth at her fingertips told her it still oozed blood. She laughed in relief that the wound wasn't worse. "I owe you a bandage, but I don't have enough clothes left for a penny doll, let alone a full-grown girl."

"It'll keep. I just hope we don't have to ride out any rapids. Sooner or later this river has to spill into a lagoon, and when we get there, we'll need to get ashore and hotfoot it back to the village. Until then, hang on tight and don't worry about your modesty. It's too dark for me to see anything anyway."

He pulled her closer to him and impulsively kissed her. She returned his kiss. "Guess you're my hero," she murmured.

"I don't know about that. Well, that one was just because I couldn't help it. This one is to celebrate escaping."

The log they rode began to buck and pitch. They clung on desperately. Overhanging trees kept the river channel mostly in darkness, but at intervals the high banks widened and a little light filtered down, along with a driving tropical rain. "I don't like this," Ann said.

"If you see white water or hear the roar of rapids, let me know. We'll have to try to get to shore somehow."

But luck rode with them. After an endless rushing time, the water suddenly smoothed out, and they felt their speed fade. "The lagoon!" Jack said. "Come on, Ann. Let's get ashore before some swimming critter decides we're on the menu."

They pushed off from the log and breaststroked until Ann felt yielding mud beneath her bare feet. It was thick and miry, and the reeds on the shelving shore clustered like a barrier, but she and Jack dragged themselves out of the water. The day was a little brighter here, but still the hard rain pelted down. "Where are we?" Ann asked.

"Maybe halfway back to the Wall. Lord, I'm tired, but we've got to keep going. We're on the right side of the lagoon, anyway. If we follow the shoreline, sooner or later we're going to hit the path that Kong broke when he carried you away from the Plain of the Altar. Wish I had—"

"Come on," Ann urged. "Let's get away from here before Kong arrives."

Overhead the clouds began to break. The rain swept away, leaving only a heavy drizzle, and at last they had enough light to navigate by. The riot of insect and animal sounds had broken out again, chirrs and wheeps, raw-throated roars of predators, screams of their prey cut short. They struck an animal trail that led in the right direction and risked following it. Day was getting on, and under the canopy everything fell into green gloom, making it difficult to see. They stumbled along as best they could. Twice they heard the rustle of some large body not far away, and both times they froze in their tracks until whatever it was lumbered away. After an interminable time, an hour or six hours, Ann couldn't tell, she asked if they could rest.

"Not for long," Jack said. "A minute or two. If you can't make it, I'll try carrying you."

"You couldn't do that," Ann protested.

"I'll carry you ten miles if I have to," Jack said stoutly.

They sat on the spongy earth, and Ann leaned against Jack gratefully. She had begun to shiver, not from cold, but in reaction and weariness. Her stomach panged with hunger—she felt famished. All the fear she had felt in the grip of Kong had vanished, but the adrenaline strength had faded with it. Now she trembled despite herself.

Thunder rolled in the distance. "It's still pouring somewhere," she whispered.

"I'm glad the storm came," Jack said. "Might wash out our scent. Ann, I didn't even ask. Are you hurt? Did that big—"

She touched his lips. "No. It was horrible being in his grasp—I felt so helpless, like a rag doll. But Kong didn't seem to want to hurt me. He was, well, gentle in a way. Tender, almost. I think he was more curious about me than anything else. He carried me carefully, in the crook of his arm. I don't know what he wanted with me. I was afraid that—" She broke off, feeling Jack's arm around her shoulders.

"Forget about Kong," he said softly.

"I'll never forget him," Ann replied slowly. "How could I? I wondered—I wonder still—well, you know what Carl's always saying about Beauty and the Beast. I can't help wondering if Kong is all beast, after all. Do you think he's following us, Jack?"

"I've been wondering the same thing. It's hard to believe that a brute beast would have sense enough to reason out the path we had to take, and we've certainly outdistanced him. I don't know. Maybe he'll go back to the village, because that's where he first found you. But he's as tired as we are, and he has to eat, too. An animal wouldn't be single-minded. It would put food first."

"He's more than an animal, I'm sure of it," Ann said. In a low voice, she added, "And in a way, that frightens me even more. I'm rested, Jack. Let's go."

They hadn't moved ahead more than a dozen steps when Driscoll suddenly lurched and fell headlong. Ann cried out and groped forward, trying to find him, to help.

"I'm all right! I caught something between my ankles—what do you know!"

"What is it?"

"A rifle," Jack said grimly. "One of our men must have dropped it here when he was running from—from something. Well, that gives me a little more confidence. Come on!"

Not long after that, they broke into a clearing, and Ann again cried out in surprise at the sight of moving lights, torches, a long way off. "Look there," she said. "In the distance."

"I see them. The rescue party."

"If Kong's coming—"

"Let me try something," Jack said. "I'm going to see if I can signal them."

Ann realized he was lifting the rifle. He fired one shot, then a second one. Around them the forest fell suddenly silent at the two reverberating reports.

Seconds passed, and then, deliberately spaced, Ann saw three muzzle flashes from the cluster of men far off, followed each time by a distant boom. "They're three or four miles away," Driscoll said. "Hope they've got enough sense to come back here instead of heading toward the mountain. We'd better move, Ann. Toward the Wall, not toward them. As tired as we are, they can catch up sooner or later."

"When they do, they're going to see that I'm underdressed," Ann remarked.

Driscoll stopped, struggled with something, then said, "Here. This ought to help." He thrust wet fabric into her hands. His shirt, she realized. Getting into it was a struggle, for it had been almost as badly ripped as her dress, but she managed the feat at last. They staggered on even as she was trying to get her arms into the sodden sleeves, and by the time she had finished with the garment's three remaining buttons, the heavy jungle again swallowed up the two of them.

Onward, onward, stumbling, clinging to each other for support. From time to time they looked back and saw figures following them, the distance continually dwindling. Jack risked one more signal shot, then said, "I don't know how much ammo I have. Better save what's left. We may need it."

Twilight was coming on, but now they could hear voices behind them. "Jack?" It was Denham, still distant. "Jack, is that you?"

"It's me!" Jack shouted. "Ann's with me, safe enough. Make tracks, Denham! Kong will be along before you know it!"

"We're coming as fast as we can! We got a late start because a big storm hit—lucky for us, I guess. Go ahead and don't wait for us. We're lugging an arsenal!"

"Then follow us. Catch up if you can, but I have to get Ann back to the Wall as fast as I can!"

"Go! We'll be the rear guard!"

A patter of running feet, a ruddy glow, and then Jimmy, the youngest of the rescue party, was there, holding a blazing torch. "Mr. Denham sent me ahead," he panted. "Said you might want some light."

"Good thinking on his part," Driscoll said. "Now we—what was that?"

They all looked back into the gathering darkness. A few hundred yards away, more torches bobbed and wavered, but the sound had come from much farther away. It was a crashing, furious sound, the sound of an enormous body forcing its way through ancient growth.

"Kong!" Ann exclaimed. "It must be Kong!" She saw Jimmy's face turn pale in the flickering torchlight, but Jack's expression was resolute.

"We run from here on," he said doggedly. "Ann, if I fall, you go on. Jimmy, you stick by Miss Darrow, understand? No matter what happens, you get her to the Wall."

"Aye, sir," Jimmy said.

They broke into an exhausted, shambling trot. Ann's mind, numbed by exertion and fear and worry, dulled to everything but the dogged necessity of lifting one foot, swinging it forward, bringing it down, lifting the other. Jimmy and Jack flanked her, each of them occasionally reaching out a steadying hand. Her feet felt raw, and she imagined them cut to shreds, but she fought to run through the pain. They reached a sharply sloping stony path, beside a torrent of water, rain-swollen, raging down in foam and fury. They steadied each other as they made their way down, then plunged into waist-high grasses.

At last Jack cried out, "Look! We made it! Just ahead!"

They had emerged onto the Plain of the Altar. Ahead of them Ann saw a shaft of golden light, streaming from the barely opened gate in the great Wall: torches, she realized, masses of them, shining on the far side, the safe side. "Oh, Jack, we're safe!" she gasped, and then fell.

Jack scooped her up. Ann was on the verge of unconsciousness, but she thought she heard again that distant crashing, and something else.

The enraged howl, the war challenge of the island's beast-god, and it was coming—for her.

★ 19 ★

Lumpy saw them first. He had hardly left his perch atop the Wall, hopeless though the vigil seemed, and when he called down, "On deck there! Here they come—and there's Miz Darrow!" Captain Englehorn felt his heart leap with hope. "Open the gate!" he commanded, and in an instant it was done. "That's enough!" the skipper shouted when the portals stood open just wide enough to admit two abreast. "Sharpshooters, be ready to give them cover!"

Lumpy and half a dozen others on the Wall with him raised their rifles. Englehorn paced. The natives had offered—something. His grasp of the language wasn't firm enough, that was the trouble. Something about Wall defenses, but he couldn't quite get it, and he trusted the rifles more than any savage foolery. In the end, he had persuaded the islanders to keep to their huts. He and his men would handle whatever threat the jungle offered.

Overhead the moon, a little past full, sailed in and out of broken cloud. The sailors on the ground held torches high, ready to offer what aid they could. "Where the devil are they?" Englehorn growled to no one in particular. "What the devil is keeping them?" He couldn't stand the wait, and he pointed to two men. "You and you, bring your rifles." The three of them passed through the gate. Englehorn had time once again to marvel at the thickness of the Wall, its width even at the summit like the waist of a beamy schooner. They emerged on the Plain of the Altar, and ahead, Englehorn spied a torch. In its uncertain light three figures stumbled toward him. "Gott sei Dank," Englehorn breathed, using the language he had not spoken since he had first shipped aboard a British vessel when he was a teenager. He unconsciously reached for his pipe.

The others caught up as Driscoll half carried Ann toward the safety of the Wall. Denham ran beside him. "Jack! By God, I told them all that if any man on earth could bring Ann back, you were the guy!"

"We're not out of the woods yet," Driscoll panted.

Ahead of them, Englehorn beckoned. "Hurry, hurry!"

From atop the Wall, old Lumpy's voice echoed down in an unaccustomed tone of command: "Lively, you mudhens, lively! Can't you see they're all wore out? Get 'em inside, lively!"

Driscoll couldn't suppress a chuckle. "Aye, aye—sir!" he croaked. Hands were reaching out, and they helped him and Ann through the open gate. Inside, Denham thrust something into Driscoll's hand. "You first, then her!" he said.

Driscoll took a long pull of whiskey, then passed the bottle to Ann, who took a quick gulp and pushed the bottle away, coughing. Driscoll's head was spinning, not from the alcohol, but from sheer exhaustion. With his voice nearly breaking, he said, "I got her. I got her, Skipper."

"Good man," Englehorn said. "Everyone inside? Close that gate!"

Lumpy had climbed down from his perch up on the Wall. "Good man, Skipper? Like hell! Great man! We're proud o' you, Mr. Driscoll!"

The sailors clustered around Ann, who lay on an improvised pallet of shirts and blankets. "I'm all right," she insisted, but they would not let her rise. "Jack, make them let me up!"

"Avast, you mugs," Driscoll said with something between a laugh and a sob. He pulled Ann up and held her close. "Ann's no weak sister. She pulled through all that like a trooper!"

"Listen," Denham said, "Lumpy and his marksmen ought to get back to their posts. Kong's coming."

"Nuts," Driscoll said. "He's miles away. We left him in his lair on Skull Mountain—"

"You heard him out there," Denham said in a challenging voice. "He's coming. We've got something he wants, and he's coming to claim it. We have to be ready. Jimmy, I want my bombs handy, you hear?"

"Got half a dozen right here," Jimmy returned.

"Good. Jack, I know you're worn out, but now you can take care of Ann. We'll get you on a boat and back to the ship, and when Kong does show up, we'll take care of him. No, don't say a word! You know me. When I start a thing, I finish it."

"I'll take her back to the ship," Driscoll said. "But as for Kong—"

"The Beast has seen his Beauty!" Denham exclaimed, pounding his right fist into his left palm. "He'll come, I tell you! Sure, the instinct of the Beast would be to stick to his lair in the mountains, but his memory of Beauty will draw him like a magnet, and when it does—"

Lumpy's voice cut down through the night, making Driscoll jump: "Kong! Kong!"

"Make sure that gate is barred!" Denham ordered. "You sharpshooters, hold your fire! I'll take him down with my bombs!"

On the far side of the gate, Kong's cry of rage resounded through the darkness. An instant later, Driscoll saw the gates themselves shudder, showering down ancient dust, as a great body threw itself against them. "Protect Ann!" he yelled.

"Can't get a shot at him!" Lumpy shouted. "He's protected by the overhang!"

"You men get down here!" Englehorn ordered. "Get Miss Darrow to safety!"

Lumpy didn't need a second order. He led the men down, and they made their way to the protection of one of the smaller walls, where they formed a rifle-bristling phalanx in front of Ann.

Driscoll heard the ominous creak and crack of wood. He couldn't believe his eyes. The gigantic portals bowed inward, slowly, relentlessly. The gate gave way, inch by inch. Kong must have exerted all his force, all his rage, all his power. Zigzag cracks appeared in the heavy bars, and the gap widened. The patch peeled back and fell away. Kong pounded the top of the door, shattering its wood beams and forcing back the top of the frame, creating a gap big enough for his huge hands to find a purchase.

The fingers closed as he threw all of his weight into one mighty push. To the left and right, the beams holding the gate closed shattered with a sound like cannon fire. Kong rammed the gates again with such force that the left door flew open, almost torn from its hinges. Kong stood in the gap for a moment, eyes glaring in the torchlight. Now nothing stood between the king and his subjects.

The sailors in the cleared space fell back, raising their weapons.

"Nobody fire!" Denham shouted. "Let him through!"

The islanders came spilling out of their huts, wailing, shrieking. Driscoll glimpsed the old woman, stalking forward, holding a torch that smoldered with a curious green flame, chanting something. He grabbed her by the waist and swung her out of harm's way. "This way, grandma!" he shouted, pushing her toward Ann. She turned a fierce face toward him, and with a start, he realized that she was not as decrepit as he had thought, but still vigorous, still strong. He had knocked the torch from her hands. She tried to reach for it, but someone kicked it aside as the sailors grabbed her and pulled her back.

Kong's lunge came so suddenly that no one could react. He seized a sailor, lifted him high, and dashed him to death. The crewmen fell back as Denham, holding two bombs, fairly danced in a frustrated effort to find a vantage point.

The sailors retreated, seeking the cover of the native huts. The islanders themselves scattered, shrieking, "Kong! Kong!" in wild dismay.

Driscoll realized that they had left Denham alone. He barked, "You men get Ann to the boats. I'm going to help Denham. Somebody give me a couple of those bombs!" Morgan thrust two of the corrugated iron spheres into his hands, and Driscoll yelled, "Go! Don't let him see her!"

The ancient witch doctor tottered forth, shrieking at Kong, who cruelly crushed him like an ant before seizing the lifeless body, biting it in two, and dropping the bloody fragments. Kong tore the roof off one hut, examined the scattered ruins, and smashed the next one as the islanders fled. Hunting, Driscoll thought. Hunting for Ann!

One after the other, Kong snatched unfortunate natives from their shelters. Massacre followed, raging, insensate massacre.

A high angry voice, a woman's voice, screaming. The old woman—the sailors were forcing her to the beach, along with Ann, but she gave them away with her shouts. Kong's head jerked up, and he set off after the retreating sailors in a spraddling run.

"Come on!" Driscoll yelled to Denham. They leaped fallen masonry, dodged among the houses, barely keeping pace with the enraged Kong. The sailors had reached the boats, and they were piling in, but the old woman stubbornly fought them, tearing free, turning to face the onrushing Kong with her hands upraised. She shouted something in the island tongue, over and over—

Incredibly, Kong paused. The hesitation gave a winded Driscoll and Denham time to draw close.

"Hey, Kong!" Denham yelled. The heavy head swung around, the eyes burning with fury. Kong's lips writhed away from his teeth as he turned to lunge for them.

Driscoll saw Denham draw back his arm and yelled, "Cover your faces! Down, everybody!"

Denham threw his first bomb.

It landed almost at Kong's feet. A billow of choking vapor burst from it, washed over the great dark form of Kong. The moonlight silvered the smoke. Kong roared and burst from the fog like a nightmare.

Denham danced back and hurled the second bomb. The bomb struck a few feet in front of the lumbering Kong, billowed out its gas, and Kong's impetus took him into the spreading cloud. His deep roar broke into a spasmodic cough, and Kong staggered through the smoke, unsteady on his feet.

"What did I tell you?" Denham exulted. "Got another one, Jack? Toss it to me!"

Driscoll handed it over and stared unbelieving. Kong swayed, wiping his streaming eyes. Denham walked to within mere feet of him and threw the bomb, then ran back to escape the fumes.

The missile struck Kong on the chest, burst open, and the liquid inside soaked Kong, fuming into streamers of gas that he could not escape. Kong feebly growled, struggled on for a step, two, swayed, and then crashed to the earth with a sound like a stout tree falling.

"Come on, you men!" Englehorn shouted from the surf line. "Now's our chance to get out of this!"

Denham gave no sign of having heard him, but, keeping carefully upwind, approached the fallen Kong. Driscoll cursed and ran forward. "Come on. Are you crazy? Are you hurt?"

Denham didn't even look around. He coughed, turned his face away from the drifting vapor, and replied, "Me? Not a bit! Come on, we've got him now!"

"We've got to get back to the ship!"

At that, Denham turned on Driscoll. "Get the crew to bring back chains, anchor cables, anything that will hold him!"

"What!"

Denham gestured. "He'll be out for at least six hours. Plenty of time to build a raft and float him out to the ship. We'll chain him in the hold—the one I had installed just in case we got a chance like this! It's steel-lined, it'll hold him—"

"Nothing can hold that!"

Denham bubbled with energy. "One thing can, the thing that any human can teach any animal—fear! He's always been king of his world, but now he's got something to learn. Chains will hold him, and fear will hold him, I tell you! This is the most sensational find anybody could make."

Englehorn and a few sailors made their way up from the shore. "What's keeping you?"

Denham laughed. "Skipper, don't you see? Don't you understand? We've got the biggest capture in the world! There's millions in this, and I'll share with all of you. Listen! A few months from now, it'll be up in lights on Broadway. Not a movie! A living spectacle the world will pay to see. King Kong!" He paused, his eyes sparkling, and Driscoll saw that come hell or high water, Denham was going to get his way. "King Kong—the Eighth Wonder!"

★ 20 ★

The crowd jammed four full blocks above Times Square and spilled over into the middle of Broadway. Traffic cops shook hopeless heads and wearily motioned taxicabs into the side streets above and below. Where the crowd pressed thickest, filling the whole street, a sign hung high announcing to the world in fiery letters:

KING KONG
The Eighth Wonder

Beneath the sign, silk hats from Park Avenue jostled derbies from the Bronx, Paris gowns rustled against off-the-rack frocks, sweaters rubbed dinner coats, slanted caps from Tenth Avenue scraped tip-brims from Riverside Drive.

The Social Register was there, along with a delegation from the underworld. Artistic young women from Greenwich Village were there, and their earnest younger sisters from Columbia Heights. Newsboys, peddlers, traveling salesmen, clerks, waitresses, stenographers, debutantes, matrons, secretaries, and ladies of the evening all swelled the throng. The whole town was there, pushing for the attention of the ticket taker and meanwhile staring up at that teasing, mysterious sign:

KING KONG
The Eighth Wonder

From under a tilted cap, Tenth Avenue asked, "Say, what is this thing Denham has to show, anyway?"

Park Avenue, from beneath his own silk hat, replied, "Some kind of gorilla, they say."

A Bronx derby jerked around, its owner's face red. "What's that? You callin' names, bright boy?"

The woman holding his arm said, "Don't be a dope. He said Denham has a gorilla. They say it's bigger'n an elephant."

"Yeah?" asked someone else. "So does it do tricks, or what?"

"I don't know," the Bronx woman replied. "But I got the word on what it is from a friend who's datin' a stagehand who—"

A few feet behind them, one of the upper crust murmured to her escort, "My dear, what a rabble!"

And behind her, Riverside Drive growled, "Didja hear that? Twenty bucks I pay for a seat, and she calls me a rabble!"

Ann Darrow saw none of this. Around back, shepherded by Jack Driscoll, who looked distinctly uncomfortable in white tie and tails, she made her way to the stage entrance. An old doorman there tipped his hat and beamed at her. "You're looking splendid, Miss Darrow!"

Ann blushed, though she had to admit she was a very different Ann Darrow from the terrifying time on Skull Island. She wore a Paris gown, a confection of shimmering, virginal white net, reaching all the way down to her silver-buckled toes. Only her white shoulders and arms were uncovered, and her honey-gold hair.

Driscoll urged her through the door, and they found themselves in a long, dark corridor. "I don't know about this," Driscoll muttered. "Denham's too damn cocksure of himself."

"But they say the show's sold out for the next six months," Ann reminded him. "And he's in business to make money."

"Yeah," Driscoll admitted. "But the whole voyage back was screwy. Why did Denham insist on taking that old lady from the island?"

"I don't think she gave him much choice. Besides, she seemed to calm Kong down," Ann pointed out.

"Her and her herbs and her torches. Well, Denham's got her stashed somewhere tonight. He won't let anybody talk to her, not even the skipper."

Ann touched his arm. "I think Kong would have died without her. She was the only one who could feed him for the longest time. And she wouldn't let Carl hurt Kong."

"Yeah, not much. But Denham was rough enough with him when we first made port, when they were building the cage and all. He broke the big guy, all right."

"I feel sorry for him," Ann whispered.

"For Denham?" Driscoll asked in surprise. She didn't answer.

Driscoll paused at the end of the corridor. To the right was a dressing room. Straight ahead lay the stage. Ann clasped his arm. "Let's not go out onto the stage, Jack," she said. "I don't like to look at him, even if he is chained. It makes me feel the way I did back on the island, on that night when—" She broke off.

Driscoll put a comforting arm around her. "I wish you weren't even here. But Denham insisted. Said he needed both of us for the publicity." He grunted. "Beauty and the Beast. Sometimes I think he's cast me in the role of—here, this room's empty. We can wait in here."

He led Ann into the dressing room and turned on all the lights, even the glaring incandescent bulbs around the makeup mirrors. Driscoll shook his head. The glamour of Broadway somehow escaped him, especially back here, in a brightly lit room that smelled of stale greasepaint and sweat. Ann sank gratefully into a chair and looked at herself in the mirror. "Carl did dress me up nicely, though."

Driscoll paced. "I'm worried. He says it's safe as houses, but if that's so, where's Denham's wife and kid? I noticed he didn't bring them down for the big premiere. Next week, he says, when the excitement dies down."

"I'm glad we're here," Ann insisted. "I don't mind, if it helps Carl. I owe so much to him. And besides, it helps us, too."

The restless Driscoll perched a hip on a corner of the makeup table and shook his head. "Maybe! Sure, it'll give us a nice nest egg to get married with, and—I don't know. Something's going to go wrong. I don't know what, but something. I've got a hunch."

Denham's jaunty voice burst out from the door. "A hunch! What's a hunch worth, Jack?" The laughing director tapped on the door frame. "May I?"

Ann smiled. "Come in, Carl."

Denham swung through the door, and Driscoll reflected that he had changed as much as Ann. A Denham in a silk top hat, a tailcoat, and an impeccable gardenia did not in the least resemble the man in khaki who had dashed to within feet of a gigantic menace to hurl a bomb. Now he was a shrewd Denham, a showman in his element, ready to reap his hard-earned profits.

Denham shook Driscoll's hand. "Hello, Jack. You look swell in that monkey suit. Stand up, Ann, let me have a look at you. For the love of mike, will you look at this gorgeous creature? I'm glad we sprang for that outfit!"

Ann's eyes sparkled. "It was terribly expensive!"

Denham laughed. "We can afford it, sister! Ten thousand dollars from tonight's box office, and the same tomorrow and every day after that for the rest of the summer!"

Despite himself, Driscoll whistled. At that rate, he and Ann together would receive a thousand dollars a night, for as long as the show ran. In a week, he'd have earned more than in a year at sea.

Denham slapped his shoulder. "And this is just the beginning, kids! Every bank in town wants to back me on a movie now—I can write my own ticket. With the footage I brought back from Skull Island, and with the script I've got in mind, you two are going to wind up as movie stars yet!"

"Not me," Driscoll protested.

"Yes, you, you mug!" Denham returned. "Hey, don't worry. It takes no talent at all—just a great director, and don't tell me you don't have one of those, because if you do, I'll punch you in the snoot!"

In the corridor, the doorman called, "Mr. Denham! Do you want me to let these newspaper fellows in?"

"Publicity!" Denham said. "Come on, kids!"

Driscoll stayed protectively close to Ann. In the hallway, a cluster of reporters clamored, holding up cameras, demanding statements. Denham raised his hands. "Okay, okay! Sure, boys, you'll get your story! Sure, I know you, all of you—the *Sun,* the *Herald-Tribune,* the *Times*—you get rid of that idiot of a movie critic yet? The *World-Telly,* yes, I see you, too. I see you've brought your photographers along."

Driscoll whispered to Ann, "Have you ever been interviewed, honey?"

Ann shrugged. "Just for a job. But I'm better dressed for this one, at least!"

Denham was waving them forward. "Gentlemen of the press, meet my star, Ann Darrow! And this big guy is Jack Driscoll, the heroic first mate of the *Wanderer.* They're engaged."

One of the photographers fired off a flashbulb and whistled. "Boy oh boy! Driscoll, you knew what you were doin' when you rescued this doll!"

The *Times* man held a pad and pen. "Mr. Driscoll, we hear you had your share of trouble on the island."

Driscoll started to shake his head, but Ann said, "Don't make any mistake about that. He saved me from Kong's den, and he was all alone when he did it. The other men in the rescue party all died in the attempt."

Driscoll's collar felt tight, and he ran a finger around it. "I didn't do so much. And the guys who died were just as brave as I was, maybe braver. I caught some good breaks. Anyway, Denham's the one who actually captured Kong. The rest of us were retreating, but fast. Denham was the only one with nerve enough to stand his ground and bring the big brute down."

Denham shook his head. "No, no, boys, don't bring me into this. Ann's your real story. If it hadn't been for Miss Darrow, we'd never have got near Kong. She drew him back to the village, where we had a shot at him. My movie will tell the whole story—Beauty and the Beast."

"That's a great tagline!" one of the photographers said, getting another shot of Ann.

"Beauty and the Beast," Denham repeated. "Next year at this time everyone in the world can see the greatest movie ever made, and that's the title. A Carl Denham production, boys!"

"How about some pictures of the Beast?" another man yelled from the back of the crowd, and the newspapermen all clamored along with him.

Denham held up a hand. "Okay, okay, in just a minute. Look, I'll take you right out on stage and let you shoot away. Just as soon as the curtain goes up, while I'm out announcing Ann and Jack. You'll have the first pictures of Kong ever made available to the civilized world. And you can get as many shots of Miss Darrow and Mr. Driscoll as you want, right alongside of Kong."

"This is going to be good!"

"Shut up, Lyons," another man said. "Look, Denham, don't let this guy pull his usual stunt of crowding out the rest of us. The *Sun* can't hog this story."

Lyons turned on him indignantly. "Me? Hey, don't worry. My boss don't like animal stories. He won't do much with this."

"Not much more than four columns!" the second photographer shot back.

Lyons started to protest, but his partner, the reporter from the *Sun*, shushed him and said to Denham, "Look here, I've heard this Kong is over twenty feet tall. Is he tied up good and tight?"

"You scared?" someone shouted from the back.

The reporter growled, "No, but I'm wearing my best suit. I don't want it mussed up."

Denham shook with laughter. "Don't worry. Take a look for yourself." Driscoll and Ann moved aside as the herd of reporters and photographers pushed past, into the wings. They gasped at what they saw out behind the closed curtain.

Driscoll followed, drawn to the sight himself. He felt a strange pang. Kong stood there, a king no longer.

He crouched in a gigantic steel cage, weighed down by a tangle of heavy chains. They led from his hunkering body to ringbolts in the steel floor of the cage. Manacles bound his wrists and his ankles, with more chains snaking from them to secure anchors. His great head was free, and he swung his gaze toward the men. Driscoll saw deep sorrow in those astonishingly human eyes.

Denham was talking to the reporters: "He can roar like a pride of lions, but he's been quiet for days. And if those arms of his weren't bound, he'd be drumming on his chest right now, challenging us to a fight."

Music rose from beyond the curtain. Denham craned and beckoned. "Ann! Jack! Come on. The curtain goes up in five minutes, and I want you onstage with me when it does. You gentlemen of the press, wait until I call you out—then shoot all the photos you want."

Driscoll became aware that, beside him, Ann had pressed her palms to her face. "Oh, no," she said weakly.

Denham smiled reassuringly. "Come along, sister. We've knocked the fight out of Kong since you last saw him. He's harmless."

Reluctantly, Ann joined Denham, her eyes never straying from Kong. Driscoll hovered just behind her, uncertain, feeling more and more that this whole thing was a bad idea.

"I hope that ape is really tied tight," Lyons mumbled.

The reporter with him shook his head. "Got to be. Denham wouldn't take any chances, not with a dame like that at his side. She's a gold mine."

A few of the photographers raised their cameras, but Denham waved them off. "Not yet! The overture's almost over. Get over to the wings, and I'll call you out in a minute!"

The press crew retreated, slowly. Driscoll took Ann's hand. It was cold.

"Chin up," he whispered to her.

"I wish I were back in my hotel room," Ann returned. "It's nine blocks away!"

Driscoll grinned. "Denham booked me into the one right across the street."

"Too close for comfort," Ann said.

The music swelled to a climax, and Denham gave them a wave and a wink. He parted the curtains and stepped before them. Driscoll could hear the murmur of a packed house die down expectantly, and then Denham's voice boomed out: "Ladies and gentlemen!"

In the cage, Kong moved restlessly, jangling his chains. Driscoll felt Ann shiver. He put a protective arm around her waist, and she leaned against him.

Denham's voice rolled on: "I am here tonight to tell you a strange story—so strange that no one would believe it. But seeing is believing, and we—my associates and I—have brought back the living proof of our adventure, and you will see this proof with your very eyes! It was a terrible struggle, and in it twelve of our party met grisly deaths." Driscoll heard the newspapermen muttering: "Twelve? I heard nine!"

"No, twelve. I talked to an old sailor named Lumpy, and he gave me the names."

"What happened to them?"

Evidently Denham couldn't hear the whispering, because he forged ahead: "You will be in no danger, ladies and gentlemen! Now, a little later, you're going to see some film tonight—not a finished movie, but shots of the most incredible animals the world has ever known, just a taste of what will come later.

"But before I tell you any more, ladies and gentlemen, I am going to let you look for yourselves. Prepare yourselves for the greatest sight your eyes have ever beheld! One who was a king and a god of the world he knew, but now he comes to civilization a captive, an exhibit to gratify mankind's insatiable curiosity.

"Ladies and gentlemen, look upon Kong, the Eighth Wonder of the World!"

Driscoll squinted as the curtain rose, spilling in the blinding glare of six dozen spotlights. Only dimly could he see the audience, packed tight, leaping to its feet, erupting in astonished shouts, gasps, frightened stifled cries.

Denham stepped back, his arm raised theatrically, smiling a showman's triumph. In the cage, Kong stood, the chains jangling as his head swept back and forth, surveying the scene before him.

Carl Denham held out his hand, and Ann took an unsteady step toward him. Nearly shouting to be heard, Denham said, "Please! Now, ladies and gentlemen—please, silence for a moment—and now I want to present to you the most courageous woman I've ever known, the heroine of our story, the Beauty who lured the Beast! She has lived through an experience, my friends, unlike anything any woman ever dreamed of, and she has come back to tell you about it! Please welcome the newest star of Carl Denham Productions, Miss Ann Darrow!"

Uncertainly at first, then with growing enthusiasm, the audience applauded. When the tide of sound ebbed, Denham waved Driscoll forward. Driscoll, feeling hot and more and more uncomfortable, looked out stony-faced as Denham continued: "And with her, ladies and gentlemen, with Ann Darrow, is Mr. John Driscoll, the bravest man I've ever known! The first mate of the *Wanderer,* John—Jack as we know him—had the courage to trail Kong to his lair, to rescue Miss Darrow, and to stand at my side to defeat this mighty foe and bring him in chains to New York! Ann Darrow! Jack Driscoll!"

Again applause washed over the stage. Driscoll felt sweat crawl down his face.

Denham gestured again. "Now, in a moment I'll tell you the whole story, and you'll see some astonishing movie footage. First, though, the gentlemen of the press have requested some photographs, and here they come, out on stage. You, the first civilized audience to see Kong, will please kindly bear with us while we take the first photographs of Kong."

The newspaper crew spread out, and sure enough, Driscoll noticed, Lyons pushed forward and grabbed an ideal vantage point. Denham beckoned Driscoll and Ann close to the cage, and Driscoll felt Ann trembling. "Stick it out," he whispered to her. "It'll be over in a couple of minutes."

Denham took Ann's hand and Driscoll backed away. Behind them, Kong looked down, his lips moving, his eyes blinking. The flashguns popped, and Kong started, rattling his chains.

"Now you, Jack. Come on. Pose with your fiancée."

Unwillingly, Jack followed Denham's direction. He put his arms around a shivering Ann and stood while the flashguns went off again.

Behind him, the chains jangled and, unexpectedly, Kong roared. Driscoll pulled Ann away, and in the auditorium the audience leaped from their seats. Denham, though, seemed to be ready for this. He shouted, "We heard that challenge on Skull Island, ladies and gentlemen, and we met the challenger and defeated him! You're perfectly safe! The cage and chains are made of chrome steel! Kong will stay where he is!"

"Get some shots of that," one of the reporters said.

Driscoll and Ann backed away. Kong was on his feet, his muscles straining, pulling at the chains that restricted his movements. No longer roaring, he growled, a deep, resentful, reverberating sound.

The flashes went off once more. Then the photographers turned and aimed their cameras at Ann and Jack again. "Close-ups," one of them explained. "Ready? Big smile—for the society page!"

The flashguns flared, and Kong's roar, frenzied and angry, rolled out like thunder. Denham pushed forward. "Stop it! Holy mackerel, he thinks you're attacking Ann! Hold it! Hold it!"

With a cataclysmic effort, Kong reared. His head struck the top of the cage and jarred it loose. For a moment, Driscoll didn't understand, and then he saw that Kong's struggles had broken the chains holding his arms. A few links still dangled from the manacles, but he now had the freedom to stand, to use those mighty hands.

Kong reached down and seized one of the chains securing his feet. He wrenched it free, ringbolt and all, and then the other one. He broke the waist restraint, and now the steel bars of the cage were all that held him.

Panic threw the audience into a shouting frenzy. People shoved, fell, clambered over the backs of seats trying to get away from the stage.

Driscoll swept Ann into his arms and broke through the crowd of startled newspapermen. He raced down the corridor, through the stage door. Behind him he heard the tortured screech of bending steel. "Come on," he said. "Across the street, to my hotel!"

"Put me down," Ann gasped. "We'll go faster if I can run!" Driscoll set her down, and without any hesitation, Ann ripped the expensive gown, freeing her legs. They rounded the corner and threw themselves into the revolving door of the hotel.

Driscoll heard screams and looked over his shoulder. Kong had beaten down the doors of the theater and, stooping, burst out onto the sidewalk, snarling in rage. A policeman drew his pistol and emptied it, to no avail. Kong made his way toward the hotel lobby.

But Driscoll had thrust Ann into an elevator. The doors mercifully closed before Kong had crossed the street.

★ 21 ★

Behind the locked door of Driscoll's room, Ann sank upon the bed, visibly shaking. "I can't stand it, Jack! It's like a horrible dream—like being back there—on the island."

Jack felt the same way, but for Ann's sake he forced himself to give her a reassuring smile. "We're safe here. I won't leave you, honey. They'll get him. It's only a matter of time. Everything's going to be all right."

Jack was amazed at the strength in Ann's thin arms as she embraced him and sobbed on his shoulder. With a more genuine smile, he patted her shoulder. Then he turned his head, hearing an excited female voice, high and nasal, coming from the next room. "Sounds like Denham's caused the most excitement this old town has had in years."

Ann wiped her eyes. "I'm not surprised at that. No one could have—"

The voice next door grew even louder and more agitated, and now Jack could tell the woman was on the phone. Her voice blared with the intensity and clarity of someone in the early stages of a drinking binge: "Yeah, Johnny! It's Mabel. You bet I'm glad you're back. After last week I thought I'd never hear from you again. I can't believe I actually did that. . . . Talk louder, Johnny! There's fire engines going by. . . . You want to what tonight? Talk louder!"

Jack turned his head. The drone of sirens came from the streets below, insistent and drawing nearer by the moment.

"We ought not to eavesdrop like this," Ann said.

Jack leaned back and grinned. "I don't think it's our fault, honey. Mabel must not know how her voice carries. She could almost talk to old Johnny without a telephone, couldn't she?"

They could both clearly hear Mabel through the door as she raised her voice even higher, as though she were talking over the uproar of a boiler room: "You just wait until you see me in my new outfit. . . . All right . . . Sure, I'll be there. . . . Say, when did I ever break a date with you, Johnny boy? Besides that time . . . Oh my God!!! Johnny! Jo— No!" The last word became a rising, piercing shriek. A sound of shattering glass, and then the woman's voice became a glissando of terrified screams, fading in a cascading echo coming not from the neighboring room but through the slightly opened window.

Ann leaped from the bed, her eyes wide, fixed on something behind Jack. She threw an arm across her eyes.

Driscoll jumped up, too, but barely had time to turn around as the window behind them blew in with the force of a typhoon. The musky stench of the matted hair on Kong's enormous hand flooded into the room as the giant creature reached through the empty window frame. Kong's nightmarish visage filled the window across the room. His eyes blinked and leered at Ann.

Driscoll picked up a heavy wooden chair and attempted to strike Kong's treelike arm. Kong must have noticed him, and flicked his arm in a side-sweeping arc with enough force to send Driscoll flying into a wall. The jolt brought an electric flash of yellow light, and that dissolved into a gathering darkness. Jack tried with all of his might to stay conscious as he slowly sank to the ground. Before his world went black he could see a long shadow envelop Ann.

Ann fainted dead away as Kong's hand closed on the bed, jerking it toward the window before finally lifting Ann gently through. Kong cradled her in one arm with that curious care he had shown her on the island and climbed higher into the night.

He had learned on the island that height meant security. Now he strove for height, climbing what seemed to him like a vertical cliff reaching to the very sky. Pillars of light waved through the night, passed him by, came back to pin him in their glare. Kong ignored them, as he ignored the unfamiliar sounds from below. Higher he climbed and higher still, until he came to a ledge where he rested for a moment. Above him towered a narrowing cliff, and, still tenderly holding Ann, Kong assaulted the final ascent, a strong night breeze buffeting him, bearing the unfamiliar scents of civilization.

The sirens blared below as Kong stood in the shadows atop the building. For the first time since his capture, he could move freely, feel the wind on his face. It invigorated him, but the strange odors it contained confused him. He grunted as his broad nostrils sniffed. He expelled the peculiar air with a snort. The ground felt strange under his feet, and the shapes all around him cut a jagged, unnatural horizon. Nothing flowed like the intertwining jungle trees and vines of his home. Every structure stood straight and rigid, outlined in glowing squares and dots of light. Kong remembered great hives of insects in certain parts of the island and wondered if these were the same: he could see tiny creatures moving within some of the hives not too far away.

More lighted creatures moved in straight lines along the ground far below him. Kong had avoided the hives on his island, knowing the insects could deliver annoying stings. No matter, he would swat them away as he always had.

Suddenly, a beam of white light blinded him, followed by a distant popping sound. He felt irritating stings on his legs and body, as though the swarm of insects had surrounded him. Kong angrily swatted at the air with his free hand, the other protectively cradling his treasure. He bellowed in exasperation and pounded a fist against the ground. Surprisingly, his hand shattered the surface and went right through it with a crash. He hastily pulled it out and proceeded to climb down the opposite side of the building.

As he reached street level, the sound of blaring horns and screaming people reached a crescendo. The lights became part of strange creatures that moved swiftly along the ground. Again he heard that popping sound, and again multiple stings assailed his body. Kong swiftly seized the closest moving creature. It had a hard cold feel to it, different from any other enemy he had ever grappled with. He had no time to dwell on such things, but lifted the heavy thing off the ground and hurled it clear across the street in an attempt to crush the lights in a row of windows.

Again and again he hurled these strange creatures at the rows of squared lights in an attempt to drive what was in them away. As he turned the corner, he encountered the blinding glare of a multitude of glowing, insectlike eyes. Something huge barreled toward him, screeching some unintelligible challenge. Kong turned to face his advancing foe and roared as he drummed his chest with his one free arm. Suddenly, the precious thing he held in his hand began to shift its position. He had no time to find a safe place to hide her as he had on the island before his battle with the flesh eater. He only had time to plant his broad feet. Putting all his weight behind his free shoulder, he braced himself for the collision—

Ann Darrow awoke to see the bright lights, hear the blaring horn and screeching brakes of the bus as it collided with the monster holding her in its grip. She clung on tightly as Kong staggered backward before recovering his balance and advancing on his adversary with the same unconquerable fury that she had seen on the island. With three crashing blows he caved in the top of the bus, almost flattening it to the ground. When the horn became stuck and blared continuously, Ann could sense Kong's fury redouble. He lifted the front of the wreck and sent it spinning across Broadway, taking out light posts and cars all along the street. Spilled gasoline flared with a *whump*, bursting into flickering light and heat. The street had become a living hell.

Ann barely had time to recover before going on the ride of her life. The hand that held her swung in a wide arc as Kong advanced rapidly down Broadway. The movement caused Ann's head to spin. She glimpsed cars that pulled to the side as the people leaped out and ran screaming. The fire, the sirens, the screams, all vanished behind them.

Ann could not yet fully grasp her situation. Suddenly she felt herself being thrust amid the thick, bristling fur in the crook of Kong's arm. Then she felt a cool rush of wind, mixed with a sudden feeling of weightlessness. The world below her fell away and the stars danced dizzily in the night sky above her. Ann weakly cried the name of the one who had saved her before: "Jack!" He did not answer, and as the darkness engulfed her, so did despair.

★ 22 ★

Jack Driscoll staggered to the window just in time to see Kong's shadowy form ascend the side of a building and swing out of sight.

"Denham!" he shouted in frustration and anger. "Denham! Where are you? Can't you stop this brute you turned loose on the city?" He threw open the door and hurried down the hall to the elevator.

In the streets below, he saw that New York was mobilizing for a fantastic pursuit. From all directions, police cars raced toward the hotel, their sirens screaming for clear traffic lanes. A hundred police nightsticks rapped the pavements and aroused a hundred more. Driscoll could only hope that even far south on Centre Street a dozen motorcycle cops, with tommy guns, were careening out of headquarters, and that in their wake rolled a squadron of the department's cars.

Driscoll wondered how the brute had broken loose. Those chains should have restrained even an army tank! Jack felt a moment of despair, but he could not let himself give up hope, not now, not after everything he and Ann had survived on the island. He had saved Ann once before, and there had to be a way to do it again. Driscoll caught sight of Denham, surrounded by policemen, as the director ran breathlessly around a corner in front of the hotel, pointing ahead. "He went up the side of the hotel, Officer! Don't shake your head at me, you half-witted flatfoot. He did! I tell you, that beast can climb smooth marble!"

Jack pushed through the cops surrounding his employer, yelling, "Denham! He got her."

Denham stopped short and, lifting his clenched fists, let loose a torrent of profanity. One of the policemen hiked up his coattail and hauled out a revolver, his eyes darting feverishly as if he expected Kong to materialize out of thin air. The police radio cars screeched in six at a time in the cleared lanes.

Denham ran dry at last. "Which way did he take her, Jack? Did you see?"

"No, but he shouldn't be hard to—look!" yelled Driscoll.

The packed throng turned as one as Kong appeared two blocks down, swiping a mighty arm at an automobile. It went tumbling, its shattering windows reflecting the red and blue glare of a neon sign.

"Ann!" cried Jack, as he could see the white patch of her form in the crook of Kong's left arm. The policemen fired their revolvers.

"Stop, you idiots!" thundered Denham. "He's holding a woman! You're going to hit her!"

A sergeant bawled, "You heard him! Cease fire!" He rushed to a fire truck that had pulled up to the curb. "I'm commandeerin' this vehicle, sonny. Come on, pile on, men! Okay, waterboy, follow that ape, and don't use your siren!"

Jack Driscoll scrambled aboard, and Denham, too, a moment before the truck screeched off in pursuit.

"Keep going!" yelled Driscoll to the driver as they neared the intersection. "He was heading east, toward Sixth Avenue. Go a block past where we saw him and stop."

The truck whipped into the turn, sped on, and then shuddered to a stop. Denham leaped down, but he saw no trace of Kong.

Then a man in a taxi driver's hat stumbled across the street, his face ashen. "It—it—there! That way!" he shouted, waving a frantic arm eastward, toward the dark shadow of the elevated tracks. The man's eyes were wide, and his mouth worked soundlessly before he began to scream, "It jumped! I swear, I seen it! It jumped from that building there, to the El tracks, and from the tracks to the building on the other side! What was it? What—"

"Scatter," shouted Driscoll. "Circle the whole block!"

To the east, yellow headlights in front of screaming sirens converged. The hunt was on.

"Come on, Jack!" Carl Denham mounted the fire truck and ordered the driver to speed on, but the man sounded the truck's siren instead as other yellow headlights raced forward. They stopped abruptly. A stuttering string of motorcycles followed, and close behind another car stopped as well. Denham grimaced, seeing the chief of police emerge from one of the cars. The others were looking for Kong, but this man was looking for him—and saw him.

He grabbed Denham's arm and pulled him from the fire truck, his face contorted in rage. "You're the cause of this, Denham! I told your boys that this show of yours would end in disaster, but they went over my head. How many strings did you have to pull to get that beast into my city?"

"You're not gonna stop him by shaking my teeth out," Denham said, pushing forward. He saw from the corner of his eye that Jack had stepped down from the fire truck too and stood at his right hand, looking ready to take on the whole police department. Good man, Jack Driscoll, Denham thought.

The chief let go of Denham's sleeve but stared in fury at the director. He waved his arm wildly and shouted, "Look!"

Denham did, and saw debris everywhere. Huge holes ripped into the sides of buildings showed where Kong's hands had taken hold before swinging from one brick- or stone-lined window to another. The top of one structure had been partially caved in from the weight of his footfall. Pieces of overturned cars lay strewn like confetti after some macabre parade. Fires had erupted everywhere, and the fire trucks had gone into action. A low growling rumble echoed ominously up the street.

And the ambulances had spilled emergency medical workers into the streets. They rushed from huddled form to huddled form, sometimes stopping to treat an injury, sometimes feeling for a pulse and finding none before moving on. The police chief's face was livid. "Look at those bodies, Denham. Innocent, hardworking people who had no stake in your get-rich-quick schemes, or your fame. It'll take weeks to clean up this mess, and God knows how much it will cost! I hope you're proud of yourself. If I were able, I'd cuff you and have you in front of a judge by morning. But we all got a message from the mayor telling us not to haul you in until we bring that monster down. Another one of your cronies?"

Before Denham could answer, Kong loomed from the darkness three blocks down the street, eerily illuminated by the surrounding fires. The giant saw the crowd, bellowed a challenge, and charged with unimaginable speed.

Driscoll's reactions were quickest. He shot to one side, an outswept arm catching Denham and throwing him to the ground. Denham raised his head and saw Kong's gigantic foot crush the chief's car. A swipe of Kong's arm cleared a whole squad of motorcycles, sending them and their drivers tumbling wildly end over end. He then turned and smashed the fire engine. He tore off an entire axle and flung it into the fourth story of a nearby building. "If I only had a camera!" Denham growled.

Kong paused to pound his chest, then with a grunt started quickly down Sixth Avenue, back the way he had come. Behind him the street seemed to writhe in agony. Denham pushed himself to his feet. The fires raged higher. The wounded lay moaning. The dead lay still.

Driscoll said, "Come on. We can't let him get out of sight." Denham pounded after him, hearing the chief, who had been knocked aside by a blow of Kong's fist, calling after them to stop.

They did not. Like Driscoll, Denham valued Ann's life even more than his own. He had glimpsed the soft, white-clad form of Ann Darrow in the monster's grip and had seen that Ann was not moving on her own. Her motions were that of a juggled rag doll. And she hadn't uttered a sound.

Denham could only hope they weren't already too late.

★ 23 ★

Following the surreal hulk of Kong to the east, Driscoll and Denham found themselves running sideways into a squadron of vehicles that had been screaming down Fifth Avenue. The cars careened to a stop, their brakes screeching. The motorcycles swung in front, on either flank, and in the rear, of a fire truck, falling into formation like destroyers around a battleship. A shaking policeman was pointing south, yelling something unintelligible, but again Kong was nowhere to be seen.

Denham recognized the mayor and the commissioner in the back of the center car. It jumped the curb, the back door flew open, and a familiar voice barked, "Denham! In here, man!"

Denham gripped Driscoll's arm and dragged him into the car. The driver didn't even wait for them to close the door before gunning the engine, and nearly pitched the two men off their backward-facing seat.

Denham pushed himself back upright and said wryly, "Surprised to see you here, your honor."

The mayor of New York met his gaze and snapped, "Not any more than I'm surprised to see you—alive."

Denham knew what that meant. This man had pulled strings for him, and Denham had greased the palms of other politicians and had made extravagant promises to them just to get permission to exhibit King Kong in the city. Someone would have to pay.

But Denham had no time to think of that now. He realized there was nothing he could do to reverse what had happened, what was happening now, or what was going to happen. Forces larger than he had now taken such power from his hands. In Denham's own mind, if only he could help save Ann, at least one person for whom he was directly responsible, then maybe he could in a small way redeem—

"We've got to save the girl!" yelled Driscoll. "That's the point!"

"We need to get ahead of him!" barked Denham. "If we had some idea of where Kong will head—"

"I can make a guess," Driscoll growled. "It'll be someplace high up, as high as he can get. Kong is used to mountains. He lived in one. The higher he is, the safer he feels. There's just one building in New York that towers over the others, and that's the building we'll find him on. On the very top of it!"

"The Empire State Building," the mayor said slowly. "It's the pride of the city. If that thing damages it—"

"Impossible!" said the blunt chief inspector.

"Driscoll's right, though," Denham shot back. "Kong will head for high ground. That's our best bet, if we can beat him there!"

"I guess it's our only bet," the commissioner snarled. "Okay, driver, let's go. Floor it."

But the driver couldn't speed through the crush of people filling the streets, jostling and pointing and shrieking, "There! Down there!"

Denham turned in his seat, craning to look over his shoulder. Kong appeared far down the street; again he crouched for a brief instant on the roof of a building and again disappeared. Cameras flashed. The mayor rolled down his window and yelled to a cop, "Confiscate those cameras! Every one! Now!" Denham smiled grimly to himself. That was a politician for you: Make it go away. Make people think they hadn't seen what they knew they had. The cover-up had already started.

The driver sounded his horn, wrenched the wheel, and finally found an opening. Down a one-way street the wrong way, then a screeching turn on two wheels, then another. Denham held on with both hands, still turned to look toward their destination. Ahead, the spire of the Empire State Building pierced the night sky in a blaze of white light. They reached the building's corner just in time to witness a scene which Denham would have sworn no one of them could believe, even as they sat watching. From a roof on the upper side of the street, Kong leaped. His black, monstrous body curved in a long arc, clear across the street to the skyscraping structure opposite. And then he pulled himself up, from window ledge to window ledge, until he turned the corner of the building and vanished.

Driscoll, Denham, and the commissioner quickly emerged from the car. The mayor stayed in the car and yelled an order, and the driver backed the vehicle, spun it in a tight turn, and left a cloud of exhaust and the reek of burning rubber behind.

The others reached the corner of the block and could see the beast-god high overhead, climbing from setback to setback as if he were scaling the cliffs of Skull Mountain. Six blatting motorcycles screeched in from the darkness, policemen leaping off them and raising their machine guns.

"No! Don't shoot," ordered the commissioner. "He's still got the girl."

There was no mistaking that. Denham could see the small, pale form of Ann. She seemed to be awake now, thank God, and appeared to be gripping the hair on Kong's shoulder.

"Send some of those tommy guns up the elevators," the commissioner ordered. "He'll never be able to climb to the top. We'll maybe catch him on the roof of one setback or another, have a clear shot."

Driscoll struck down the commissioner's pointing arm. "You'll never catch King Kong on any roof!" he shouted, his voice furious. "He's going to the top of the mountain, I tell you."

"Easy, Jack," Denham said, laying a hand on his friend's arm.

Jack shook him off. "It's true. Look! There he goes, up again."

Kong was now so high that his figure seemed smaller than that of a man, and still he climbed. A black silhouette against the chalky walls, he drew himself from ledge to ledge until he rose into the bright flood-lights which swept around the crest of the building. Still he ascended.

"That means the end of the girl," a police sergeant muttered. "If we shoot him up there, she's gone."

"Wait a minute," Driscoll shouted. "There's one thing we haven't tried."

The commissioner looked at him.

"The army planes," Driscoll explained, "from Roosevelt Field. They might find a way to finish Kong off and leave Ann untouched."

"It's a chance," said the commissioner. "Call the Field, Mr. O'Brien. Burn up the wires."

"I'm going up into the building," Driscoll announced, loosening his collar. "I'll take a try at Kong's mountain myself."

Denham felt a surge of energy. Risking it all had always given him a zest for life. He said, "I'll go along, Jack."

The commissioner motioned to half a dozen police officers armed with submachine guns, and they followed.

"Let me take one of those things," Driscoll demanded when they were inside the cool corridor of the building.

The commissioner raised an eyebrow. "You know how to handle one of these, son?"

Denham laughed. "Say, Driscoll can handle any shootin' iron on earth. The boy's good, really good. Let him have one!"

"Hand it over, Sarge," the commissioner ordered, and the man gave the weapon to Driscoll.

Denham sweated out the long ride up. They reached the last bank of elevators at last, and to his frustration they could go no farther. The doors out to the observation deck were locked, with no key, no custodian, to be found. Denham rattled the doors and growled, "Oh, for the love of Mike—"

"Quiet! Listen!" Driscoll whispered.

Denham paused with his hand on the door. From far off he could hear the drone of a plane. No, of a squadron of planes.

"The good old army!" Denham said, trying to laugh. "We've got to get these doors open, men. We can't stay cooped up in here!"

Six planes came into sight, wings tipped with green and red lights. They cruised at an altitude of three or four thousand feet, Denham judged, far above the pinnacle of the skyscraper. Then Denham tensed.

The planes were diving, like birds of prey. One after another, they hurtled down beneath the paling stars.

Ann Darrow had been fully alert almost from the beginning of Kong's relentless climb to the top of the Empire State Building. The rush of fear and the realization that she would not be harmed by Kong balanced against each other as she rose to complete consciousness. Now they were at the summit, as high as they could go. All around them lay New York, limned in lights. Above them the stars were fading as a faint glow of dawn washed into the eastern sky.

As Kong gently placed Ann on the ledge at his feet, the cold and the rush of the wind at this extreme height stung her, keeping her senses heightened. He loomed above her, impossibly large, scanning the sky.

For what? She couldn't even guess.

And then Ann first noticed the dull hum of airplane engines above them in the night sky. Kong's sharper ears must have detected them. As he had set her atop a dead tree to defend her against the flesh-eating dinosaur, he now tucked her safely at the base of the Empire State Building's pinnacle to face a new challenge.

Ann caught sight of the planes just as they tipped their wings and began a coordinated dive.

Kong roared thunderously. Ann had heard that roar before: it was a battle challenge. As on the island, the very air vibrated with its fury. The drum note of his fists upon his chest rose to a wild tattoo. He stretched to his tallest stature.

The first plane came down in a long swift slide, momentarily illuminated by sweeping searchlights. It roared past, just beyond the reach of Kong's extended fingertips. Another followed, then another, a whole squadron of them. They flashed by just above Kong.

Ann pushed herself up. What were the pilots doing? And then it came to her, with a shock: They're looking for me! The planes climbed and circled, and then they dived again. The lead plane swooped down. For a split second it appeared to hover in front of its beast adversary, the broad canvas wings poised like those of some giant pterodactyl from the island. Then it curved upward and shot away.

But this time, in the instant before its turn, the plane's machine gun poured burning lead into Kong's chest. The other planes dived after it, relentlessly spitting fire into Kong's back and sides. Kong bellowed his rage, his arms flailing wildly, vainly reaching for the strange tormentors, flashing past maddeningly out of reach.

Ann closed her eyes and covered her ears, huddling against the metal of the dome atop which Kong stood. The pilots hadn't seen her, must have assumed that Kong had dropped her. Bullets screamed as they spanged off the metal dome, and Ann shrank away from them. Then, as abruptly as it had started, the gunfire stopped. Kong's oppressors peeled away to circle at a safe distance, as if to gauge the effect of their assault. Ann couldn't even hear them, for the wind swallowed the scream of their engines. The beast's roars slowly subsided, and he turned to look down at her.

In the strange silence, the slow cones of the searchlights from the street below swept over Kong, over the planes. As one light lifted the veil of darkness from Kong's shadowy figure, Ann saw with a shock that his expression had an odd touch of reproach and regret, like that of a child accused of some wrongdoing and not knowing what it was. His gaze was—

Ann had never seen that expression on a man's face. Oh, she had received plenty of lascivious looks on the streets of New York. But

Kong's features were strangely innocent as he slowly reached down one finger to caress her. She realized he wanted her, but not in the manner of a city wolf.

His oddly human eyes shone with—with adoration, with a pure and innocent worship.

Perhaps he thought he was protecting her. For a brief instant Ann felt a rush of—pity? Affection? Loathing? She could not tell. In her exhaustion and heightened state of fear, a heartbeat away from shock, her emotions fluctuated wildly, and she had the strange feeling of hovering between life and death. She could not for that moment tell if she was experiencing reality or a dream.

It was then she felt the warm drip of viscous blood flowing down Kong's arm, off his fingers and onto her skin. Fear, terror she could not control, suddenly erupted within her, and Ann began to shriek hysterically, even as part of her mind told her no one would hear her voice.

The scream of airplane engines exploded in her ears, and immediately Kong's roars challenged them as once more Ann heard the thudding drumbeat of his fists upon his chest. The blaze of multiple machine guns tore the night to fevered chaos. One of the planes ventured too close to Kong's straining arms.

The giant struck, struck hard, and ripped the tail section from the aircraft. Ann heard a momentary cry of terror from its crew as the plane spun down, like some wounded bird, in a death spiral. Halfway down it crashed into the wall and burst into flames as it bounced off. Then it was gone, and the night fell strangely silent. Again Ann heard only the sound of whistling air and saw only the methodical searching of the lights.

Ann screamed no longer. Now in the relative quiet she could hear Kong's low moaning, his soft gurgled cough. A plane swooped past, and in the wavering glare of a searchlight, Ann saw the bullets rip into

Kong's hide. She saw his coarse hair jerk and rip off his body in bloody clumps.

The great beast staggered. He brushed Ann as he painfully slid off the parapet, straining to gain easier footing below, on the circular roof space where Ann lay. Kong turned slowly, as though to pick her up.

He stopped, staring down at Ann with a puzzled, hurt look. He fought to stand erect, but weakness forced him to hold the spire with both hands as he began to cough again. Kong then gazed about himself and seemed unable to comprehend the flow of his blood, the creeping numbness in his limbs. As he alternately moved his arms to inspect himself, Ann could clearly see the many wounds in his torso, the crimson punctures over his heart. Ann knew Kong was dying.

From high in the dawning light, the planes swooped down again. With one last look at Ann, Kong rose up. His roars broke into a harsh, rending cough, but he still straightened to his greatest height. He thumped his chest as wildly as ever, in a fierce, unconquerable gesture of final defiance.

One after another the planes screamed down, each poised in turn for a murderous instant, and then curved away. The rattle of the machine guns drowned out Kong's bellowed challenge. Suddenly he swayed, and in spite of his gripping feet, began to topple. As he painfully caught himself in an effort to regain his balance, his gaze met Ann's for one last time.

His eyes were heartbreakingly weary, but in them was a look she had not seen since he was on the island, the king of all he surveyed. Then Kong turned to face his attackers.

Indomitable, he fought to the end. With his last bit of strength he leaped for the last plane as it flashed past. He missed, but his mighty spring had carried him clear of the setbacks below, and out above the street.

Ann could never quite understand or explain what happened next.

All fear left her, and with crystal clarity she saw Kong hang, motionless, as though time had stopped. She imagined him in the same regal loneliness that had been his upon the summit of Skull Mountain. Once again a king and a god, gazing upon the world he knew. King Kong. Ancient. Eternal.

Then time moved again. In the next instant, he was gone.

★ EPILOGUE ★

"We can see them from here!" Driscoll exclaimed. He led the way through a window to the farthest corner of the cramped roof of the topmost setback. A policeman, his revolver drawn, followed, along with Carl Denham. Above them, on the ledge of the uppermost platform, they saw Kong's massive form stagger.

Driscoll could tell at once that Kong had been mortally wounded. The great creature was moaning, reeling. Then Jack saw Ann, lying prone in a softly glowing white dress stained with dark patches. Blood.

His heart stopped. High above, the nimble airplanes renewed their dance of death as they dove toward Kong in another grotesquely graceful ballet. Their barking guns ripped into Kong's body. "Duck!" Driscoll yelled, and he, Denham, and the policeman flattened themselves against the meager protection of a corner. Slugs bit into it, kicking up a gritty spray of fragments. Jack turned his face away from the drift, trying to keep the wind from whipping grains of concrete into his eyes.

Unexpectedly, the machine-gun fire fell silent, and the planes swept away to gather themselves for their final attack. A reek of sulfur dissipated in the breeze. Above them, Kong barked a deep, gurgled cough and swayed unsteadily. The end was very near.

Suddenly, Ann began to move. "She's alive!" Driscoll yelled to Denham. But he had no time to relax.

Denham grabbed Driscoll's arm and yelled, "Stay down, Jack! They're coming back, all five of 'em!" In the growing light of dawn, Driscoll saw the planes wheel around and peel off for their dive.

"God help that woman," growled the policeman.

"God help me, too!" Driscoll shot back. "I'm going after her. Kong can't fight off those planes and keep his eye on Ann at the same time, and I can't leave her there alone!"

Denham said nothing, but he followed, and after a moment of hesitation, so did the policeman.

As the new barrage of machine-gun fire began, Kong's last stand shook the airship mooring mast. Driscoll, in the lead and taking the stairs inside the spire three at a time, lost his footing and fell to his knees. A slug ripped through the thin metal skin of the building and passed just above his head. Jack ignored it—if it didn't kill him, it didn't matter. He scrambled to the top and burst through the doors only to encounter—

The whistling wind.

Driscoll took in a deep breath of the chilly morning air. Kong was gone. As he looked up he saw Ann blankly staring at something he could not see.

"Ann!" Driscoll rushed forward and almost fell. His foot had skidded in a splash of blood and fur, and now he saw that blood had spattered everywhere.

Ann stared at him with a terrified, empty gaze, and for a moment, Jack thought she had been hit. Then she weakly called his name and reached out for him. Driscoll gently lifted her to her feet and helped her off the ledge where she had lain.

As soon as they were in the stairwell, Ann began to sob. "Oh, Jack!"

Driscoll held her, close and warm. "It's all right," he murmured. "It's all right now."

As they embraced, he knew he need say nothing more.

Denham and the policeman had just arrived. Denham took a moment to raise his eyebrows at Jack, who answered his unspoken query with a nod: Ann was unharmed. Denham stepped out onto the narrow platform at the base of the spire, the policeman at his elbow.

The cop was gasping for breath. He holstered his revolver and stared at the bullet-ravaged facade of the tower, at the blood and tufts of fur spread everywhere. "Looks like a battlefield. You know, the size of that thing—I never thought the aviators'd get him."

"The aviators didn't get him," Denham replied slowly.

"What?"

"It was Beauty killed the Beast."

The cop gave him a long, uncomprehending look. Denham sighed. Below somewhere, the gargantuan body of Kong lay on the street. The carnage Kong had left was something that Denham would have to answer for. Denham thought fleetingly of his wife and son—good thing he had not brought them to the show, as he had first planned. They were better out of this.

With mingled feelings of relief and despair, Denham looked off into the new dawning day. He could not help wondering if his long nightmare was over—or if it was just beginning.